"I took a home test this morning—well, three, actually."

Now Jason sat forward. "And?"

Piper sucked in a big breath and pushed the words out too fast. "I'm pregnant, Jason." For a moment the word made no sense. He felt light-headed. She kept on talking. "I mean, I'm completely, ridiculously, surprised about this. I kept wondering, how did it happen? I honestly never in a million years..." She kind of ran out of steam about then.

"Piper."

"What?"

And he was on his feet, circling the coffee table, pulling her out of her chair and up into his arms. Miraculously, she didn't object. Instead, with a long sigh, she sagged against him.

He cradled her close and whispered, "We're having a baby."

Dear Reader,

A little happy hour good cheer on a rainy Friday night. That's all librarian Piper Wallace is looking for. But as fate would have it, she's going to get so much more, including a little quality time with a hot younger man. No, Piper's not looking for love. In fact, she's put love in the Never Again category.

But just for one night? She's never done that before, and she tries to be open to new experiences. Really, what could go wrong?

Rancher and chain saw artist Jason Bravo has always had something of a secret crush on the pretty librarian, starting way back when she first began working at the local library. He was thirteen then. Now he's a grown man—and he is not passing up his one chance with Piper.

The deal is that they'll both walk away when their one night is over. But a deal like that is made to be broken. Especially when a good man refuses to give up on the woman of his dreams.

I hope Jason and Piper's story keeps you turning pages, that it makes you smile and sigh and maybe shed a tear or two.

Happy reading, everyone.

Christine

TAKING THE
LONG WAY HOME

CHRISTINE RIMMER

HARLEQUIN

**SPECIAL
EDITION**

HARLEQUIN®
SPECIAL
EDITION™

Recycling programs
for this product may
not exist in your area.

ISBN-13: 978-1-335-59458-7

Taking the Long Way Home

Copyright © 2024 by Christine Rimmer

For questions and comments about the quality of this book,
please contact us at CustomerService@Harlequin.com.

TM and ® are trademarks of Harlequin Enterprises ULC.

Harlequin Enterprises ULC
22 Adelaide St. West, 41st Floor
Toronto, Ontario M5H 4E3, Canada
www.Harlequin.com

Printed in Lithuania

MIX
Paper | Supporting
responsible forestry
FSC® C021394

Christine Rimmer came to her profession the long way around. She tried everything from acting to teaching to telephone sales. Now she's finally found work that suits her perfectly. She insists she never had a problem keeping a job—she was merely gaining "life experience" for her future as a novelist. Christine lives with her family in Oregon. Visit her at christinerimmer.com.

Books by Christine Rimmer

Harlequin Special Edition

Montana Mavericks: Brothers & Broncos
Summer Nights with the Maverick

Montana Mavericks: What Happened to Beatrix?
In Search of the Long-Lost Maverick

Montana Mavericks: Six Brides for Six Brothers
Her Favorite Maverick

The Bravos of Valentine Bay
Almost a Bravo
Same Time, Next Christmas
Switched at Birth
A Husband She Couldn't Forget
The Right Reason to Marry
Their Secret Summer Family
Home for the Baby's Sake
A Temporary Christmas Arrangement
The Last One Home

Montana Mavericks: Lassoing Love
The Maverick's Surprise Son

Visit the Author Profile page at Harlequin.com for more titles.

This one's for my older son Matt
and my grandson, Milo.

Matt, you're a wonderful father and a fine man who
takes loving care of his family. You step up to help
whenever it's needed. Plus, you're smart and funny
and thoughtful, too. A mom couldn't ask for more.

And, Milo, how have the years passed so swiftly?
Wasn't it just yesterday you were running through the
sprinklers in the backyard? Watching you grow up
is an honor and a pure delight.

Chapter One

People always thought of libraries as quiet, even peaceful. But in Piper Wallace's experience, no way.

The Legos at the Library event was in full swing when four-year-old Bobby Trueblood stuck the plastic spaceman in his mouth and swallowed—or tried to. Piper, newly promoted to the top position of library director, saw him do it.

As Bobby grabbed his throat and attempted to cough, Piper stepped in close, bent down to his height and spoke to him calmly. "Bobby, can you breathe at all?"

Frantic, Bobby shook his head, held his throat with both hands and continued his desperate, soundless effort to cough.

"Okay," Piper said softly, "I'm going to help you get that spaceman out of there..."

A few feet away, Lacey Beaufort, the children's librarian, had noticed the problem. "I'm calling 911," she said in a near whisper and whipped out her phone.

Moving directly behind the little boy, Piper dropped to one knee. "Bobby, I'm just going to put my arm around you now..." She drew his small, heaving body back against her and tried like hell to remember her first aid training.

Slap it out first, right?

Dear God in heaven, she hoped so.

With her fist just above his navel, Piper bent him at the waist. As he continued desperately clutching his throat and struggling to draw even a bit of a breath, she struck him five times between his shoulder blades with the heel of her right hand, being careful with each strike to pound upward in an effort to help him expel the object.

Nothing. Poor Bobby continued to hold his throat and shake his head.

About then, his mother, Maxine Trueblood, turned and saw what was happening.

"Oh, my Lord!" Maxine shouted in horror. "Bobby! Bobby, are you all right?!"

Bobby was most definitely *not* all right. Lacey had the 911 dispatcher on the phone now. As for Piper, she moved on to perform abdominal thrusts. Wrapping her other arm around the boy, locking her right hand on her left wrist, she squeezed sharply in and up, five times in succession.

The fifth squeeze finally did it. The small plastic figure shot out of the child's open mouth, hitting seven-year-old Milo Nevins in the chest.

"Holy smokes!" exclaimed Milo as Bobby finally sucked in a long, wheezing breath.

"It's out," Lacey reported to the 911 dispatcher. "...Yes, that's right. The toy is out. And he's breathing now...Yes. That's what I said. He's getting air, breathing normally. The obstruction is out." She listened for a moment and replied, "I think he's all right, just really shaken up...Yes. Of course. I'll tell them..."

About then, Maxine scooped her son up into her arms. The little boy grabbed his mom around the neck and started crying.

Piper rose to her feet. "He'll be okay," she reassured

the terrified Maxine. She asked Lacey, "Are they sending an ambulance?"

"Since he seems fine, no. But he should go straight up to the hospital in Sheridan so that they can look him over."

Maxine nodded. "Yes, okay. We'll go right now." She was crying by then, too. Her other child, a little girl, clung to her coat and sobbed right along with her mom and her brother. In the meantime, two other mothers had moved in close. One offered a travel packet of tissues as they both patted Maxine's back and whispered reassurances. "Thank you," sobbed Maxine, holding Bobby on one arm while swiping at her own tears with her free hand. And then she spoke directly to Piper. "Thank you so much!"

"Of course," Piper replied. "Bobby is going to be fine." She said that at full volume, for everyone to hear. Then she turned to Lacey. "I'm going to walk them out to the car…"

The other moms stepped out of the way and Piper moved in. With a light hand at Maxine's back, she guided the sniffling mom forward.

As they left the children's section, Lacey continued to assure the crowd that Bobby was all right. Faintly, when Piper, Maxine and the two children went through the reception atrium toward the main entrance, Piper heard Lacey announce the next group of entries. She kept moving forward, guiding the shell-shocked mom and her kids out the wide glass doors into the stormy mid-April afternoon.

It was cold out there and pouring down rain. At least Maxine, Bobby and the little girl were wearing hooded coats. Piper hadn't stopped for hers. "Would you like me to go with you?" she asked as they reached Maxine's battered Subaru.

Maxine drew a slow breath. "We'll be all right. I can manage."

"You're sure?"

"Yes. He's okay now. We'll be fine—and I don't know how to thank you. If you hadn't known what to do…"

"Happy to help." Piper pulled Maxine into a quick side hug. "Now, let's get you guys out of the rain, huh?"

Maxine blinked and looked Piper up and down. "But what about you? You're dripping wet."

"I'm fine." Piper lifted the little girl up into her car seat and buckled her in as Maxine did the same for Bobby.

Two minutes later, Piper stood shivering in the downpour watching the Subaru leave the library parking lot. Once the car disappeared from sight, she whirled and ran for the shelter of the building.

Inside, she ducked into her office to grab her purse and the change of clothes she kept in the closet there just in case. Because you just never knew at the Medicine Creek Library.

A couple of years ago, Tootie Gracely, technical services librarian, had bumped into Piper in the staff room and spilled half a strawberry smoothie down the front of Piper's sky blue silk dress. Another time someone had left an enormous wad of bubble gum on the chair at the reference desk. Piper's tan pencil skirt had not survived the incident.

Which was why she was always prepared for a wardrobe disaster.

Today, after ten minutes in the restroom, she looked—well, better than she had any right to expect, given the circumstances. She'd changed into slim gray pants, a white shirt, a gray jacket and black pumps. She'd also mopped up her smeared mascara, put on fresh lip gloss and smoothed her wet hair up into a ponytail. As for the green wool dress she'd worn out into the rain, she left it in her office to deal with later.

Drawing her shoulders back and aiming her chin high, Piper reentered the children's section just as Lacey announced a new group of winners.

Half an hour after that, Legos at the Library wrapped up. Everyone declared the event a big success, even if little Bobby Trueblood *had* gotten a plastic spaceman temporarily stuck in his throat.

The really great news was that Maxine had called from the hospital and left Piper a message full of thanks and relief. Bobby was fine. The doctor in the ER had examined him, delivered a gentle lecture about what *not* to put in his mouth—and sent the Truebloods home.

Potential tragedy averted. Bobby Trueblood had come through his ordeal in good shape. And hey, it was Friday. Piper had the weekend off.

Tonight of all nights, she wanted to blow off a little steam. She wanted some happy-hour good cheer, to enjoy a drink at Arlington's Steakhouse bar in the company of friends and colleagues.

And if she couldn't get a group together on the spur of the moment, no problem. Just one friend or colleague would do it. Because if happy-hour good cheer wasn't happening, someone to confide in would be great.

That morning, she'd received a second invitation to share information from one of her 23andMe DNA matches—and this was no second-or-third-cousin kind of match. This was someone she'd given up on years ago.

Way back in her teens, she'd put all that hope and heartbreak behind her. So much so that, when the match was miraculously made, she couldn't bring herself to deal with it. A few days after the notice from 23andMe, the match himself had reached out for the first time.

How hard could it have been to respond to the guy?

Harder than she'd ever imagined, definitely. Her mother had been on her case about it way too much the past month or so. So far, she'd backed her mom off.

But now she was at the point where she would love to have a friend to talk to about the situation. Tonight, a drink and a long conversation with someone she trusted, well, that would be even better than going out with a group to celebrate Bobby Trueblood's continued good health.

As it turned out, none of her coworkers could join her tonight. And when she called a few friends, she got regretful refusals, which didn't really surprise her. Most of her friends were in their late thirties to early forties. They had spouses, kids of varying ages and jobs, too. They juggled hectic schedules as best they could. That night, no one could get away.

Piper put on her red raincoat, grabbed her soggy green dress and hurried out to her Volkswagen Tiguan. Behind the wheel, she turned the car toward home.

But halfway there, she changed her mind.

She wanted to go out. And why shouldn't she? Widowed four years ago with no children, Piper had zero reason to rush home. Plus, she made it a point to be open to first-time experiences. Really, tonight was as good a night as any to try happy hour solo.

Five minutes later, she was parking on the street outside Arlington's Steakhouse. Inside, she refused the host's offer of a small table to herself and claimed an empty stool at the bar, where she ordered a cosmo.

As she slowly sipped her drink, the fiftyish cowboy to her left mounted a half-hearted attempt to pick her up. She answered politely but took care to give the man zero encouragement. After a few minutes of awkward conversation, he gave up and left her alone.

She turned around on her stool. Every table in the bar area was occupied. She waved and smiled at a few people she knew. They waved back, but none of them approached her or signaled her over.

Which was fine.

Except, well, she did feel a little uncomfortable. Everybody else seemed to be on a date or out with friends.

Sipping a cosmo alone? It felt kind of sad now she was doing it.

Fair enough, she thought, and sat up straighter. She would finish her drink and be on her way—and in the meantime, she would people-watch.

For the next few minutes, she casually observed a couple at a two-top not far from the bar. They were adorable, kind of shy but obviously crushing on each other. Pretty young, too. They looked barely old enough to order a real drink.

She turned her powers of observation on another couple at the next table over from the shy lovebirds. No flirty, excited glances were zipping back and forth there. Those two hardly looked at each other, let alone spoke.

The cowboy she'd discouraged a few minutes before got up from his stool. "Have a nice night." He tipped his hat to her.

She gave him a smile. "You, too." He headed for the door. Piper resumed her people-watching.

"Hey, Mrs….er, Piper. How are you?"

Hiding a grin at the way he'd stumbled over what to call her, she smiled at the young man who stood behind the stool the older cowboy had vacated. Piper had known Jason Bravo for fourteen years. She'd met him when she first came to work at the library.

Jason was in middle school then, wasn't he?

Back then, he used to check out books on things like woodworking and saddle making. She'd been twenty-six at that time, a librarian for two years and absolutely thrilled to have snagged a position in her hometown library.

Jason had been a good kid, one who'd grown into a fine, handsome man—and thoughtful, too, stepping up now to check on her, to make sure she was okay on her own.

"Piper?" He watched her face expectantly.

She realized she'd failed to respond to his greeting. "Uh, hi, Jason. Good to see you. And yeah, I'm…fine."

He gave her the kind of smile that should probably come with a warning label. "You don't sound so sure about that."

"Sorry, just thinking back."

"To…?"

"My first year at the library. You were in middle school then, right?"

"Eighth grade," he replied without even having to think about it. For a moment, they just looked at each other. Finally, he asked, "Want some company?"

Why not? "Have a seat."

He claimed the empty stool, signaled the bartender and asked Piper, "Another drink?"

"Sure."

The bartender poured Jason a beer and quickly whipped up a second cosmo for Piper.

Jason took off his hat, hung it from one of the hooks under the bar and then raised his glass. "Are you waiting for someone?"

She tapped her drink to his. "No, I'm on my own."

"You like drinking alone?"

"Not exactly. But tonight, all my friends had somewhere else to be. I almost went home, but then I had this idea that I…" She shrugged. "It doesn't really matter."

"Sure, it does—come on. Tell me." He had thick, dark hair and blue-gray eyes. And that smile of his made all her menopause-adjacent hormones sit up and take notice.

Don't be ridiculous, she reminded herself. *He's a nice boy just trying to look out for you.* "I, uh, do my best to be open to new experiences, that's all. Tonight, I decided to try drinking alone at a bar."

He laughed then. The rich, deep sound tugged on something forbidden down inside her. "And how'd that work out for you?"

She sighed. "Well, it's not something I'm going to be doing on a regular basis. Honestly, it's lonely and it made me a little bit sad. But I needed to get out, you know? It was a rough afternoon at the library."

His gaze stayed locked on her face. "What happened?"

"Well, today was our Legos at the Library event. Everything was going great. Until Bobby Trueblood tried to swallow a plastic astronaut…"

"That's scary. Is he okay?"

"He's fine now, but I had to perform the Heimlich maneuver. And I was terrified while it was happening…"

"Of course you were." Jason leaned a fraction closer.

His big shoulder brushed hers and a little shiver vibrated through her. He raised his beer again. "To you, Piper. You saved the day."

"I wouldn't go that far."

"I would. And I'll bet Bobby would, too."

"He's okay. That's what matters—and the sheer relief that he came through it just fine had me wanting to get out with friends, to uh, celebrate life and all that. And then when no one could come out with me, I decided to try the whole being-alone-at-a-bar experience."

He chuckled. "Being-alone-at-a-bar. That's a thing?"

She gave a silly little snort-laugh and felt comfortable enough with him right then that she wasn't even embarrassed. "It's not a thing to anyone but me and as I said, it's not fun in the least. I am never choosing to be alone at a bar again—I mean unless I desperately need a drink for some reason. I kind of settled on people-watching, trying to make the time go faster." She tipped her head at the couple who looked like they wanted to be anywhere but together and whispered, "I believe they're fighting."

He watched them for a moment. "Never seen them before. But you're right. They don't look happy."

"You think maybe he cheated?"

"Hmm." Jason took a moment to consider the possibilities. "Nah. She probably wants to go to counseling to work on their issues and he's one of those guys who doesn't believe in that crap."

"Harsh," she said with a grin.

"Hey, it was just a guess." He tipped his head at another couple and then leaned close again to ask, "That blonde and the guy with the mullet. What about them?"

Piper gave a half shrug and whispered, "She loves him despite his unfortunate grooming choices."

"What? You're judging a man's mullet?"

She assumed a remorseful expression. "You're right. That was over the line."

Jason looked at her as if… Well, as if he found her fascinating. Was he actually flirting with her?

No way.

And that second cosmo? It made her bold. "Jason Bravo, are you flirting with me?" The words were out of her mouth before she could think how silly they might sound. "Um, I mean, you wouldn't, right?" Shutting her eyes, she drew a slow, calming breath and muttered, "Just shoot me now…"

He leaned close again. "Of course I'm flirting with you."

"But…why?" she asked because tonight she couldn't seem to keep all the uncool things from popping out of her mouth.

"You're a very pretty woman and flirting is fun."

How did he do that? Every time she put her foot in it, he managed to make it all okay. It was lovely of him. "You have salvaged this evening for me. Thank you."

"Anytime." Those dusky blue eyes seemed to suggest things she knew she shouldn't take seriously. He asked, "How's your mom? Haven't seen her in a week or two."

"Same as always." Piper's mom, Emmaline Stokely, was opinionated, outspoken, lively and fun. An artist, Emmaline painted psychedelic landscapes and made boho jewelry. She also took surveys and babysat other people's pets among other things, all in the interest of making ends meet in her own special, creative way. "I think she's deep into a new series of landscapes. When she's lost in her work, even I don't see much of her."

"She's remarkable." Jason was an artist, too. He not only ran the family ranch alongside his mom and dad and younger brother, but he was also a talented chain saw carver. Piper's mom always spoke highly of his work.

Piper made a noise of agreement to the wonderfulness that was Emmaline. "She's one of a kind, all right."

"That she is." One side of his fine mouth quirked up. "She told me once that for the first nine years of your life, the two of you lived on the road in a Volkswagen bus."

"It's true. She homeschooled me in that bus. I met a whole bunch of interesting people, very few of whom were anywhere near my age. Then my grandfather died, and we came home to help out my grandmother."

"And you stayed?"

She nodded. "I fell in love with Medicine Creek. I wanted to go to a real school and have a 'normal' life. Mom seemed to know how much I needed that. So she sold the bus, and we moved in with my grandmother."

The bartender asked, "Can I get either of you another drink?"

"No more for me." Piper gave him a smile. "Thank you."

Jason said, "I'll have one more." He asked Piper, "Hungry?"

"Really, I should get going."

He pinned her with those beautiful eyes of his. "Got a menu?" he asked the bartender.

"You bet."

So they ate sliders and sweet potato fries, and another hour flew by. Her sad, solo evening had magically turned wonderful. Now, she didn't want the evening to end.

But really, it was time to say good-night to this beautiful, attentive man who was several years too young for her—not that it mattered how young or old he was. Piper wasn't getting anything going with a man. Not now. Probably never.

Jason put his hand over hers and said, "Don't."

Her breath caught. And suddenly her heart was racing.

With the hand he hadn't captured, she picked up her water glass and drank it down. "What's going on here?" she whispered, her voice oddly breathless.

He leaned in again and she wondered how in the world any man could smell that good. Like red cedar shavings, saddle soap and…something else. Ferns, maybe, something moist and green and fresh.

Their gazes locked.

And she asked, "Jason, are you trying to pick me up?"

His eyes didn't waver. "Oh, you bet I am. The question is, will you say yes?"

She should pull her hand away. But she didn't. "Hmm. This is not the kind of situation I normally find myself in. To be brutally honest, I'm boring."

He just shook his head. Slowly.

She insisted, "No, really. I am. I always say I'm open to trying new things, but the truth is, I'm a creature of habit. I like my routines."

"Such as?"

"Well, every Thursday, without fail, I eat lunch at Henry's." The diner was a Medicine Creek landmark.

"Henry's is great. Everybody loves Henry's."

"But Jason, *every* Thursday?"

"Absolutely. Why not?" He looked at her so steadily.

She asked in a shaky whisper, "Do you pick up women in bars all the time?"

He laughed then, a low, rueful, oddly tender sound. "No. To tell you the truth, I'm more of a relationship kind of guy."

For most of her life, Piper had considered herself a relationship kind of girl. She'd grown up wanting what her grandparents had shared—that special someone, her very own soulmate.

But not anymore. Never again. "I hope you find what you're looking for, Jason."

"You're saying you're not interested?"

"In a relationship…with you?"

"Well, I was thinking more that we might see each other again."

Was he kidding? He must be. But she answered him honestly. "Nope. Not going there. I'm single and happy that way."

He drew a slow breath. "So, then, Piper. Do you think you could be interested…just for tonight?"

The question shocked her. She was, what? Thirteen on the day he was born. And the age gap aside, going home just for the night with any man was not, and never had been, her style.

She blurted, "I've never done that, had a one-night stand."

He leaned a fraction closer. "First time for everything."

The breath had mysteriously fled her lungs. She dragged in air. And shocked herself by admitting in a goofy little squeak, "Okay, I'm intrigued."

"Good. And right now, I think I should probably up my game a little." He gave her a slow grin.

She frowned. "What does that mean?"

"This…"

She gasped as his soft lips touched hers. And then she sighed.

Because Jason Bravo definitely knew how to kiss. So much so that it didn't even occur to her to pull away.

The bar and everyone around them receded. It was just the two of them sharing a lovely, leisurely kiss. A light kiss—but so sweet. He didn't touch her, except with those wonderful lips of his.

"Wow," she whispered when he finally pulled away.

His gaze tracked—from her mouth to her eyes and back to her mouth again. "Piper, come home with me. I'm out at the family ranch, the Double-K. I have my own place there."

She wanted to say yes. She wanted that so much.

And why shouldn't she?

They were both grown-ups, after all.

And they were both single…weren't they? "Got a special girl, Jason?"

His gaze remained steady, focused on her. "Absolutely not."

She stared at him. He was fun and kind and she knew she could trust him.

Plus, he was one hot cowboy.

"All right," she said. "I'll follow you to your place."

He insisted on picking up the check. At the door, he helped her into her raincoat and offered his arm. She took it, grinning to herself, thinking that the kiss they'd shared back there at the bar might get a few busybodies whispering.

Not that she cared, really. She'd been raised by a single

mom who never let the opinions of others dictate her behavior. If Emmaline ever learned that her only child had spent a night with Jason Bravo, her response would be a proud smile and an enthusiastic *Good for you, my love.*

It was still raining out. Piper pulled up the hood of her raincoat. They were both parked right there on Main. He walked her to her car and then ran through the rain to his big pickup.

When he eased out onto the street, she followed him.

In no time they left the lights of town behind. Overhead, the clouds were a curtain of gray blotting out the stars, obscuring the peaks of the mountains. The rain came down hard enough that the windshield wipers could hardly keep up with it.

Twenty minutes or so from town, they turned off the highway onto a well-tended gravel road. By the time she pulled to a stop behind him at a wide, wooden gate, she was feeling pretty nervous, second-guessing the wisdom of this completely uncharacteristic decision she'd made.

Going home with Jason Bravo? This was not like her at all.

He got out, opened the gate and signaled her through under a big iron sign depicting two Ks back-to-back—two Ks for the Double-K Ranch, which had belonged to his mother, Megan Kane, before she married Nate Bravo. Piper knew this because she enjoyed reading books about Wyoming history—including *Brands of the Bighorns* by Chester T. Sedgwick, which offered detailed accounts of all the local ranches and their owners over the years.

Once through the gate, she pulled to the side and waited as he drove through, got out of his truck again, shut the gate and then jumped up behind the wheel to lead the way once more.

They passed a Victorian-style house on the left. From there, the road wove through a stand of cottonwoods. When they emerged onto open land again, Jason pulled to a stop in front of a two-story log cabin with a pair of small one-story wings branching off to either side. At the back of the house she could see what looked like an attached barn.

Jason jumped out of his truck and jogged to her side window. She rolled it down. "This is it," he said, the rain running off his hat, making a stream of water between them. "Pull up beside the deck."

He stepped back and she drove forward, stopping a few feet to the left of the deck steps. A moment later, he pulled open her door for her.

When she stepped out of the car, he said, "You'll ruin your shoes." And then he put one arm at her back, the other under her knees and scooped her high against his broad chest.

She laughed in surprise. Clutching her purse in one hand, she grabbed him around the neck with the other as he carried her up the short run of stairs and under the shelter of the overhang above the door.

Once he reached the doormat, he set her on her feet. She pushed back the hood of her coat and blinked up at him as a sense of complete unreality assailed her. She was about to have a one-night stand with Jason Bravo. Never in her life had she imagined this might happen.

He gazed down at her from under the dripping brim of his hat. "You okay?"

She gave him a big smile. "Yes, I am."

"Come on in." He unlocked the door, ushered her ahead of him and flipped a switch on the wall. The rustic chandelier overhead lit up the big living area.

"Your house is beautiful, Jason."

"It's pretty simple," he said. "A couple thousand square feet. Great room in the middle, bedrooms to either side."

"But what's with the attached barn?"

"I have my workshop back there."

"Ah. So that's where the chain saw art happens?"

"Yeah. You want a tour?"

She did, but getting a tour of his workshop would make tonight feel more like a date. This was not that and boundaries mattered. "Better not."

He tossed his hat onto a rough-hewn bench by the door and then took her face between his big, wet hands. "Please don't change your mind."

She gazed up at him, breathless. "I won't."

He seemed relieved. "Good."

Her poor heart was going a mile a minute. "Do I look terrified?"

One corner of his mouth ticked up. "No way. Not you."

"Liar," she said, feeling nothing short of fond of him right at that moment.

"Piper…"

"Hmm?"

"I can't believe you're here."

"I understand. Because neither can I."

He took her mouth, gently at first. And then more deeply, more…hungrily. His lips went from cool and rain-wet to scorching hot.

She gasped at the wonder of that kiss and let her purse

drop to the rug at their feet. Talk about being open to new experiences…

Twining both arms around his neck, she silently vowed to give herself up to him and to the magic of this one special night.

Chapter Two

Utterly limp and completely satisfied, Piper stared dreamily up at Jason's beamed bedroom ceiling.

"That was…" She raised her voice a little to be certain he could hear her in the other room. "Jason, I have no words!"

Idly, she twined a long swatch of her hair around her index finger like she used to do back when she was a kid. Before tonight, there had been only two men in her life—her college boyfriend, Brandon. And her husband, Walter. Until Brandon almost killed her and turned her love to hate, she'd been head over heels for him. As for Walter, he was the opposite of her college lover. Walter was quiet and safe. He'd died of a heart attack when he was only forty-one.

As gloriously naked as when he went in there, Jason emerged from the bathroom. The man was every bit as gorgeous coming toward her as he'd been when he walked away. Without a word, he lifted the blankets and got back into the bed with her. His expression was much too serious.

"Jason. What's wrong?"

Bracing up on an elbow, he looked at her solemnly. "I should be asking you the same question. I can't believe you're not upset."

She let out a slow, happy sigh and twirled her hair some

more. "I just had four orgasms in three hours. I'm swimming in endorphins right now. I don't think I could be upset if I tried."

For a moment, she thought he might give her a smile—but no. His eyes remained serious, and the corners of that wonderful mouth refused to tip up.

"Okay," she conceded. "I get it. It's not good that the last condom broke."

He touched the side of her face, a light caress that warmed her deep down inside. "You did say you're not on birth control…"

"Jason, I promise you. I'm not going to get pregnant."

"Are you telling me that you can't have kids?"

"It's possible that I can't—more than possible. I'll go further. It's very likely that I can't."

The skin was all scrunched up between his eyebrows. "You don't know for sure?"

"No, I don't. But I do know that it's not the right time in my cycle for me to get pregnant. My period just ended. Also, Walter and I were married for eight years. We never once used birth control and I never got pregnant in all that time." She waited for him to say something. But he just kept on looking at her.

Assuming he wanted more details, she went ahead and overshared. "We, uh, always agreed we wanted children, Walter and me. Now and then, we would talk about checking into fertility tests and all that, but we failed to actually do anything about it."

The truth was, she and Walter had talked about a lot of things. But there'd always been a lack of urgency between them, a certain distance that at first had felt so sane and real and comfortable. Walter had been safe, and safety was what she'd needed at the time. She hadn't let herself admit until quite a while after her husband's unexpected death that she'd never been in love with him.

"So, really," she concluded, more than ready to be done with this particular conversation. "A broken condom is not a big deal to me. If by some impossible miracle I really did get pregnant, I would be thrilled. I would love to have a baby and the prospect of being a single mom doesn't bother me in the least. My mom had me without a man around and it worked out just fine."

He looked at her as though he wasn't sure what to make of her. "You're way too calm about this."

She waved a dismissing hand—and then realized that he might be worried about STDs. "Listen, I mean it. I'm not pregnant and I promise that you won't be getting any sexually transmitted diseases from me. Until tonight, I haven't had sex with another person in years—since a good while before Walter died, to tell you the embarrassing truth."

He gave her a slow nod. "I haven't been with anyone since my last relationship ended almost a year ago—and she and I always used condoms."

"Okay, then. We're good, I'm sure." And she truly wanted to be finished with this conversation. Talk about awkward—and what time was it anyway? "Listen. I really should pull myself together and head back into town."

She didn't wait for a response from him, but instead slid to the edge on her side of the bed and slipped out from under the covers. It felt weird being naked now that the good times were done.

But so what?

"Be right back," she said as she headed for his bathroom. Once she'd used the toilet and freshened up a bit, she returned to the bedroom to find him back in the bed, sitting against the carved headboard, the sheet pulled up to his waist, the ridges and hollows of his broad chest and lean belly on glorious display.

Her clothes were right there on the bedside chair. She got busy putting them on, starting with her white lace bikini panties and matching bra. Piper loved good lingerie. All her underwear was pretty. Good lingerie made her feel attractive and feminine, whether any man ever saw it or not. She stifled a smug little grin as she realized that tonight of all nights, wearing nice underwear had been an excellent idea.

Jason watched her as she buttoned up her white shirt. When she reached for her gray trousers, he said, "I want to see you again."

That couldn't happen. They had an agreement and she fully intended to stick by it. "Jason, you are amazing. Tonight was perfect. But, sweetie, we agreed. It was just this one time."

His gorgeous face looked carved from stone. "Please don't talk to me like I'm a child."

She winced. "I'm sorry. It's just…listen. I had a beautiful night and I promise I do not see you as a child. I see you as a very sexy man—and I do have to go."

For a long, painful string of seconds, he just looked at her through those eyes she knew would be haunting her secret dreams. Then he pushed back the covers and swung his feet to the floor. "All right, then." He reached for his own clothes. "I'll put on some pants and walk you out."

* * *

Outside, the rain had stopped.

Jason pulled open the door of her little SUV for her. He knew better than to try to kiss her. She thought she was done with him. He got that.

They had an agreement. He wasn't going to break it—at least, not right now.

"Good night," she said as she settled into the driver's seat and reached for her seat belt.

"I'll be happy to follow you to the gate and open it for you, so you don't have to get out of the car."

Her eyes were wary. "Is there something complicated about getting it open?"

He shook his head. "It's a simple butterfly latch, but you'd have get out of the car twice, to open the gate and then again to shut it behind you."

"No problem. I can manage."

"All right, then. Night, Piper." He closed her door.

She met his eyes through her side window. As she granted him a quick wave, he resisted the wild need to fling the door wide again and drag her back out and into his arms.

With a nod, he stepped away from the car. A moment later, he was watching her taillights disappear into the stand of cottonwoods between his place and the main house.

Overhead, the last wisps of storm clouds drifted way up there in the starry sky. To the west, Cloud Peak poked up toward heaven, more threads of cloud caught on the crest. All was right with the world.

Just not with Jason.

He heard a whine and his dog, Kenzo, a German She-prador, came wiggling out from under the deck. "Hey, boy!" Kenzo trotted on over. Jason knelt to scratch him behind the ears and tell him what a good boy he was.

Back in the cabin, Jason knew he wouldn't sleep. A month ago, he would have headed out to see if the night calver needed him. But calving season was winding down on the Double-K and it wasn't cold enough to worry about any newborn calves freezing before they could latch on.

With Kenzo at his heels, he walked on through the house to his workshop in back, where a beautiful red cedar stump waited for him to discover what waited inside. Kenzo lapped up a long drink from the water bowl in the corner and then flopped down near the door that led back into the cabin as Jason geared up, grabbed a hatchet and started peeling bark.

An hour or so before dawn, he and Kenzo reentered the house. He fed the dog, put on his work clothes and went out to join his dad and his younger brother, Joe, for morning chores.

As it turned out, his mom's cousin Sonny and his wife, Farrah, had driven up yesterday from Buffalo. This morning, Sonny pitched in with the chores, too.

Sonny and Farrah and their kids used to live and work full-time on the Double-K. The kids were grown up now and on their own. About a decade ago, Farrah had inherited a motel in nearby Buffalo from her mom. Nowadays, the couple ran the Cottonwood Inn for a living.

They still showed up to pitch in whenever they were needed—and sometimes, like this weekend, they left a manager to run the motel and came out to the ranch for a visit. Both Sonny and Farrah liked the motel business. But they also missed life on the Double-K.

After the chores were done, the men converged on the

main house for breakfast. Jason's mom and Farrah had done the cooking this morning.

Jason took his turn washing up in the half bath off the front hall and joined the group around the breakfast nook table. He hadn't realized how hungry he was until he started shoveling it in—hungry and kind of tired, too. Even with more than one cup of coffee, he wouldn't mind heading back to his place for a nap after the meal. Staying up all night was starting to catch up with him.

The talk around the table was the same as always—about moving cattle and what equipment needed repair. He kind of tuned it out in favor of recalling the night before. Smiling to himself, he pictured that sweet dusting of freckles across Piper's pale shoulders and all that long, red hair on his white pillowcase.

He'd had fantasies of Piper since the first time he set eyes on her when he was thirteen and she came to work at the Medicine Creek Library. She'd been single then, though right away she'd started going out with Mr. Wallace, who taught history at the high school. They'd gotten married eventually. He was a nice guy, Walter Wallace. But not good enough for Piper.

Nobody was.

And never in a thousand years would Jason have guessed that last night might ever really happen.

But then he'd walked into Arlington's, taken a seat at a four-top in the bar area with a few guys he grew up with and ordered a beer. He was just about to pick up the check and head back to the ranch for the night when Piper appeared and hopped up on a stool in the middle of the bar.

All of a sudden, he'd had zero desire to leave. He'd stayed right where he was, half-heartedly holding up his end of the conversation with the other guys, keeping an eye on his favorite librarian while trying to be cool about it.

She always looked so pulled together—not like a city girl, exactly. But close, in her trim gray pants, matching jacket and white button-up shirt. Everything tailored and crisp. And with little black pumps on her narrow feet, too. She had that red hair pulled up in a high ponytail and he tried not to let himself imagine wrapping that tail of hair around his hand, or maybe taking it down so it fell loose and messy on her shoulders.

But he did imagine. In detail. It was a longtime habit with him, imagining doing sexy things to Piper Wallace.

And when the cowboy beside her had gotten up to go, Jason saw his chance and took it…

"Wild night, huh?" Joe was watching him—and wearing a smirk. Twenty-three now, Joe thought he knew everything.

Jason set down his coffee cup and looked his little brother square in the eye. "I got no idea what you're talking about."

Joe smirked all the harder. "Noticed that little VW SUV sitting out in front of your place till all hours last night."

"And this is your business, how?"

Joe could be a smart-ass, but he was a good guy at heart. He knew when he'd stepped in it. Backing down, he put up both hands as though Jason held a gun on him. "Okay, okay. You're right. I didn't see a thing."

"Boys," said their mom. "Not at the table."

Both Jason and Joe chuckled at that. It was one of Meggie Bravo's hard-and-fast rules when they were growing up—no fighting at the table. "Sorry, Mom," they replied in unison, just like when they were kids.

And the talk turned to the new research on sunn hemp as an alternative to alfalfa.

All the rest of that day, as he checked on the last of the newborn calves and pitched in to move cattle to fresher pastures, he thought about Piper.

And that night in bed, he faced the truth.

Yeah, he'd agreed that last night was the only night he would share with her. And at first, it had seemed only right to let some time go by before trying to get her to see things a different way.

But hell. Life was too short. No man could afford to sit around on his ass waiting for the right woman to see the light.

Now that he'd had a little time to think it over, he realized that the least he could do would be to check in with her. No matter what she'd said last night about it being the *only* night, well, a woman had a right to change her mind. He needed to tell her again that he really would like to spend more time with her—and as soon as she was ready to look at the situation in a more hopeful light, well, all she had to do was give him a call.

He made himself wait until Tuesday to seek her out at the library.

And he got lucky, too. He walked in and she was right there near the entrance hugging Mrs. Copely, who had been the director for years until her retirement last December, when Piper had stepped up to fill her shoes.

Piper caught sight of him over Mrs. Copely's shoulder. She didn't frown or anything, but she didn't look all that happy to see him.

Mrs. Copely let Piper go. "Well, I'll be on my way. Just had to stop in to see how you were doing."

"It's always good to see you, June."

Mrs. Copely sighed. "I miss you all. But Andre and I are heading off on another cruise next week. The Caribbean this time."

"Sounds wonderful."

"We do enjoy a little travel—but we'll be back in plenty of time to help out with the live auction in July."

"We're counting on it," said Piper.

Mrs. Copely spotted him as she turned to go. "Jason Bravo! How are you, young man?"

"Real good, Mrs. Copely."

She grabbed him in a hug, and he was engulfed in her powdery scent. June Copely was a big woman. When she hugged you, you felt it. "It's such a perfect coincidence that I walked right into you, Jason." She took him by the shoulders and beamed a giant smile at him. "Piper and I were just talking about the annual auction this summer." She looked over her shoulder at Piper, who nodded and smiled back.

He shot Piper a look—mostly to make sure she stayed put until he could have a word with her. She forced a smile for him, too.

Mrs. Copely said, "Jason, do you think you might possibly consider donating one of your chain saw sculptures to this very important cause?"

"I would be honored, Mrs. Copely."

"Wonderful!" She clapped her plump, age-spotted hands. "Do you have a card?"

"Of course." He pulled out his battered wallet and handed one over.

"Fantastic." She took the card, went on tiptoe and kissed his cheek.

He said, "I'll make sure Piper has my number, too."

"Please do." Mrs. Copely lifted the flap of her shoulder bag and slipped the card inside. "And now, I am out of here. I'll be in touch." With a perfectly executed pageant wave, Mrs. Copely sailed out the main doors.

"I'll give you all my information," he said to Piper before she could rush off.

"Of course." Her smile was reluctant. "This way." Turning, she set off toward the children's section.

He fell in step behind her.

Today, she wore a yellow skirt and a short blue-green jacket. Her little pumps were blue with pointy toes. And her hair, contained in a loose, low knot at the back of her head, made his hands itch to undo that knot so he could run his fingers through the long red strands.

At the children's section, she veered right. It wasn't far to the office with her name on the door. "Come on in," she said, and stood to the side, ushering him forward. "Have a seat." She shut the door and gestured at the pair of guest chairs on the far side of her desk.

"Thanks." He took one.

She circled around and sat in a big, black swivel chair, placing the expanse of her tidy desk between them. "It's very generous of you to donate one of your carvings. Thank you, Jason."

"Always happy to contribute to a good cause." He pulled another card from his wallet. She reached across the desk for it—and he changed his mind.

Slipping the card back into his wallet, he took out his

phone. "Just give me your number. I'll send you a text. That way we can easily keep in touch."

"Jason. Just call the library and ask to speak to me."

"I mean your cell number."

She bit her lip and asked in an adorably worried tone, "What are you doing?"

He got it. She really didn't want to give him her number. "All right, Piper," he said wearily as he pulled out the damn card again and handed it over.

"Thank you."

"Sure."

She popped to her feet. "Well…"

He kept his butt in the seat, though he'd never been the pushy kind. Until now. With her. He cast about for a friendly, neutral topic of conversation—just to kind of get the ball rolling.

There was a handmade card on her desk. A stick figure with spiky brown hair and a wide, red-crayon smile adorned the front of it. "Cute. Looks like it's handmade just for you."

She was smiling again—somewhat cautiously, but still. A smile was a smile. "Bobby Trueblood sent me that."

"Ah. The boy you saved at the Lego event."

"Yes, well. He's doing great. They came in yesterday, Bobby, his mom and his little sister. He was smiling and talking a mile a minute. No ill effects from almost swallowing a plastic astronaut."

"Glad to hear it."

She nodded. "He's the sweetest little guy…" As her voice trailed off, she looked at him reproachfully. "Jason. We had an agreement."

He went for it. "Go out with me."

"Please. We've been through this."

"I was thinking a picnic. Saturday. I'll pick you up at noon. Wear jeans and sturdy shoes or boots. And a swimsuit underneath. I'll bring everything we need, and I know the perfect spot along Crystal Creek."

She just stood there, staring down at him, waiting for him to give up. The woman had no idea how long he could keep on like this.

Forever. Longer.

But it wasn't working.

He knew it was time to go. "Hey. Can't blame a man for trying." He got up. "You haven't seen my workshop. Now that I'm contributing to the auction, I would appreciate your help deciding what to donate. Plus, I've finished a new carving I'd like you to see. Just drop by when you can. Evenings are good, any night the rest of this week. My days are mostly about what needs doing on the Double-K…"

"I understand," she said. Whatever the hell that meant.

And he supposed he'd struck out enough for one day. "See you, Piper."

"I'll walk you out." She started to come around the desk.

He put up a hand. "No need. You take care, now."

Piper watched his fine backside walking away from her. The man had the broadest shoulders and the narrowest hips.

And she really needed to stop thinking about Friday night.

When the door shut silently behind him, she sank to her chair and tried not to get wistful about that picnic he'd wanted to share with her. She wished things were different. She truly did.

But one night was the deal they'd made. Better to stick to that. All the reasons *not* to say yes to him still applied.

However...

It was good of him to donate one of his carvings to the auction. And as the library's director, she had an obligation to show her appreciation for both his work and his generosity.

That evening she stayed late preparing for the upcoming board meeting. The Medicine Creek Library got a lot of backing from town leaders and from the chamber of commerce. They were an independent library, but they had the enthusiastic support of the community and some big private donors. With everyone helping out, they were able to run a great program.

Much of the credit for the library's longtime success went to June Copely, who'd been the director for decades. Piper knew she had big shoes to fill, and she worked hard to be as productive and innovative as her predecessor.

June had overseen the renovations accomplished last year by the hit home improvement TV show *Rebuilt by Bartley*. The project had expanded the library—and not only by adding more space for books, but also by making the library more beautiful, more welcoming, with a more open, inviting floor plan.

Really, Piper owed so much to June. And June was thrilled to have gotten Jason on board for the auction. Piper needed to be sure that Jason felt appreciated for his contribution and that meant she really should accept his invitation to visit his workshop.

That night, she got home around ten, ate a light meal and went straight to bed.

Wednesday, she woke up thinking of Jason—the kind

of thoughts she really shouldn't be allowing herself to have of him. Sexy thoughts. Fond thoughts.

And curious thoughts, too.

Beyond her obligations as director, she did want to see that workshop of his. And he'd said that he had a new carving he wanted to show her.

What kind of director would she be if she failed to gracefully accept the invitation of a respected local artist who'd agreed to donate his work to an important fund-raising event?

She had his card, but he'd said just to drop by any evening. Why not tonight?

After work, she went home and changed into jeans and a pair of comfortable walking shoes. It was a little after seven when she got to the gate with the ironwork Double-K sign above it. Nobody came out to see what she was up to as she opened the gate and then closed it once she'd driven her car through.

When she reached the cabin, a black dog sat on the front deck. The dog barked twice, then trotted down the steps toward her, tail wagging. The animal seemed friendly, so she dipped to a crouch.

"Hey there," she said.

The dog dropped to his haunches and tipped its head from side to side with a low, questioning whine. Cautiously, she offered a hand, palm up.

The cabin door opened and there was Jason in heavy-duty orange pants, a worn Cheyenne Frontier Days T-shirt and steel-toed boots. "His name's Kenzo. He's cautious, but friendly."

The dog sniffed her hand and allowed her to give him a quick scratch under the chin.

"It's good to see you," Jason said.

Her heart kind of juddered in her chest and then skipped a beat or two as she went up the steps to meet him. He watched her come toward him, his eyes never leaving her face.

For a moment, they just stood there a foot apart, staring at each other.

He broke the spell. "Come on in…" And he turned and led her into the house. She followed him across the living area into the open kitchen. From there, they went through a door on the back wall and directly into a barn with bright industrial-style lamps overhead.

They descended the five steps to ground level, where sawdust was thick on the floor. There were rough tables of varying heights and tools everywhere—on the shelves that lined walls and also hanging from hooks. She looked around at tree stumps of different sizes and admired a gorgeous five-foot carving of a rearing dragon and another of an eagle taking flight.

"Still working on those two," he said, noting the direction of her gaze.

He picked up a remote from a workbench, pushed a button and the garage-style door on the opposite wall rumbled up onto a grassy space. It was still light out. About twenty yards away a barbed-wire fence stretched away in both directions. In the pasture beyond, cattle grazed.

"Now the weather's getting better and daylight lasts longer, I'll be doing more work outside," he explained. Then he sent the door rolling down again. Dropping the remote back onto the bench, he turned toward another door to the right. "This way…"

Beyond that door were finished carvings, a lot of them.

"I carve on-site for people at times, and I take commissions to carve what the buyer wants," he said. "But whenever I get the chance, I carve whatever I see waiting in the wood."

"They are beautiful, Jason." And they were. She admired a giant owl and a couple of frisky-looking bear cubs.

He gestured to the right. "Any of the carvings along that wall are available for the auction. I would also be happy to carve something on request."

"I was thinking it would be nice to let June Copely choose…"

"Works for me. Have her give me a call when she's back in town."

"I will, I…" The words died in her throat as she spotted a red cedar mermaid near the wall to her left, a mermaid who appeared to emerge from the wood, her tail curling around the base of the stump, her long hair trailing down the curves of her bare back—a mermaid wearing Piper's face.

Piper took a slow breath and made herself look at him squarely. "When did you carve that one?" Her voice came out brittle sounding as she gestured toward the mermaid.

His gaze never shifted but stayed locked on her face. Apparently, he didn't have to check where she pointed to know which carving she meant. "That's the one I wanted you to see. I started it after you left the other night and finished it before dawn on Sunday morning."

She went ahead and stated the obvious. "It looks like me…"

He grinned. "You noticed."

"You see me as a mermaid?"

"No. I saw a mermaid in that hunk of wood. And I happened to be thinking about you at the time, picturing your face." He stuck his hands in the pockets of his heavy-duty pants. "Maybe I went too far. Should I have asked you first?"

"No. Of course not. I'm flattered. It's very beautiful, Jason."

"Thank you."

"But…"

He frowned. "Whatever's bothering you, just say it."

"Well, I would appreciate it if you didn't offer it for the auction."

His expression relaxed. "Don't worry. I wasn't planning to. That one's mine. It has…personal significance."

She dragged in another slow, careful breath. "Jason, I…"

"Yeah?"

What was there to say, really? Yes, he'd invited her to see his workshop, but she shouldn't have come. Even considering that June would have wanted her to come—uh-uh.

She should not be here. "I know you were working. I should let you get back to it, so I'm going to go." When he said nothing, she turned for the door that led back into the workshop.

He followed behind her all the way to the front door, where she paused and faced him. "Your work is so good."

"Thank you." His expression gave her nothing.

"I'll have June call you…"

"All right."

"Great. Good night, then."

He nodded.

She turned and got out of there.

Chapter Three

Jason watched her drive away.

She'd seemed pretty eager to leave.

He didn't get it. He wanted to be with her. And when he looked in her eyes, he saw that she wanted to get closer to him, too. Was that just wishful thinking and an overactive imagination on his part?

Maybe.

But the fact remained that he wasn't ready to give up on her.

The next day was Thursday. And thanks to their conversation at Arlington's Friday night, Jason knew where to find her on Thursday at lunchtime.

"Jason!" Mona McBride greeted him with a big smile. Mona, her husband, Henry, and their daughter, Sadie, owned the diner jointly. As of last December, Sadie was also the fiancée of Jason's second cousin, Ty Bravo.

"Hey, Mona!" Jason gave her a wave and hung his hat on the tree by the door. The place was packed.

Mona said, "It might be a few minutes…"

"Not a problem." He'd spotted Piper seated alone at a deuce in the back corner near the swinging doors to the kitchen. "You know what, Mona? I'll just go say hi to Piper Wallace, maybe join her if she doesn't mind."

"All right, then. Be with you in a flash." Mona bustled off to take an order.

He headed on back to join his favorite librarian, who had her nose in a book and seemed oblivious to the noise and bustle around her. "Is this seat taken?" he asked when he reached the empty seat across from her.

She glanced up to grant him one of those looks—the ones she'd perfected from years at the library. This particular look said, *You are skating on very thin ice, young man.* "Make yourself comfortable," she said, heavy on the irony.

"'Preciate it, Piper. I was worried I might never get a seat."

That brought a knowing grin from her. "Oh, I'll bet you were."

Mona appeared. She offered him a menu. When he shook his head, she turned to Piper. "What'll you have?"

Piper closed her book and slipped it, spine down, between her purse and the wall. "Avocado BLT, wheat toast, with cucumber salad and iced tea."

"Done," replied Mona. "Jason, do you need a minute?"

"No. That sounds good. Give me the same, but I'll have fries with the sandwich."

"You got it." Mona marched off.

Once it was just the two of them again, he leaned forward. "Tell me you've changed your mind about going out with me."

She didn't reply, only gazed at him steadily.

Hey. It wasn't a no. He leaned even closer and whispered, "Piper. I like you. I want to spend more time with you."

She looked at him solemnly for several seconds. "Jason…" She said his name slowly. Thoughtfully. And then nothing.

He waited. That went on for a while—the two of them, just sitting there staring at each other, with all the noise and bustle of the busy restaurant going on around them.

Then Zeb, the dishwasher, who also helped out wherever he was needed, came hurrying over with Jason's place setting and two iced teas.

Piper gave Zeb a smile and waited for him to go before leaning across the table and admitting, "All right. I admit I've been thinking about you, too."

Jason quelled a giant grin. "Did you just give me a yes?"

She hesitated. That couldn't be good. And then she said very quietly, "I would be open to friendship."

Friend-zoned? Not what he'd hoped for. Not by a long shot. "Any chance of more?"

"Jason, it wouldn't be wise."

"Who cares?" He kept his voice low with effort, so that none of what they said would escape the confines of their booth. "I want you. I really do get the feeling that you want me. I can't stop thinking about last Friday night."

She started to speak. "I…"

Their food came. Mona set the plates down with a flourish. "What else can I get you two?"

"This is great," he replied.

Piper said, "It looks perfect, thank you." As soon as Mona left them alone again, Piper whispered for his ears alone, "I like you, too. And Friday night was…" She seemed at a loss for the right words.

He suggested, "Life-changing? World-shaking? Like

nothing that has ever happened before in the history of time and space?"

She laughed and suddenly he was the happiest guy alive. And then she tried to be serious. "Yes. It was so good. But it's over now and I meant what I said. Being more than friends won't work for me."

Being just friends didn't work for *him*.

He sent a quick glance around the diner. Every booth was full and so were all the classic bolt-down stainless steel stools with the green pleather seats that lined the long counter. The noise level was high enough that they could make their own private world in the corner booth.

"What are you afraid of?" he dared to ask.

She sat back from him. "Jason, I didn't say I was afraid." He kept his big mouth shut that time and was rewarded with, "I've had two serious relationships. Neither worked out. I have no interest in trying again."

"Give me a chance to change your mind."

She shook her head, ate a bite of her sandwich and set it down. "I don't think so…"

Again, she hadn't given him a real no. "So, then. You've had two serious relationships. I've had three."

Piper tipped her head to the side and made a thoughtful sound. "As I recall, you used to come into the library to study with Jennifer Rosario when you two were in high school…"

"That's right. Remember that time you caught us kissing in the US history section?"

"I do remember." She sipped her tea and added with a grin, "You two weren't the only ones."

He ate a French fry. "Jenny was so embarrassed. She worried that you would think less of her."

"I didn't. I always liked Jennifer."

He nodded. "Everybody liked Jenny. She used to make friendship bracelets, the ones with the beads strung on colored embroidery floss. She gave them out to everyone because she was everybody's friend."

"Didn't she move away?"

"Yeah. She and I broke up senior year. She moved to Cody, met another guy and got married. But back in high school, I really thought it was true love with Jenny. I told her so. I swore that I would love her forever."

"Did she say it back?"

"Yes—but it didn't work out."

Piper seemed to be studying him.

He went on, "After Jenny, I decided I needed to wait, to be certain, before ever saying those three words again."

Piper asked, "And since then?"

"I've had two more serious girlfriends since Jenny. I never said the words, though. It never felt right."

Piper seemed thoughtful. "I said the words to my college boyfriend." Her eyes were far away, focused on another place, another time. "And to Walter. I still feel guilty about that."

"About saying I love you to your husband?"

"No. About marrying Walter in the first place. He made me feel…safe. Too safe, really."

"You're saying he was the wrong guy for you?"

"I don't think there is a guy for me. I think I'm one of those people who's just happier on her own."

"There's someone out there for everyone, Piper."

"Jason, you are entitled to your opinion."

He studied the delicate shape of her face for a long, appreciative moment before asking, "What about if we try friends with benefits?"

"No. I did mean what I just said. The whole relationship thing is not for me."

"Friends with benefits isn't a relationship."

"Maybe not. But it's close enough that I don't want to go there. Honestly, I don't know what my problem is. Maybe I'm somehow doing relationships wrong. Or maybe it's that I grew up with my mom for my role model—and she never had any desire to get married and settle down. For those first nine years, when we lived on the road, traveling around the country to art fairs where Mom sold her paintings, we made our own rules—and that's why I think, somehow, I'm missing the couple gene. Or whatever it is that makes people want to find the 'one' to spend forever with. I'm happy being single and I don't need a husband or a lover or any other kind of special relationship with a man to make my life work."

He focused on the last of his sandwich as he decided how to respond. Finally he said, "So, then. Friends, and that's all?"

"That's right. Jason, I do like being with you. I like talking to you."

"And I like doing those things with you." *And I would love to do a lot of other things with you*, he thought but had the good sense not to say.

"So, then," she replied in a brisk tone, "if you want to be friends, I'm in. But I will completely understand if you say no." She poked at a cucumber with her fork. "I mean, it doesn't sound all that exciting for you."

She was so wrong. It sounded just great to him. Simply getting her to agree to see him again—as friends, if that was all she was ready for—would constitute a step in the right direction.

The right direction for what?

Hadn't she made it painfully clear that friendship was as far as the two of them could go together? And could he settle for that in the long run?

Doubtful. There was just something about her. Since last Friday night, this thing with her had become more than a crush for him.

He was half in love with her. And that scared him— because she really did seem determined not to let him get too close.

He pushed his plate away, dug in his pocket and laid enough bills on the table to cover both of their meals and a decent tip.

She was watching him closely. "What'd I do wrong?" she asked softly.

"Not a damn thing."

"But…?"

He eased his napkin in at the side of his plate. "I've been pushing for any way to get closer to you. But you're right. I'm not sure that being 'just friends' with you is going to work for me. I need a little time to think it over."

"Oh. Well, of course. I understand…"

He was about to get up and get out when he remembered the broken condom. "Listen." He leaned in and kept his voice very low. "I meant what I said the other night. Piper, I *will* need to know if you're pregnant."

She scoffed. "I told you that there is no way I could be."

"I remember what you said. And I'll still need to know for sure."

"All right. Let me, uh, check the calendar?"

"Sure."

She took her phone and poked at the screen a few times. "Okay, so my period is due in ten days, on May fifth, and—"

"Wait. That can't be right. Last Friday night you said your period had *just* ended."

She shot him a cool glance and whispered, "Stop. Really. I am not pregnant—but yes, you have a point. *Just* is a relative word. I meant recently, but looking at the calendar now, I see that it wasn't as *recently* as I implied on Friday night."

"Bottom line, the chances are greater than you thought that you could be pregnant and—"

"Jason, I really had no idea you were such an expert on a woman's cycle." Was she making a joke?

Because this was not funny in the least. He explained, "Back in high school, Jenny was more than a week late once. It was a false alarm, but at the time, I got real interested in just how likely it was that we were going to be having a baby."

Beneath those sweet freckles, her pale cheeks flushed red. "I'm sorry to make light of something that must have been scary."

"Yes, it was scary. We were seventeen and not in any way prepared for parenthood."

"Listen." She spoke gently now. "How about this? If my period doesn't come right on time, I'll take a home test the next day."

"That'll work. You still have my number?"

"Yes. I have that card you gave me."

"And you'll call me—either way."

"Yes, Jason. Of course I will."

Piper tried not to anticipate hearing from Jason again. But she did.

And when he failed to call, she felt let down. It was totally unreasonable of her to feel that way. He'd chased her until he tired of her unwillingness to give him a chance. She couldn't blame him for giving up and leaving her alone.

Really, it was for the best. They had too much chemistry to go the friends-only route. And getting something romantic going with him would be such a bad idea. As soon as her period made its appearance, she would call him and tell him he had nothing to worry about. And that would be it.

But then the day came.

And her period didn't.

She felt like a fool. She never should have agreed to call him if her period was a single day late. After all, she was forty years old. There were a number of reasons her period wouldn't necessarily appear like clockwork every time. She should have insisted on waiting at least a week more before having to contact him.

But she'd named the terms of this agreement and she would stick by them. Tomorrow morning, she would take a home test and then call him to let him know that the test was negative.

So why was she so…on edge about the whole thing?

She felt like a teenager all over again—and not in a good way.

All day long, she kept popping into the restroom just to check for spotting. It was nerve-racking to be so obsessed with a biological function.

She got home at six. Still no period. By eight in the evening, she couldn't stand it anymore. She needed to talk to someone trustworthy, so she gave her mom a call.

Emmaline answered on the second ring. "Hello, my love. How are you?"

"Are you working?" Her mom often painted late into the night.

"Nope. I'm all yours. Talk to me, Piper."

So she went ahead and put it right out there. "My period's late—well, not really late. But it's due today and it hasn't come yet."

As usual, her mom cut right to the point. "Are you saying you have reason to believe you might be pregnant?"

"I suppose it's possible," she grudgingly confessed. "Barely. It was one night last month. I'm not on any kind of birth control."

"But you did use a condom…"

"Yes, of course. We used condoms and one of them broke."

"I see—and one night with whom?"

"You're so nosy, Mom."

"Oh, yes I am." She could hear the shrug in Emmaline's voice. "I am the nosiest."

"Fine. I spent a night with Jason Bravo."

"Wow. I adore Jason."

"Yes, Mom. You've mentioned that."

"He's smart, sensitive and really good with his hands—not to mention he can make beautiful things with a big hunk of wood and a chain saw. Allow me to congratulate you on your excellent taste in one-night stands. I'm so proud of you."

Piper couldn't help but smile. "I knew you would be."

"And, sweetheart, you've always said you wanted children."

"I have, yes. I *do* want a child. I'd just reconciled my-self to the fact that it wasn't going to happen."

"So, then, one way or another, it's all good. If you're not pregnant, life goes on as planned. If you are, every-thing changes and isn't that fabulous?"

"You make it all sound so simple."

"It is simple. Huge. But simple."

When they said good-night twenty minutes later, Piper felt pretty good about everything.

The good feeling didn't last, though. She went to bed and couldn't sleep. At 3:00 a.m., she realized that she needed to get to a pharmacy as soon as one opened and buy herself a home test.

Six hours later, a few minutes after she'd called the li-brary to say she was taking a family day, the doorbell rang.

Her mom, in paint-spattered skinny pants, a big white shirt and polka-dot sneakers, her curly, white-streaked red hair tied back pirate-style with a green satin scarf, greeted her with, "Hello, my love. You look exhausted. Rough night?"

"You could say that."

"It's the not knowing, right? You need to find out."

"I do, yes."

"And that's why I made a quick trip to the State Street Pharmacy." Cheeks dimpling with a proud smile, Emma-line held up the white bag with the drugstore logo on it. "Ten home tests."

Piper blinked at the bag. "Do I need ten?"

"It seemed like a nice, even number—plus, if you doubt the results, you can wait a few days and take another. And another. Until you're satisfied that you are, or you aren't."

"Get in here." Piper grabbed her hand, yanked her inside and hugged her good and tight.

"Let's go upstairs and get started," Emmaline said briskly when Piper finally released her.

"I don't know…"

Her mom frowned. "What? Just come out with it."

"Mom, I love you harder than ever for showing up this morning with just what I needed, but some things I have to do on my own."

Emmaline took Piper's hand and put the bag in it. "You want me to leave?"

"No, I don't."

"How about if I hang out down here while you pee on one of those sticks in the privacy of your en suite?"

"Would you?"

"Of course. You go on up. I'll be right here when you need me."

An hour later, Piper dropped to the little teak stool in the corner of her bathroom and put her head in her hands. By then, three used test sticks littered the counter between the twin sinks.

"I do not believe that this could have happened," Piper moaned into her hands. "A baby…"

I am having Jason Bravo's baby.

"It's okay," she whispered to the bathroom floor. "It's more than okay. I've always wanted a baby…"

It was true. Because the reality of the life inside her? That part was nothing short of astounding. It was so wonderful it felt like it couldn't be real. And that had her feeling slightly queasy.

She picked up one of the used sticks and stared at the

result window. *Pregnant.* Her breath caught again at the enormity of that one word.

A baby. She was going to be a mom.

Doing it alone? Not a problem. It was a giant shock right now, true, but underneath the astonishment, she could already feel joy welling.

A baby.

She'd never realized how much she wanted a child.

Until now. Until it was happening.

A baby, a little person to help grow up. They would be a family of two—well, three, counting her mom.

Emmaline chose that moment to tap on the bathroom door. "Piper? How are you doing in there?"

Tossing the stick back on the counter, Piper put her head in her hands again. Her stomach churned with equal parts shock and joy.

There was another light tap on the door. "It's been over an hour. Just say you're all right, my love."

Swallowing down a big lump of combined terror and excitement, Piper got up, went over there and swung the door wide. "Come on in."

Her mom saw the sticks. "You took three? You're supposed to wait a week between tests for the pregnancy hormones to build up again. Did you read the instructions?"

"I did, yes. And you're right. But after the first one, I was a bit stunned. I kept thinking I had to be sure, somehow. So I took another one. And then another. And guess what? They all three came out the same."

Emmaline picked one up, peered in the little window and let out a whoop of delight. "This one's positive!"

"Exactly."

"So all three…?"

"Yeah, Mom. It looks like I'm pregnant. It really does."

Emmaline beamed at Piper and held out her arms. "Come on, now. Give this future grandma the sugar!"

Piper swayed forward.

Emmaline gathered her close and kissed the side of her head. "This is wonderful news. Wonderful!"

Piper held on tight and breathed in Emmaline's familiar scents of lemony shampoo and mint from the artist's soap she used to wash off stubborn ink and paint. "I can't believe this is happening," she whispered raggedly. "I just can't…"

Her mom took her by the shoulders and looked straight in her eyes. "What? Talk to me. You're not happy?"

Piper blinked in surprise at the question. "Yes! I'm happy. Very. But I'm also kind of wondering if this is all some crazy dream. For years, I've been telling myself that the chance to have a child has passed me by…"

Emmaline took both her hands. "Let's go downstairs. I'll brew you some of that masala chai you love, and you can relax. Catch your breath."

Piper nodded. "Chai. Yes. All right."

Downstairs, Piper took a stool at the island as her mother got busy with the electric kettle. When the tea was ready, they carried their mugs to the living area and sat on the sofa together.

Emmaline got right to the hard part. "How much does Jason know?"

"Well, he was there when the condom broke, so pretty much everything. Except that three home tests just came out positive." She took a careful sip of the hot chai.

"He's young."

"Yes, Mom. He is. Too young for me."

"I didn't say that."

"That doesn't make it any less true."

"Wait. Think again. Look at it this way. It's a fact that women tend to outlive their men. But probably not if the woman is at least a decade older. And ageism is a crock anyway. As long as two people are both functioning adults, more power to them. Jason is a good man. He's very grounded. And he's superhot, too."

Piper tried not to groan. "Mom. Please."

Smiling way too sweetly, Emmaline shrugged. "I'm only trying to make you see that Jason just might make a good match for you."

"No. Wrong. I don't need a good match. I don't even want one. I'm perfectly happy to raise my baby on my own, the same way you did."

"Of course you are, but that doesn't mean you wouldn't be happier with the right man beside you."

"I don't get it. What's up with you? Where is this coming from?"

"You're not me, my love. You really do want to connect."

"As though you don't?"

Her mom smiled so sweetly. "Of course I do."

"You're making zero sense. You have to know that."

"What I'm trying to say is that *you* want a family."

"I have a family."

"You know what I mean. A family that includes a man you can count on, one you adore."

"I can count on myself, my friends—and on you, Mom. I am fully self-supporting. There's nothing a man can give me that I don't already have."

Emmaline smirked. "Well, there's at least one thing that springs instantly to mind."

Piper groaned. "I can't believe you went there."

"Sorry, I couldn't resist." Emmaline put on her sweetest expression. "And back to the main point. We came home to stay when you were nine years old because you wanted friends your age and you wanted a settled-down life in this charming hometown of ours. Don't lie to yourself. You also want a partner in this settled-down life."

"I had a partner. He died."

Emmaline scoffed. "We both know that Walter was a terrible disappointment to you."

Piper gaped. "Wait a minute. I thought you liked Walter!"

"He was a perfectly nice man, but not the man for you. Nothing about your marriage was what a marriage is supposed to be—and don't pretend you don't know what I'm talking about. There was no spark, no passion. You were only going through the motions. And I get it. After Brandon, you—"

"Mom. Please can we *not* talk about Brandon McAdams?"

"Fine. My point is, don't kid yourself. You are not me. You don't want to be a single mom and you *do* want the right man. Yes, you've been disappointed. Twice. But please don't give up now."

Piper wished she might be magically transported to anywhere but here—someplace she wouldn't have to think about the things that had just come out of her mother's mouth. "You never said a word about all this before."

"You weren't pregnant before. Now you need to make important decisions and you should be honest with yourself and with Jason when you do. Piper, you're going to have to tell him."

"Of course I'm going to tell him. Give me a little credit, will you?"

"*When* are you going to tell him?"

"As it happens, I promised I would reach out to him by today. And I will."

"Good. And you should also respond to the request you got from your father. How long has it been since he got in touch with you?"

Piper gulped. "Which time?"

"He's tried to contact you twice?" Emmaline wore a disbelieving frown. At Piper's nod, she asked. "How recently?"

"A few weeks." Piper glared down into her nearly empty mug and wondered when her mother would get off her case. "I never should have let you talk me into signing up with 23andMe in the first place."

"Of course you should have. And you did. And after all these years, you've found your father. He's reached out to you twice now. Reach back."

"It's too late."

"As long as you're both still breathing, it's never too late. And I just don't get it. You know it's not his fault that I had no idea where to find him."

"Of course I know that."

"And you wanted desperately to know all about him when you were younger."

"Well, I'm over it now."

Emmaline pinned her with a hard glare for an endless string of edgy seconds before finally throwing up her hands. "I don't believe you. But be that as it may, even if *you're* over wanting to contact the man who contributed half your DNA, how can you deprive your baby of a grandfather?"

Piper had no comeback for that one. "Okay, Mom. I know you're right—but come on. One huge and intimidating task at a time, okay?"

Emmaline sighed. "Of course." Her tone was conciliatory now. "And I apologize for piling more on your already full plate. Sometimes I do get a bit carried away."

"Yes, you do. But in this case, you're not wrong," Piper said grudgingly.

Emmaline hooked an arm around her and kissed her on the forehead. "More chai?"

"No. I really should call Jason. I guess."

"Could you be more ambivalent?"

She shrugged and answered honestly. "Probably not."

With a low, wry chuckle and a shake of her curly head of hair, Emmaline picked up their empty mugs and carried them to the sink. Piper trailed after her. She felt lost, cast adrift, all her usual calm confidence blown to bits by that one word in three test stick windows.

Her mother put the mugs in the sink and turned to her. "Shall I stay?"

"Thank you. For everything. But no. Reaching out to Jason is another one of those things I need to do on my own."

Emmaline touched her cheek. "You're brave and strong and good." She guided a straight swatch of hair behind Piper's ear. "Beautiful, too."

Piper almost smiled. "Brave? I'm not so sure. But as for the rest of it, I take after my mother." They both reached out for one last hug and then Piper followed her mom to the door.

"Call me," Emmaline commanded. "Whatever you need."

"Thanks, Mom. You're a champion."

Emmaline reached for the doorknob just as somebody knocked. She pulled it wide.

It was Jason, in a crisp Western shirt and dark-wash jeans. He swiped his white hat off his head. "Emmaline. Hello." He spotted Piper behind her mom. She felt an actual *zap*, like an electric shock, as their eyes met.

"Hello, Jason," said Emmaline. "Have we got some news for you…"

Chapter Four

Two minutes later, Emmaline had driven off, leaving Jason and Piper facing each other in her open doorway. He wasn't sure how to proceed here.

"Come in." She gestured him forward into her small entryway and then indicated the coatrack in the corner. "You can hang your hat there." He hooked the hat on a peg and followed her into the great room, which had a fireplace on one wall, light-colored furniture and a quartz-topped island that marked off the kitchen area. "Have a seat." She swept out a hand toward the sofa. "Can I get you—"

"I'm good, thanks." He eased around the wood-topped, iron-framed coffee table and sat.

She perched on the chair across from him. More awkwardness followed. He wasn't sure what to say. She sat there so straight and careful, like she had no more idea where to start with this than he did.

He drank in the sight of her, in old jeans, black Keds and a sage-green T-shirt with Make America Read Again printed just above the soft curves of her breasts. Her face was scrubbed clean of makeup. Her hair, loose and messy, trailed over her shoulders.

Finally, he said, "I, uh, guess I got a little impatient. I should have waited for your call."

She waved a hand. "It's okay. Really. I was about to call *you*."

"Yeah?" That made him smile.

She nodded. "I took a home test this morning—well, three, actually."

Now he sat forward. "And?"

She sucked in a big breath and pushed the words out fast. "I'm pregnant, Jason..." For a moment, the words made no sense. He felt light-headed. She kept on talking. "I mean, I'm completely, ridiculously surprised about this. I keep wondering, how did this happen? I honestly never in a million years..." She kind of ran out of steam about then.

"Piper."

"What?"

And he was on his feet, circling the coffee table, pulling her out of her chair and up into his arms. Miraculously, she didn't object. Instead, with a long sigh, she sagged against him.

He cradled her close and whispered, "We're having a baby."

She stiffened in his hold. "Wait." Her slim hands came up to push at his chest as she craned her head back to meet his eyes. "No..."

He didn't get it. "No, what?"

"Jason, *I'm* having a baby."

Okay, fine. Yeah, *she* was the one having the baby. But he'd helped—and he intended to continue doing so. Unless... "Are you saying you were with someone else?"

A strangled laugh escaped her. "No! Just you. Only you."

He bit the inside of his lip to keep from grinning in relief. But then his urge to smile over this situation vanished. Because if there wasn't some other guy in this equation, then what was she getting at here? "I understand that for the next eight and a half months or so, you'll have to do all the work in this deal. But still, the baby is mine, so we're *both* going to be parents."

She blinked. "Oh! Well, I get that you might feel responsible."

"I am responsible, every bit as much as you are."

"Yes, but I'm just saying, I promise, you don't have to be involved at all."

As if. "Stop it, Piper. Of course I will be involved in raising our baby. This is a lifetime partnership we're talking about here."

Two frown lines appeared between those jade green eyes. "What does that even mean?"

"It means that no matter what happens between you and me, we will always be the parents of this child— both of us."

She pushed harder at his chest. "Please let me go." He dropped his arms to his sides and went back to the sofa. She sat down again, too. "Now," she said. "Let's just… slow down a little here."

"All right."

"I mean, first of all, we don't want to get ahead of ourselves. Maybe I got a false positive today…"

"Three times?"

"I'm just saying that we can't make assumptions or jump to conclusions. Please."

"How many more tests do you plan on taking?"

"Well, I was thinking I would make an appointment with my doctor, get a test there, just to be sure. Maybe next week?"

"Fair enough. I'll go with you."

"Jason, I..." She seemed to run out of words.

He leaned in and braced his elbows on his spread knees. "Be straight with me. Do you honestly have any doubt that you're pregnant?"

She swallowed. Hard. "No. No, I don't. But that doesn't mean we shouldn't be absolutely sure. And really, it's not as if we know each other all that well. We should arrange for a paternity test."

"If I'm the only one you've been with, then I don't see how a paternity test is necessary."

"Jason, I just think that you need to know. For certain."

"I do know for certain." When she scoffed at that, he added, "You're not a liar, Piper. Maybe I don't know you that well on some levels. But I *have* known you for four-teen years. And I know that you are honest. Everyone in town knows that about you. No way you would tell a man you're having his child if you weren't."

She looked so damn miserable. "I just... I guess I as-sumed you wouldn't be that eager to take on the endless responsibilities of being a father."

"Well, you assumed wrong."

She folded her hands together and stuck them between her knees. "I'm sorry. This is a lot, you know—and I've insulted you, haven't I?"

"I'll live. And I get it. Look, we both just found out. It's a shock for me, too." He wanted to comfort her, but he knew better than to try that again at this point. "Do you want me to go?"

She slid him a wary glance and answered carefully, "I would appreciate a little time to...process all this."

"All right." He wanted to ask for her number again but decided against it. She'd refused to give it to him more than once already—and if she failed to reach out, she wouldn't be all that hard to track down. He got to his feet.

She rose, too. "You have your phone with you?"

"Out in my truck, yeah."

"Hold on just a minute?"

"Sure." He waited as she went to the kitchen area and got her cell off the back counter. "I do still have your card," she said, as though to reassure him that she hadn't tossed it in the trash. "But I haven't entered your number yet."

"No problem." He rattled it off.

She typed it into her phone. "Okay. I have you in my contacts. I'll just send you a quick text." Her thumbs flew over the keys. "There. So now you can reach me anytime you, uh, need to."

It lightened his mood a little, that this time she'd given him the number without his even asking. "'Preciate that."

"No problem." She looked at him expectantly.

It took him a moment to realize she was hoping he would go. He headed for the foyer.

"I'll make the appointment with my doctor today," she said, "and text you to let you know where and when."

"Thank you." He grabbed his hat and went out the door.

Once in his truck, he took his phone from the console. She'd texted, It's me, Piper.

He smiled as he put her in his contacts. She was the strangest bundle of contradictions. Forty years old, if he'd done the math correctly, smart and capable and well educated. The kind of person who would always keep her head in a crisis and know what to do in any emergency. At the same time, as a woman, she was wary as a high school virgin at a keg party.

His amusement lasted until he'd rounded the corner

onto the next street. About then, he had to pull to the shoulder, put it in Park and take a few slow, deep breaths.

A baby.

Piper Wallace was having his baby.

He'd been crystal clear that he needed to know if it turned out she was pregnant. But had he actually believed it would happen?

No.

He gripped the wheel to keep his hands from shaking as he decided that he really needed someone to talk to.

A few minutes later, he parked around the corner from Cash Enterprises on Main Street, got out his phone again and texted his second cousin Tyler Ross Bravo. You busy? I'm around the corner from your office.

A minute later, Ty replied, Come on in.

Ty and his dad—the "Cash" of Cash Enterprises—ran the business together. They were mostly in property and land deals.

Ramona Teague, their longtime secretary and receptionist, smiled at Jason when he walked in the door. "Go right on through." She tipped her head toward Ty's office.

Jason tapped on Ty's door. From the other side, his cousin called, "It's open."

When Jason pushed the door wide, Ty was getting up from behind his big desk. They greeted each other with a quick hug and some backslapping. Then Ty gestured toward the sitting area across the room. They got comfortable there.

"Coffee? Something stronger?"

"No. I just need advice."

Ty chuckled. "And you came to me for that?" Divorced from his first wife, Ty had two kids and a fiancée, Sadie

McBride. For a year or two after his divorce, Ty had run a little wild, hooking up with a different woman just about every weekend. But those days were over now. He and Sadie were living together, and Ty was the happiest he'd ever been.

"Yeah, well." Jason was nodding. "You'll be an old married man before you know it. These days, you're downright dependable. I figure you're the one to give me solid feedback when I need it."

"Damn. You make me sound dead boring." Ty was grinning. He shrugged. "Probably because I am. And I like it that way. I would marry Sadie tomorrow, but she wants a summer wedding out at the Rising Sun." The Rising Sun had been in the Bravo family for several generations. It was jointly owned by three Bravo cousins—Ty's dad, Jason's dad and Zach Bravo, who lived on the ranch and ran the Rising Sun Cattle Company. "So then," said Ty. "What's going on?"

Jason thought of Piper. How reserved she could be. She wouldn't want her business on the street. Plus, it was way too soon to tell anyone that she was pregnant. Still, he had to talk to someone and he trusted Ty to keep a confidence. "This conversation has to stay between the two of us."

"As long as it's got nothing to do with Sadie or my kids, you got it. I'm a vault." Ty stretched out an arm along the back of the sofa.

Jason got to the point. "Piper Wallace is pregnant—and it's mine."

His cousin leaned forward, cleared his throat and sat back again. "Well."

Jason groaned. "That's it? That's all you got?"

Ty slanted him a wary glance. "I suppose I need to

admit up front that I already knew something was going on with you and Piper."

Jason did not like the sound of that. "How?"

"You were seen with her at Arlington's a while back. And then Sadie told me that her mom told her that you and Piper had lunch together at Henry's about a week and a half ago."

"You're saying everybody's talking about us?" Piper wouldn't like that. And if she didn't like it, Jason didn't, either.

"No. Everybody is *not* talking about you. It's just that they're bound to notice that you and Piper have been hanging out together. I mean, from what I've heard, she hasn't been out with anyone since her husband died. So it's news that she's seen around town with you, who just happens to be quite a bit younger than she is."

"So what?"

"No judgment—but face it. Nobody would have picked you as a match for the hot librarian."

Jason leveled his coldest stare on his cousin. "Are you *trying* to piss me off?"

Ty put up both hands. "Hold your fire, man. No offense. Lighten up a little."

"Yeah, well, show some respect."

"Got it."

Jason rose, went to the window and looked out at Main Street. A couple of cowhands, a skinny long-haired guy in a ball cap and a woman with a take-out bag from the Stagecoach Grill went by. Still staring out the window, he laid it right out there. "I have a thing for her, okay? I always have. When I was kid, it was a crush, something I never thought would be more than my own secret fantasy. But now, since that night she and I got together at Arlington's, it's turned into something more. I don't care if she's older. I just don't." He turned and faced his cousin. "I care about *her*."

Ty got up and joined him at the window. "You want my take?"

"That's what I'm here for."

"All right, then. The way I see it, more power to you. Yeah, she's a little older than you, but… Hey, man. We've all seen her ass." As Jason considered popping him a good one, Tyler stepped back and put his hands up again. "Honestly, cousin, I mean that in a way of complete respect and admiration. The truth is, I get it. There really is something about her. Come on. You're not the only one who ever had a crush on her."

"Are you telling me that *you*—"

"I'm just saying she made all of us willing to go the library back in the day."

"You are not helping," Jason grumbled. "And right now, I have no clue why I came to you for advice."

Ty laughed out loud then. "Sorry. I never could resist yanking your chain. And we both know I'm no expert on women, let alone on love. Took me way too many years to get it right with Sadie."

"But you did," Jason said. "You finally did. I admire that you worked it out, that you found a way to get what matters. I honestly do."

Ty clapped him on the shoulder. "What can I tell you? Except to say, figure out what you really want, get out of your own damn way and go for it. If Piper's the one for you, show her, make sure she knows it. I mean, no, you can't make a woman love you. But you can take a chance. You can put yourself out there. You can show her who you really are and prove to her that you're there for her, that she can count on you to step up for her no matter what goes down."

Jason let all that sink in for a minute. "Damn. That's really good advice."

Ty gave him a slow smile. "Glad I could help."

Jason did want to find a way to get closer to Piper—and not only as her baby daddy. Too bad he had no idea how to make that happen. After all, aside from the night they met up at Arlington's, she'd resisted every attempt he'd made so far. He returned to the Double-K that day with no clear idea of what his next move should be.

That night, he ate at the main house with the family. It was him, his mom, his dad and Joe. His sister, Sarah Ellen, was in Ohio, a student at Ohio State. She'd found a good-paying summer job there, so she wouldn't be home much this year except maybe for Christmas, or whenever she could steal a few days for a visit.

He loaded up his plate and dug in. The food, slow-cooker chicken, melted off the bone. And he'd always liked his mom's garlic mashed potatoes.

It was relaxing, listening to the murmur of voices around the table. Being with the family helped to take his mind off the phone in his shirt pocket that hadn't rung once all day.

He thought of the carving he was working on, a ten-foot-tall grizzly bear commissioned by a guy who owned a dude ranch in Jackson Hole. When it came to chain saw art, bears were real moneymakers.

"You're quiet, Jay," said his mom. Meggie May Kane Bravo was like that, observant. Attentive to him, to his siblings and his dad. And she could work circles around all of them. The Double-K had come down to her through her father. "Everything okay?" she asked.

"It's all good, Mom," he lied. "Pass me the chicken, please?"

She gave him that look, the one that said she knew he had something on his mind. But she didn't press. She handed him the platter and he helped himself to more.

He'd just picked up his fork again when his phone buzzed. As a rule, phones were forbidden at the dinner table.

Too bad. This was a special situation—or so he hoped. He didn't go so far as to check to see who'd texted him while he was sitting right there at the table. He might be a grown man, but in Meggie Bravo's house, even grown men lived by her rules.

Instead, he sent her an apologetic glance and said, "Sorry, Mom. Excuse me, I need to check this."

To his left, his dad was hiding a smile.

His brother muttered out of the side of his mouth, "We got a damn rule-breaker around here…"

Meggie held Jason's gaze for a moment. "All right," she said at last in a tone of great patience.

He tucked his napkin in at the side of his plate and pushed back his chair. Out on the front porch, he pulled the phone from his pocket and smiled when he saw he had a text from Piper.

I have an appointment with my doctor on Thursday at four in the afternoon.

He called her.

She answered on the second ring. "Hello, Jason."

"Hey. Just got your text. How about if I pick you up and we go together?"

"Better not. I'll be leaving from the library. And really, there's no need for you to be at the appointment anyway. I'll call you Thursday night—but I won't have the results then. It takes a couple of days for the lab to run the test. We probably won't know until Monday."

He almost let it be, almost agreed that he would wait for her call. But he couldn't quite keep himself from asking, "Are you embarrassed to be seen going to your doctor with me?"

"I…" A soft sigh escaped her. "Jason, I'm sorry. I should be braver. Believe me, I know that, given who raised me." She had it right about that. Emmaline Stokely could not have cared less what fools said behind her back.

"So you're nervous about it, about everybody talking?"

"I am. After all, I'm the director now. People have… expectations of the library director."

"You're good at your job. Your personal life is your own."

"I know, but—"

"Look, Piper. Chances are, they're all going to find out anyway. Might as well just go ahead and do what we need to do. Sneaking around will only make the situation worse. It's not anyone's business but ours and everyone else will just have to get over it."

"You're right. I know it."

"Piper, it's my baby, too." He said it gently, as a reminder. "I really do want to be there with you. I want to be at every doctor's appointment. My cousin Ty missed the ultrasounds for both of his kids. I'm not missing those. And I'm going with you to the birthing classes, to all of it. And when the baby comes, I'll be your coach.

"That's why there's no way around it, people are going to know eventually—that you're having a baby and that your baby is mine."

She said nothing for several seconds. He kept his mouth shut with effort. Finally she chuckled. It was a soft, rueful sound. "You couldn't just be one of those guys who's happy to walk away, now could you?"

"If I was one of those guys, you wouldn't have gone home with me that night."

"Hmm. Fair point."

He said, "You do know the blood test result is highly unlikely to be any different than the home test you took."

"Yes. I know. But it's very early. We don't know what might happen. Something could so easily go wrong and then we'll have gotten everyone talking when no one ever had to know."

"And then you would be, what? Relieved?" He kept his tone neutral, but it took effort.

"No! No, I wouldn't be relieved. I meant what I said that night we were together. I never in a million years expected to get pregnant, but I want this baby, I do. So much." He could hear the yearning in her voice. It did his heart good.

"I want our baby, too. Please let me go with you to the doctor."

Again, she hesitated. But when she did speak, she gave him the answer he needed. "All right. Pick me up at the library Thursday at a quarter to four."

Piper was just about to leave her office Thursday afternoon when the text came through from Jason.

I'm here. Waiting by the circulation desk.

She reminded herself that he was going to be involved and she needed to stop worrying about what people might think.

On my way, she replied.

Shrugging into her lightweight jacket and hooking her purse on her shoulder, she drew herself up to her full five-foot-five-in-practical-pumps and headed for reception.

He was right there waiting, heartbreaker-handsome in a fresh-looking plaid shirt tucked into dark-wash jeans. He had his hat in his hand and his dark hair was wet from a recent shower.

Behind the circulation desk, Marnie Fox, one of the assistants, pushed a stack of children's books across the desk toward the little girl on the other side. "Enjoy," she said.

"Thank you," said the child and gathered the books into her arms.

Marnie turned to Jason and asked way too hopefully, "What can I help you with?"

About then, he spotted Piper. "Thanks," he said to Marnie. "I was waiting for Piper and here she is."

Marnie blinked. "Oh! Well, I see…"

Which was a perfectly normal reaction, Piper reminded herself. And even if it hadn't been, so what? Jason had it right. People would think what people would think. Piper would keep her chin up and do what had to be done, same as always.

Piper nodded at Marnie. "See you tomorrow."

"Have a good night." Marnie waved as Piper and Jason started down the wide hallway to the main entrance.

Piper's doctor, Levi Hayes, was new in town. He'd taken over for old Dr. Crandall, who had finally retired.

Piper checked in with the friendly receptionist. Then she and Jason took a seat in the waiting room with a couple of young moms and three kids who were playing with blocks at a low central table.

One of the women smiled and nodded at her. Piper was pretty sure she was a regular at the library.

Jason leaned close. "Nervous?"

"A little."

"Are you just getting the blood drawn?"

"That's about the size of it. I think there's a brief consultation with Dr. Hayes."

"Want me to go in with you?" His eyes, more gray than blue in the bright waiting room light, seemed full of mischief right then.

"I think I can manage that part on my own."

He didn't push. Apparently, just being there in Dr. Hayes's office with her was enough for him right now. It wasn't as though having blood drawn was an event a prospective father longed to witness.

And really, it was kind of nice having him here. Now that he'd pushed her to live her brand-new pregnancy out in the open, she found that a lot of her nervous tension and worry had dissipated. It was the right way to go.

She touched his hand. He met her eyes.

"Thanks," she said. "For keeping after me until I agreed you could come with me today."

"You're welcome." He leaned closer. "After we're done here, how about getting something to eat? We can go to the Grill or to Arlington's. Or drive up to Sheridan if you'd rather."

He smelled amazing, of soap and something woodsy. *We are doing this out in the open*, she reminded herself.

She was going to be a mom and Jason wanted to be their baby's dad. He intended to be a real dad, the kind who was there for his child. That her baby would have a real dad was a good thing—a wonderful thing, something she'd never had as a child.

"Let's go to the Grill," she said.

"Sounds good to me."

It was only a little past five when Piper and Jason arrived at the Grill.

They got a small table by the big window in front. As they ate, she asked him about himself. He said he'd always wanted to live and work on the Double-K. "It's a good life, a healthy life. You get up early and you work hard and what you have you know you helped to build with your own two hands."

"Did you go away to college?"

"Yeah. I went to Santa Monica College in Southern California. It's a two-year community college. I took mostly art classes and got to spend a lot of time with my grandma Sharilyn. She's my dad's mom. She lives in Los Angeles with her second husband. Hector—the second husband—is a real sweetheart. He's nothing like Grandma Sharilyn's first husband, my dad's father, who was known as Bad Clint."

"So you're saying, your grandfather was as bad as his name implies?"

"According to my dad, he was the worst."

"You never met him?"

"Nope. Bad Clint Bravo died of blood poisoning after being bitten in a bar fight when my dad was fourteen."

"That must have been hard on your dad."

"He doesn't talk a lot about his father, but I think he was mostly relieved when Bad Clint died."

"So then, your grandmother ended up raising your dad alone?"

"No. My dad went to live with my great-grandfather. Then, when my dad grew up, he moved to LA and became a private investigator. My mother went after him there."

"You mean, she went to Los Angeles to find him."

"That's right. The way they both tell it, she finally convinced him they were made for each other. They've been happily married for almost thirty years."

"Well, all right, then. Here's to your mom and dad." She raised her glass of sparkling water.

He tapped it with his.

When they left the restaurant, he asked, "Do you need to get your car at the library?"

"No, I knew you would be picking me up, so I walked to work."

He drove her home. She started to invite him in, but then kept her mouth shut about that. They probably shouldn't get too carried away with this co-parenting thing. It was very early days.

But she did have one point she needed to get his agreement on. Unbuckling her seat belt, she turned toward him in her seat.

His dark eyebrows drew together. "You have that look."

She pulled back a little. "Which look is that?"

"You're about to say something you're not sure I'll go for."

A goofy squeak of laughter escaped her. She shook her head. "How did you guess?"

"So then it's true?"

"You didn't answer my question."

He gave her a one-shouldered shrug. "You didn't answer mine."

She put up both hands. "Fine. It's like this. I don't want to tell anyone about the baby, not for a while yet. It still hardly seems real to me and, well, most people wait to spread the word for at least a couple of months. Usually three months when they're in my situation."

He shot her an oblique sort of glance. "You have a situation?"

"Yes, I do. I brought home some books from the library, and I've been researching online, learning everything I can about pregnancy and childbirth. My age is a factor. It can't be ignored. Being over thirty-five makes me what they call *of advanced maternal age.*"

"Wow. No kidding?" He seemed kind of amused.

But she wasn't joking. "I'm completely serious. In some of my reading, they used the term *geriatric pregnancy.* I can't decide which description is worse, but whatever words you use, this pregnancy is considered high risk." She put a protective palm against her flat belly.

"Piper." He said her name almost tenderly. As she lifted her palm from her stomach, he claimed it.

"What?" she demanded as he rubbed his thumb slowly across the back of her hand. It felt good, that light touch of his. It soothed her. She prompted, "Just say whatever's on your mind."

He looked at her so steadily. "My mom was thirty-five when she had me—and even older when she had Joe and Sarah. A lot of older women have successful pregnancies that result in healthy babies."

She nodded as his thumb continued to brush back and

forth over her skin. She felt so close to him right then, intimate with him in a way she couldn't remember ever being with any man before. Like they were connected somehow, as though they shared a mutual understanding, the kind that made it possible to communicate without using words.

Thoughts of that one night they'd shared filled her head. It wasn't that long ago. But right now, it felt like forever ago. She wanted to sway a little closer to him, lift her face to his. She longed to feel the sweet, hot pressure of his mouth on hers…

Bad idea, she reminded herself.

Carefully, she eased her hand from his hold.

What were they talking about?

Right. He'd said his mother was close to Piper's age when she'd had both of his siblings…

"You make a valid point," she agreed. "I'm in excellent health and I plan to take good care of myself throughout this pregnancy. Dr. Hayes said that as long as I take good care of myself, this pregnancy should be uneventful. But I still think we should wait until I'm through the first trimester before we start telling everyone I'm pregnant."

"I get it. Agreed."

Relief made her smile. "Whew. Thank you."

"Don't thank me yet," he warned, that beautiful smile of his reminding her again of all the foolish things she shouldn't do—like jump into his lap and wrap herself around him or grab his hand and drag him out of the pickup, into her house and straight to her bedroom. But then he added, "I have something I want from you."

Those hot, sexy feelings? So inappropriate. They were supposed to be talking about the important stuff now. And judging from his watchful expression, whatever he wanted from her was probably something she would be reluctant to give.

She gulped. "I'm listening."

He braced one arm on the wheel and the other across the back of her seat. "We need to get to know each other, you and me. We need to start developing a relationship—and please don't give me that look."

"What look?"

"The *no way am I doing that* look. Think about it," he coaxed. "This is not about just you and me anymore."

"Frankly, for the next few months, it *is* about you and me."

"But we need to consider how it's going to work when we finally have to tell my family and your friends and colleagues at the library that you're having a baby and I'm the baby's father."

"It's not rocket science, Jason. We can just, you know, be discreet and play it by ear."

"Be discreet? Piper, I'm going to be there when the baby's born. I'm going to be there for both of you from now on. I'm going to be a hands-on dad. My kid is never going wonder if his dad wanted him—or her."

"I get it, I do. And I think it's admirable of you to step right up like this. I agree that we'll work together. As co-parents. But honestly, we can figure that out as we go. It's not something we have to get overly concerned with right this minute."

"Maybe not when it comes to your mom."

"What does my mom have to do with it?"

"Your mom already knows about the baby. She and I get along great. As of now, she's the only one who isn't going to get a big shock when we finally let everyone else know what's going on." Suddenly, his gaze slid away. "And that reminds me. You should know that I told my cousin Ty about the baby."

It took effort, but she managed to ask quietly, "You told Ty Bravo that I'm pregnant with your baby?"

"I did, yeah. I needed a little advice, okay? And you don't have to worry. Ty's not going to go spreading the news all over town. He'll keep his mouth shut."

"Well, I hope so—and honestly, I just don't get it. Why would you tell your cousin?"

A muscle twitched in his sculpted jaw. "Come on, Piper. *You* told your mom."

"Okay, whatever." She blew out a hard breath. "So... you're saying you've changed your mind and you want to tell everybody about the baby right away?"

"No, that's not what I'm saying."

"Then, what?"

"I'm thinking, wouldn't it be better if it doesn't come out of the blue? Wouldn't it be better if it was more than a one-night stand and a broken condom?"

"Jason, it is what it is."

"I know, but it *could* be more. And why shouldn't it be more? If you and I were to start spending more time together, people would get used to seeing us as a couple. We might even find we like being together, that it's something we want to do more of."

She felt like Alice, lost in Wonderland. She'd dropped through a rabbit hole and suddenly down was up—and up was down. "But we're *not* a couple."

"I know. But we could be if you would only give us a chance. I'm asking for time with you, Piper. I want to see if we can have something good together, you and me. Maybe you'll find out we make a good team in every way."

"What are you saying?"

"Fine. I'll just lay it right out there."

"Yes! Please do."

"We need to date as parents-to-be."

Her head was spinning. "No."

"Yeah. We need to learn about each other, to come to trust each other. Because when it comes to the baby, we are going to be a team for the rest of our lives."

Well, now. That was pretty terrifying. And probably true, given how determined he was to be a real father to his child. But what good would their dating do? It seemed to her that there was a clear boundary between co-parenting and coupling up. She had no intention of crossing that line.

Did she?

No. No, of course not.

And yet, she felt so drawn to him. Even with her relationship phobia and their thirteen-year age gap that was bound to get tongues wagging, she did like him. A lot. How could she not?

He was thoughtful and kind. And way too attractive for her peace of mind. Since their night together, she couldn't stop thinking about all the sexy things they'd done, couldn't stop fantasizing about doing those things again. She remembered the sweetness and heat of his kisses, the feel of his strong body pressing close to hers…

"Well?" he asked.

She just stared at him. Because she had nothing. She needed a minute.

A whole bunch of minutes…

Chapter Five

Jason got the message. It was obvious from the look on her face that she wasn't buying what he was selling.

She asked, her tone carefully controlled, "You're serious. You want us to date because that will be best for the baby and will also get everyone in town accustomed to seeing us as a team?"

"Yeah—and don't forget that I just plain want to get closer to you."

"Jason, you've already asked me out. I turned you down, remember?" She said it so gently. Like she was trying really hard not to hurt his feelings.

He wanted to laugh and put his fist through the windshield, both at the same time. "Of course I remember. You shut me down every chance you get."

"That's not fair."

"Maybe not. But it's true."

She folded her arms under those beautiful breasts of hers. "Fine. I've shut you down. I said from the first that I wasn't interested in developing a relationship—with any guy. But now that there's a baby, you expect me to suddenly change my mind?"

Oh, hell, yes, he thought. But he said, "I just want you to think about it. I want you to give us a chance. We need time to know each other better and the people we care about need to see us together, to see that we *like* each other, that we get along, that we understand each other. That way, in a couple of months when we share our big news, they'll already know that we're good together, that we can work together."

She stared at him like she could see right through him—and she probably could. "Your logic is skewed. This isn't about other people. This is about you and me and the baby. Forget this dating idea," she said flatly.

Was he giving up? Not a chance. "Look at it this way. I want to spend time with you. We don't have to call it dating. Think of it as starting to learn how to be parents together. Consider it a chance to get everyone used to us being a couple before they find out there's a baby on the way. Call it becoming friends if that works for you. Two weeks ago, at Henry's, you did say that we could be friends."

"And you got up and walked out."

Busted. "So shoot me. I wanted more. I still want more."

"Jason…"

"Just hear me out. I'm not expecting you to be my girl. I'm only asking you to give us a chance to get to know each other better by being together—getting dinner, hanging out at your house or mine, taking long walks, sharing a picnic. I want us to find out where a little time together takes us."

She had a grim look, like she was lining up fresh arguments, finding a slew of new ways to tell him no. But before she could come back with more reasons why his plan didn't work for her, a curly-haired woman strolled by the truck on Piper's side.

It was Marilee Lewis, who ran a pet grooming and

boarding business out of her cute Victorian house several blocks away. Marilee had two perky Pomeranians on the leash. She spotted Piper through the passenger window and waved. Piper waved back.

It was after seven by then. And Jason was getting nowhere. They were having a baby together and the chemistry between them was palpable.

And yet Piper wouldn't give an inch.

He wanted to ask what had happened to her that had made her so completely unwilling to give a man even the ghost of a chance.

But he knew damn well that he wouldn't be getting an answer to that question tonight. "Listen, just think about what I said, will you?"

Her slim fingers were already gripping the door handle. "I will."

"I'll walk you to the door."

"No. It's fine. Good night."

It took effort, but he stayed in his seat. "Don't be a stranger. Give me a call."

She pushed the door open. "Good night, Jason." She swung her feet to the ground.

He watched her go up her front walk and let herself inside.

Only then did he start up the truck and head for home.

Friday, Piper had an afternoon coffee date with Starr Tisdale at the Perfect Bean, a cute little place two blocks off Main on Pine Street. Starr owned the local newspaper, the *Medicine Creek Clarion*. Piper got together with her at least once a month. Not only did Piper enjoy hanging out with Starr, but the regular coffee dates allowed her to run down the list of upcoming events at the library. Starr always put out the word on library events ahead of time and then wrote articles about them afterward.

That day, Starr brought her toddler, Cara Grace, a quiet baby who was usually happy to sit in her stroller and play with whatever toys Starr had brought along for her.

This time, Cara seemed to recognize Piper. She held out her plump baby arms and cried, "Hi, hi!"

Piper glanced at Starr for permission. As soon as she got the nod, she turned her chair sideways and took that sweetheart in her lap.

"You are so gorgeous," Piper whispered to the little one—and she was. Cara took after her mom. She had thick black hair and stunning violet eyes.

The baby giggled and offered Piper her stuffed turtle. Once Piper had kissed the toy, she handed it back.

"Stay right there," Starr instructed. "Masala chai as usual?"

"Yes, please."

Starr went to the counter and came back with their drinks and a muffin for each of them. When Cara spotted the treats, she cried gleefully, "Yum-yum!" So they took turns feeding her bites, which she ate surprisingly neatly, sitting there on Piper's lap.

"It's so satisfying eating muffins with a hometown hero," teased Starr.

Piper groaned. "Stop it."

Starr smirked and rubbed it in. "Everyone loved the way you came to Bobby Trueblood's rescue at the Lego event."

Piper sipped her chai. "And *you* know you really didn't need to put that in the *Clarion*."

"Oh, yes I did."

"Anyone could have done that."

"Piper. *You* did that. We all take first aid, but how many of us leap into action when the moment comes? Very few. The citizens of Medicine Creek salute you." Starr raised her coffee cup.

Piper groaned. "Enough with that."

Starr shrugged—and finally let it be.

As they chatted, Piper kept thinking that Starr could always be trusted to keep a secret. She would be the perfect person to confide in. And Piper really did need to talk to someone about her unexpected pregnancy and Jason's out-there idea that they should date for the sake of the baby.

But she kept her mouth shut. After all, she and Jason had an agreement. Plus, Starr just happened to be yet another of Jason's cousins. Her dad was Zach Bravo, who ran the Bravo family ranch, the Rising Sun.

Small-town life. Everybody knew everybody—and half the time they were related.

A little later, when Starr went up to the counter to get Piper another chai and more coffee for herself, Piper looked down and saw that Cara had fallen asleep right there in her lap. The little girl had her arm around her stuffie and her chin on her chest. Her thick, black eyelashes made perfect fans against her plump cheeks.

It felt good, to cradle her warm little body, to imagine how, sometime next January, Piper would have her own baby to hold. The idea both thrilled and terrified her. She would follow in her grandmother's footsteps, having her first—and no doubt only—baby at forty-one.

Starr returned with their drinks. Piper sipped her chai leaning sideways over the table, taking extra care that none of it dripped on the sleeping child.

"You look great with a baby in your lap," Starr observed in a half whisper.

"I *feel* great with a baby in my lap." She glanced down at Cara's shining black curls. "She's just a bundle of wonderful, this little girl."

When she looked up again, her friend asked, "Ever think about having one of your own?"

She answered quietly—and honestly. "I do, yes."

"It could still happen."

Piper didn't want to lie—but she didn't want to break her agreement with Jason, either. "Wouldn't that be something?"

"You would make a terrific mom."

Piper didn't know what to say. Starr fell silent, too.

Piper tried not to ask, but somehow the words escaped anyway. "Okay, what's on your mind?"

"I probably shouldn't bring this up…"

"Just say it," Piper commanded.

Starr sipped her coffee. "So." She set the cup carefully back in its saucer. "You and my cousin Jason at Arlington's together on a recent Friday night…"

Piper went ahead and rolled her eyes. "Does everyone in town know about that?"

Starr thought the question over. "Well. Not *everyone*."

Piper brushed a featherlight kiss on the crown of Cara's head as she once again considered how much to say. "Jason's a great guy."

"That's right. He is. A hard worker. A magician with a chain saw. And solid, you know? The kind of guy you can count on. You two could be good together."

Piper glanced up from the sleeping Cara and into Starr's eyes. For several seconds, neither of them said a word.

Starr broke the silence. "Anytime you need to talk, I'm here. You know that, right?"

Piper nodded. "Thank you."

"As I said, anytime."

The weekend crawled by. Piper kept worrying that her period might start. She imagined she felt that familiar heaviness in her lower belly. More than once she checked for spotting. When there was none, a wave of relief washed through her.

A baby would change her life dramatically—and in a lot of challenging ways. But not being pregnant, after all?

For her, that would be harder. Like the death of hope, somehow.

Already, in a matter of days since she'd taken those three home tests, she'd accepted her baby as part of her future, as a major component of what made her life worthwhile.

She got the call from Dr. Hayes's nurse on Monday at three. As it happened, Piper was alone in her office at the time. The nurse said the test was positive.

Piper replied, "Great. Can you hold on just a moment?"

"Of course."

Piper put the phone on mute, dropped it on her desk and then ran around the room fist-pumping and silently screaming, *Yes! Yes! Yes! Yes!*

Because it was happening. It was on! She really was pregnant. The dream she'd never had the guts to actively pursue was coming true anyway.

As soon as she hung up, she called Jason.

He answered with, "Well?"

"The blood test was positive. We're still having a baby."

He said nothing. Had he hung up?

"Uh, Jason?"

"Right here. Sorry. Piper…" He sounded tense—had he suddenly decided that he didn't want to be a dad right now, after all?

"What?" she demanded, her heart sinking at the same time as she reminded herself that he had every right to change his mind and she would have no problem doing this all on her own. "What is it?" She kept her voice level with effort. "Just say it."

He made a rough sound, low in his throat. "It's only that I'm so glad, I don't know what the hell to say."

Relief rolled through her. It made her knees feel weak—and not for any silly romantic reason. No. It was because she'd already gotten used to thinking of him as her partner in this. In a strictly co-parenting capacity, of course. And because it was better for the baby to have a dad who wanted her.

Piper laughed. It was a strange, strangled sort of sound that made her feel way too vulnerable. "I hear you," she said firmly. "I completely understand."

"Good." And then he asked, "When can I see you again?"

She didn't even hesitate. "Tonight. My house. Six thirty?"

"I'll bring takeout. Italian?"

"That sounds great."

"Flowers?" Piper smiled at him as she greeted him at the door.

Jason imagined pulling her close and kissing her for a very long time. But that probably wouldn't go over well.

Plus, he had his hands full. "I saw them as I was driving by that new flower shop on Gartner Street." He held out the big bouquet. "I thought of you."

She tried to look stern. "You shouldn't have done that."

"What?" He played it clueless for all he was worth. "You don't like flowers?"

She took them. He stepped back and admired the view. Damn, she looked fine in a calf-length skirt and a silky knit top. Her feet were bare, slim and pale, her toes painted red.

When he looked up, she was smiling. "I love flowers," she said. "Thank you."

"You're welcome. I also brought dinner, as promised." He flashed the two bags of takeout in his left hand.

"I appreciate that." She stepped back. "Come on in." He followed her across the living room and on to the kitchen area. "Just put the food on the counter," she said. He set the take-out bags next to the cooktop and she stuck the bouquet under his nose. "Would you hold this just for a minute?"

"Sure." He took the flowers again, and she went on tiptoe to bring down a vase from the cupboard.

She turned to the sink and filled the vase with water. Her red hair flowed down her back past her shoulders, so shiny, so sleek. "Here…" Reclaiming the flowers, she removed the cellophane wrapping and stuck them in the vase. "Lilies, tulips, hyacinth and carnations. All my favorites." She set the arrangement on one end of the central island.

And to hell with restraint. He made his move. "Hey." Catching her hand, he reeled her in slowly, giving her time to pull away.

But she didn't pull away. Those green eyes went wide, and her mouth went so soft.

"So. It's official," he said. "We are having a baby."

"Yes. Yes, we are."

"You'll be an amazing mom."

"I hope so…"

"I know so." He lowered his lips to hers.

Her sigh was all he needed to hear. He gathered her closer and she slid her hands up over his chest and onto his shoulders. When he deepened the kiss, she let him, her mouth opening beneath his, her fingers straying to brush the back of his neck and thread up into his hair. She tasted so good, sweet and fresh and way too tempting.

He nipped at her lower lip, testing the soft, giving flesh. She let out the cutest little moan. So he pulled her even closer, wrapped his arms around her even tighter.

The scent of her filled his head. She surged up onto her toes, pressing against him, her body curving into him, making him hard for her, making him burn for more of her…

With a low, regretful sound, she broke the kiss. He loosened his hold but didn't let go. "Co-parents," she reminded him in a husky whisper, her face still tipped up.

He pressed his forehead to hers. "Right…" He tried to sound regretful for stepping over the line. But he regretted nothing—except that he probably wouldn't get to kiss her again tonight. The tilt of her pretty chin and the resolve in her eyes told him he'd better keep his hands to himself from now on.

"I got Caesar salads and veal piccata," he said. "I hope that's okay."

"Perfect."

She dished up the food and they sat at the table near the French doors leading out to a back deck and a small, fenced yard. The bit of sky beyond the fence was clear blue. For a few minutes, they ate in silence.

Then he said, "So what's next, baby-wise?"

"Well, Dr. Hayes says I'm in excellent health." She spoke briskly, and she seemed so young right then, like a very good student, repeating what she'd learned in class that day. "He said what all doctors say to pregnant ladies— that I should get plenty of rest, try to keep my stress levels low, eat lots of fruits and vegetables and take the prenatal vitamins he recommended."

He wished he'd known her when she was a kid. He would bet she'd been curious and determined—and earnest, too, like right now. Earnest and a little bit awkward. No doubt adorably so.

She added, "Oh! I almost forgot. The first ultrasound— the early one I need because I'm over thirty-five—is four weeks from today, June 10, at eight in the morning, up in Sheridan at the hospital."

"I'll go with you."

"Okay." She cut a bite of veal and chewed it slowly. When she swallowed, she shot him a quick glance—not nervous, really. But maybe unsure.

He set down his fork and had a sip of the beer she'd poured for him. "Whatever's on your mind, just say it. I can take it."

She wrinkled her nose. "I'm that obvious?"

"Just tell me."

She drew a slow breath. "So your cousin Starr and I are friends. We get together for coffee often. We met up this afternoon. She'd heard about you and me meeting up at Arlington's that night in April."

"That surprises you?"

"No. I just find it ironic."

"What?"

"I was people-watching myself that night, remember?"

"I do, yeah."

"But I wasn't paying any attention to who might be watching me, though I suppose I should have been."

He reached across the table and put his hand over hers. "Do you think you did something wrong?"

She pulled her hand away and sat up a little straighter. "Absolutely not."

"Good. Because you didn't. *We* didn't. You should know, though, that Ty mentioned the same thing."

"That people saw us at Arlington's?"

"I'm not sure of his exact words, but yeah. Ty already knew that we'd been together at Arlington's that night. And I wasn't surprised that he knew. People talk. They always have."

"And now we've probably been seen at the Grill, too."

"That's true."

"*And* sitting out in your pickup afterward."

"Come on, Piper. We're single adults. Where's the problem?"

"Me," she said. "The problem is me."

He didn't get it. "Okay, you lost me there."

"Think about it, Jason. My mother never met a rule she wouldn't break. But as for me, I've never done anything in this town that anyone would ever gossip about—until recently, with you."

He studied her face. "I can't tell. Are you proud of yourself for being so good for so long? Or disappointed that you didn't get out and have more fun?"

She took a moment to consider his question. "I'm not

sure. Maybe a little of both. This whole thing with you has made me want to be braver."

"Braver? I like that."

"Well, good. But the age difference is a big deal to some people—especially if it's the woman who's older."

"It's not a big deal to me, Piper."

"But we're not talking about you. We're talking about everyone else in town. I mean, last Thursday you said we should date."

"And you said no way."

"Wrong. I said I would think about it."

"You only said you'd think about it so you could get away from me after Marilee Lewis spotted you in my truck."

"Okay, that's true," she conceded reluctantly. "But as it happens, I *have* given the idea some thought, and I've changed my mind."

"You have?"

"Yes. And I think you're right."

It was exactly what he'd been hoping for. "Did you just say that you think *I'm* right?"

"Don't be smug, Jason."

He suppressed a chuckle. "Sorry."

"No, you're not." The look on her face made him want to grab her and kiss her again. But somehow he managed to keep his hands to himself. She went on, "The thing is, eventually there will be talk about us anyway. We might as well take control of the narrative. And that's why I've come around to your point of view. I think we *should* date."

"Take control of the narrative." He nodded. "Yeah. I like that. A lot. Let's start with this weekend. Saturday night I want you to come to dinner with my family at the Double-K."

She blinked. "Wait. Jason. Isn't it kind of early for dinner with the parents?"

"Considering that you're already having my baby, no. Think about it. We'll be telling them about the baby in a matter of weeks. I want my family to start getting to know you *now*."

She set down her fork. "I don't know. It could be really awkward. I think it's better just to hold off on dinner with your parents until we're ready to tell them what's really going on."

"No. It's better that they be around you right now, that they start getting to know you. Look, *I* already know *your* mom. She and I get along great. I want you to know my folks, too. I really do. I want you to know them *before* it gets to be all about the baby."

"Yeesh."

"Hey." He took her hand and wove their fingers together. "It's just dinner." She looked away, but then she met his eyes again. He coaxed, "I know you'll like them."

She made a soft, thoughtful sound. "I've met your mom once or twice. And I did like her. She comes into the library now and then. She seems friendly and outgoing."

"She's great, I promise you." He brought her hand to his lips and kissed it. "Say you'll come out to the ranch with me Saturday."

Beneath the light dusting of freckles, her cheeks had flushed the prettiest shade of pink. She grumbled, "You know, you really are far too charming for my peace of mind."

"Was that a yes?"

Her gaze slid away. "Oh, all right."

He kissed her hand again. "All right, what?"

She glared at him—but then she sighed. "All right, Jason. Saturday night, I'll meet your parents."

Chapter Six

That night, Jason had trouble sleeping. He'd convinced Piper to come to dinner Saturday and now he needed to make sure the whole thing went off smoothly. He wanted to guarantee that everyone got along, that Piper liked his mom and dad, and that they welcomed her with open arms.

In hindsight, maybe he should have approached his parents first, made sure that Saturday dinner would work for them, though he couldn't see why it wouldn't. They ate at home most nights.

But what if Saturday just happened to be one of those times when they went to visit Sonny and Farrah down in Buffalo? Or maybe his dad was taking his mom out. That didn't happen too often, but now and then the two of them drove up to Sheridan to a quiet little Mexican place they liked there.

In the morning, he felt grouchy and tired from stewing all night—and also pissed off at himself for getting all tied in knots about this. He was acting like some silly kid, wanting to introduce his special girl to the family and not having a clue how to go about it.

He dragged through morning chores. Then he ate breakfast in the main house with his mom and dad sitting right there at the table with him—and failed to make a peep about Piper joining them on Saturday night.

His mom gave him funny looks. She knew he had something on his mind. But she also understood him, which meant she probably figured he would talk about it when he was ready.

After the meal, Joe and their mom rode out to check on the stock. Jason helped his dad repair one of the tractors. Around noon, he clicked his tongue for Kenzo, who got up from snoozing on the dirt floor of the tractor shed and followed him to his cabin and on through to the workshop in back.

Jason threw up the big door to let the sun in and got to work on a new carving of an Arabian rearing up from the tall, thick stump of a black walnut tree. It calmed him to concentrate on coaxing the horse from the dense wood. He found the muffled scream of the saw through his earmuffs downright soothing.

Yeah, he needed to go talk to his mom about dinner on Saturday. And he would. Very soon.

All that day, Piper felt anxious.

She never had trouble keeping her cool with library patrons. It was part of the job, after all.

That day, though, she wanted to say rude things to every single person who dared to ask her even the simplest, most innocent question. It got worse as the hours crawled by and Jason had yet to reach out, to let her know what Meggie and Nate Bravo had said when he proposed that he bring Piper to meet them on Saturday night.

Piper hadn't even wanted to go. But he'd kept after her

till she caved and said yes. Now, the more she stewed over it, the more it seemed like a bad, bad idea.

It wasn't as though she and Jason were really a couple. They were future co-parents.

Co-parents. She kept repeating the word in her head—*co-parents*, reminding herself that, though he was an amazing man, and she couldn't stop thinking about him, they weren't a couple—this wasn't that.

Co-parents. It was what they were and what they would remain.

At a little after three, Helen Linwood demanded to speak with "that new director." As if Helen didn't know Piper's name.

Today of all days, the feisty octogenarian was the last person Piper wanted to talk to. She almost instructed Libby at the circulation desk to tell Mrs. Linwood that the director was unavailable. After all, Helen would only be complaining about the same thing she always grumbled about.

But then Piper reminded herself that Helen Linwood was entitled to the respect and understanding every person who used the library deserved. The library and everyone who worked there provided an important public service paid for by the people of the community. When a patron wanted to speak with the library director, the director said yes if at all possible.

"Send her to my office, please," Piper instructed.

Libby sighed. "She's already on her way."

Helen Linwood, who wore a red straw hat on her curly silver head, a faded jean jacket over khaki pants and a pair of enormous wire-rimmed glasses, pushed open Piper's door without knocking. "Piper. There you are."

Piper rose. "Hello, Helen." She gestured at the guest chairs on the far side of her desk. "Have a seat." Helen marched over and took one of the chairs. "How are you?"

Helen adjusted her hat and smoothed nonexistent wrinkles from her khakis. "Well, I've been better."

"I'm sorry to hear that. What can I do to help you?"

Helen scoffed and crossed her arms. "I've been on the wait list for a hardcover copy of Marjorie Wade's *The Other Lover* for months, but somehow I never get my copy." The truth was, Helen wanted to borrow hardcover copies of all the major bestsellers the minute they hit the bookstores—as did a lot of other people in Medicine Creek and the surrounding areas.

Piper said, "As I might have explained to you last week when *The Secret of Samothrace* wasn't available—"

"I don't have that one yet, either," Helen huffed. "It's just not right. I get on the list good and early and yet it takes forever and a day to get my copy."

"If you would just give reading an ebook a chance, you might—"

"Good God, no. I want a *real* book—and that's not to say that current ebook bestsellers are any easier to come by than the hardcover editions. My friend Jeannetta Rossi explained to me that the library doesn't pay for enough ebook copies, either, so everyone's waiting for them, too."

It went on like that. Piper tried again gently to explain that the Medicine Creek Library did not have unlimited funds, that donations were much appreciated and would help a lot toward making sure more copies of bestsellers were available timely to avid readers.

When Helen got going on how if she had unlimited

funds, she would certainly be buying her own copies of the books she craved, Piper gave up and tuned her out.

It was that or say something she would later regret.

Because she just didn't have the patience to deal with the usual issues today. Today, all she could think about was that Jason hadn't called and what was *wrong* with her that she hadn't stuck to her guns and said absolutely not, she wouldn't be going to dinner at his mother's—and especially not as his girlfriend?

Helen trotted out her parting shot as she finally allowed Piper to usher her toward the door. "When June was director, I got my books sooner," she announced angrily—but then her silver eyebrows crunched together and she insisted, "I'm sure of it." By then, she sounded anything but sure. "I mean, I had to wait much too long even back then, but not as long as I am waiting now."

Piper apologized some more and promised that Helen would be called immediately when the books she was waiting for were ready for her to check out.

"Thank you," replied Helen, her tone softer now. "And that was rather mean of me, Piper, to imply that June was a better director than you are."

Even with all those grim thoughts about Jason and why he hadn't called yet gnawing away at the back of her mind, Piper wanted to hug Helen right then. "June was and is the best of the best. I'm lucky to have her to look up to."

Helen patted Piper's cheek. "You always were a sweet girl."

"Thank you, Helen."

"Have Libby call me the minute my books are available…"

"Of course I will."

When Helen finally went out the door, Piper checked her cell for news from Jason.

Nothing.

Oh, she should have nixed the idea of dinner with his family—nixed it and refused to budge on it no matter how long he kept after her to change her mind.

But she hadn't. She'd weakened and let him charm her into saying yes to his bad, bad idea. And now she was absolutely certain something upsetting had happened when he'd told his parents that he and Piper Wallace were a thing.

By the time he'd showered and headed back to the main house for dinner with Kenzo trotting along behind him, Jason felt good. He felt ready to tell his parents there was someone special he wanted them to meet on Saturday evening.

It was kind of funny, really. He'd been so confident, even downright cocky, while convincing Piper that she should get to know his family a little. But now that he had to propose the idea to his folks, he was having a hell of a time trying to decide what to say.

It was ridiculous and he knew it, to be all tied in knots about something so simple. It was dinner with the family. His parents always welcomed guests.

But no matter how he imagined getting the words out, they sounded abrupt and awkward when he tried to put them together inside his head.

Still, it had to be done.

In the kitchen of his mom's house, the food was on the table. His parents and his brother sat in their usual chairs. He'd just showered at his place, so he had no need to wash up.

"There you are, Jay," said his mom with a smile.

Kenzo flopped down in his favorite spot on the scuffed floor as Jason took his customary place at the table. He waited until they all had full plates in front of them before he said, "Mom, Dad. I've been seeing someone special, and I would like to bring her to dinner here Saturday night."

"Someone special?" His mom was smiling. Definitely a good sign.

Before he could tell them about Piper, Joe swallowed the big hunk of pot roast he'd just stuck in his mouth and said, "Piper Wallace, right? I heard you took her out to dinner at the Grill last week and she came by your place in the evening a couple weeks ago, didn't she?"

Jason had a very strong urge to punch his brother in the face—not because there was anything wrong with what Joe had just said. It was the interruption that got on Jason's last nerve. He'd hoped to handle this conversation himself. Smoothly, if possible.

But hey. Life didn't always go as planned. He nodded at his brother. "That's right. I took Piper to the Stagecoach Grill, and before that she came to see my workshop. I'm donating a carving for auction at the library fundraiser this summer."

"Piper Wallace," said his mother. She was frowning now—but a frown didn't necessarily mean anything bad. Maybe she didn't remember exactly who Piper was. "The librarian?"

"That's right. Piper and I have been seeing each other

for a while now. I really like her. And I want you and Dad to get to know her, too."

That frown on his mom's face? It wasn't going away. She asked, "Wasn't she married to that nice history teacher?"

"Piper's a widow," he said flatly. "Mr. Wallace died four years ago."

His mom replied, "I remember. And you were in Mr. Wallace's class in high school." It sounded like an accusation.

And the stern look on her face? Not good.

Now, he didn't know where to go with this. Should he have expected this kind of reaction? He hadn't—though maybe his own nervousness about approaching the subject should have clued him in that he wasn't as confident about this situation as he kept telling Piper he was.

"What are you getting at, Mom?"

Meggie looked away, but then she faced him again and drew herself up. "Honey, I'm just going to remind you of the obvious. She's so much older than you."

"Thirteen years, yeah. So what? Piper and I are both adults. You act like I'm still in high school."

"I didn't say that."

"Good. Because I'm not in high school anymore and I haven't been for almost ten years. I'm a grown-ass man. I can't see how my wanting to be with Piper is a problem for you."

"Well, if it's serious—"

"It is serious." Okay, maybe that was more than he'd meant to say at this point. And maybe Piper wouldn't say the same. Not yet. But it was the truth—*his* truth. And his mother might as well get used to it.

"But, Jay—"

"Meggie." His dad interrupted her this time.

She shot him a look. "What?"

"Let's not get ahead of ourselves."

"But, Nate, I just think we should—"

"—not get ahead of ourselves?" his dad suggested gently. Again.

Joe shifted in his chair. Jason glanced in his brother's direction. Joe's eyes were so wide they seemed to take over his face.

"It's fact," Meggie protested, her eyebrows pinched together, and her mouth all scrunched up. "Piper Wallace is—"

"—smart and helpful," his dad finished her sentence for her. "And did you read that great bit Starr put in the *Clarion*, about how that four-year-old boy almost choked on a plastic astronaut in the middle of some library event?"

"Yes, I did, but—"

"Piper Wallace saved that boy's life, Meggie. I'm really looking forward to getting to know her a little."

"But—"

"Oh, now, Meggie May," Nate said in a voice smooth as warm honey. "Jay and Piper are both grown adults and their choices are their own. Let it be."

Meggie bit her lip. Then she and Jason's dad did that thing they always did, staring at each other, saying things to each other without using words.

Finally, his mom nodded. "Yes," she said in a slow, considered tone. "I get it. And I know Piper Wallace is a good person."

"Yes, she is," said his dad.

Jason didn't know what to think. If he'd worried a little

that one of his parents might not be all in on Piper from the first, he would have guessed that would be his dad.

Which just proved that even people you'd known since birth could surprise you now and then. Sometimes in a good way. But sometimes not.

His mom turned her big brown eyes on him. "I apologize for trying to tell you how to live your life. I'm proud of you, Jay, and I do respect your right to make your own choices."

"It's okay, Mom." It wasn't, but right now, he just wanted to keep the peace and bring Piper to dinner.

"Piper is a fine person," she said. "And we would love to have her over for dinner on Saturday."

"Thanks, Mom." He had zero desire to stir up more trouble, but there was something he did need to say. "Look, Mom, if you're really opposed to my being with Piper, I don't want to bring her here, not until I know you're good with it."

"I…" Meggie took a moment before she answered. "I want you to be happy, Jay. Yes, I'm all right with it. Please tell Piper that we look forward to spending some time with her."

It was not the enthusiastic invitation he'd hoped for. But she'd as good as promised to treat Piper as a welcome guest. And he did want his mom and dad to know Piper before they found out there was a baby on the way.

He nodded at his mom and put on a smile. "Great. I'll ask her to Saturday dinner. Six o'clock?"

"That'll work," said his mom and the matter was settled.

Back at his place a little later, he sat on the front deck throwing a chewed-up red Frisbee for Kenzo, ruffling the dog's thick black coat and calling him a "Good boy" every time he returned with the drool-covered plastic disc.

Kenzo never tired of catching a Frisbee. Jason indulged him for more than an hour, though he knew he should have called Piper by now. It was just that he was trying to decide how much to say about the conversation he'd just had with his parents.

Jason believed that honesty was always the best policy. He made sure to live by that belief. But right now, the way his mom had reacted when he said that Piper was special to him...

He didn't want to tell Piper that. He'd worked hard to convince her that she would be welcomed at the Double-K. And she would be welcomed...

Just with reservations on his mother's part.

Really, it would be all right. He just didn't see the need to get into his mom's initial reaction to the news that he was bringing Piper to dinner.

Because why upset Piper when it was all worked out? Why scare her off?

Didn't he have enough of a challenge with her already? Here he was trying his damnedest to get closer to her while she kept pushing him away. For weeks, he'd gotten nothing but an endless chain of noes from her. And lately her favorite word was *co-parents*.

He hated that word already. It was a word that said they were connected, but only by the child they were raising. Not by their hearts, not by the life they might build together.

He damn well would be a father to his child, but he also planned to do anything and everything he had to do to see that he didn't end up a *co-parent* kind of dad. He wanted a family with Piper. He wanted his child to have what he'd had growing up—a mom and a dad who loved, trusted and counted on each other, a mom and a dad who could talk to each other without using words.

In the end, it really didn't matter that she was older than he was, or that they were going at it backward, starting with a one-night stand instead of taking a while to get to know each other first.

They could work it out. He knew they could. He would take it slow, show her day by day that she could count on him, that they could make a beautiful life together.

And right now, he wasn't going to say anything to freak her out. They would have a nice dinner here at the ranch on Saturday. His mom and dad would welcome her. By the end of the evening he would be one small step closer to earning her trust.

Kenzo came trotting back to him across the grass. The sweet mutt dropped the Frisbee on the ground at Jason's feet. It was covered in drool.

Jason chuckled. "Later for that, big guy. Let's go inside. I really need to make a call."

It was after seven when Piper's phone finally chimed with the call she'd been waiting for all day. She stared at the ringing phone there on the coffee table in front of her.

Voice mail would take it before the fourth ring. She waited till it rang three times before she picked it up. "Hello, Jason." She ladled on a little uncalled-for attitude. "What a surprise."

A silence on the other end, then, "You're pissed."

"Me? No, not at all," she lied through her teeth.

"You at home?"

"Why?"

"I'll come over there."

Now she just felt foolish. "No. Sorry. I was…well, a lit-tle nervous about what your parents might say when you told them you wanted to bring me to dinner." She gath-ered her legs up onto the sofa and snuggled her bare feet under a throw pillow. "When you didn't call, I just knew it must have gone badly."

"It didn't go badly." His voice was low, soothing. She felt instantly reassured. "I waited till dinnertime to talk to them, that's all."

She drew a slow breath and just went ahead and asked him, "So, then. How *did* it go?"

"It was fine, Piper." He sounded so sure of that. "It went great."

She breathed a slow sigh of relief. "Yeah?"

"Yeah. I told them we were going out together—dating, like you and I agreed. My dad said he's looking forward to getting to know you and my mom said they would love for you to come to dinner Saturday night."

Dating. He'd told his parents they were dating. Yes, it was what they'd agreed. But now that it was too late to take the words back, it seemed like a bad idea, after all, to tell lies to the people he loved the most.

"Don't." Jason's voice was firm and confident—like he was the mature, experienced one. And she was some shy youngster who had no idea what in the world she was doing. "Stop second-guessing. You're coming to dinner and it's going to be great. Saturday. I'll pick you up at five thirty."

She still had her doubts about this. But eventually, she would be getting to know Nate and Meggie Bravo any-way. Might as well get started on that. "I'll be ready. See you then."

* * *

When Saturday evening came, *ready* was the last word she would have used to describe herself.

But she pulled it together. She put on a pretty yellow cotton dress and the cute cowboy boots she kept in the back of her closet. She'd even made a quick trip to Betty's Blooms on State Street for a sweet little bouquet of pale pink tulips for Jason's mom.

"You look gorgeous," Jason said when she answered the door. That gleam in his eye said he wanted to kiss her. She would have let him if he'd tried.

But he didn't—which was good. Yes, they were "dating" for the world to see. But in private, they needed to remember that it was all about the baby. Sharing kisses right now would only confuse the issue for her—and for him, too.

"Ready?" he asked.

Was she? Not really. She felt on edge about this whole thing. "I have to tell you, meeting the parents? It makes me nervous. I never met Walter's parents. His father had died back when he was twenty. And his mom passed on five years later. And as for my college boyfriend…" She was babbling, she knew it. And talking about Brandon? No good could come from that. She finished lamely, "I, uh, did meet his parents…" It had been an absolute disaster.

He was frowning. "Are you okay?"

"Yes. Of course. I'm fine."

She locked her door and led the way down the front walk. At the curb, his pickup was sparkling clean, the chrome shiny bright. "You washed your truck," she said as he pulled open the door for her.

"Waxed it, too." His grin was slow and way too tempting. "I wanted everything just so for my special girl."

"You're such a romantic," she teased as she stepped up into the cab.

"You don't know the half of it—watch that pretty skirt, now."

She pulled it out of the way so that he could shut the door.

As they left the streets of town behind and headed west toward the mountains, she realized her nervousness had eased. She felt good. Happy to be with Jason on a warm, clear Saturday evening, on the way to spend a little time with his family.

At the ranch, Jason stopped his pickup in front of the main house, a sweet old Victorian-style two-story farmhouse painted white with a gray shingle roof and old-fashioned sash windows.

His mom and dad came out as Piper and Jason mounted the porch steps. Jason made the introductions. His parents seemed friendly and welcoming. His younger brother had gone into town to play pool with friends, so it was just the four of them.

Piper offered Meggie the bouquet she'd brought.

"I love tulips, thank you," Jason's mom replied.

They went in and straight through the great room into the kitchen, which smelled so good, of a juicy-looking rib roast that had just come out of the oven. Meggie put the tulips in a pretty crystal vase, and they took seats near the fireplace in the great room.

Nate offered drinks. "Piper, what'll you have?"

Was it a dead giveaway that she wanted club soda? Nobody looked at her funny when she asked for it, so she decided it was fine. Nate and Jason had whiskey with soda and Meggie had a glass of red wine.

They chatted, the getting-to-know-you kind of talk, most of it focused on Piper, which upped her nervousness a notch or two. But she was the newcomer, Jason's "special" girl, so of course his parents wanted to know all about her. Nate, tall and broad like his son, with the same thick, dark hair, but with gray at his temples, said he'd read in the *Clarion* about the incident with little Bobby Trueblood.

Piper reassured Jason's dad that Bobby was fine, completely recovered. They asked after her mom.

"She never stops," Piper said. "She's running her art center and she's also painting and making jewelry. In addition to all that, she takes surveys and gets paid to watch videos."

Nate said, "She's one of a kind, your mother."

"Oh, yes she is."

Eventually, they moved into the formal dining room for the meal.

Meggie sipped her wine. "Until last week, I had no idea the two of you were dating." She asked Piper, "How did you get together?"

Piper realized she should have expected that question. Her mouth felt kind of dry. She grabbed her glass of club soda and knocked back a big gulp.

Jason answered his mother's question. "We ran into each other at Arlington's one night."

"It was back in April," Piper said. "The scare with Bobby Trueblood had happened that day, as a matter of fact."

Jason was nodding. "I bought her a drink. We talked. It was so easy, talking with Piper. Fun. I could have stayed there all night. Didn't matter what we talked about, I never wanted to leave." His hand brushed hers under the table.

She caught his fingers, gave them a grateful squeeze. "I tried to get her number. No luck. She turned me down more than once." One side of his mouth quirked up. "But I didn't give up. Eventually I convinced her to give me a chance."

Piper pulled it together and played her part. "I was hesitant. I've been on my own for four years now and I never planned to…get serious with anyone again."

"So, it really is serious, then, between you two?" Meggie asked.

"Well." Piper cleared her throat. "Maybe *serious* is a little too strong a word."

"No, it's not," Jason contradicted her. Piper shot him a warning look. He ignored that look and went right on. "It's not too strong a word at all—and, Mom, I already mentioned that I was serious about Piper."

Meggie nodded as she turned to Piper again. "I was sorry to hear that you'd lost your husband, Piper."

"Thank you. But, as I said, it's been four years. I've adjusted to being single."

"And yet here you are, dating my son." Meggie's voice was soft, her tone friendly. But there was something unnerving—and disapproving—about the look in her eye.

Piper got the message then. Meggie didn't want Piper getting close to her son. A glance at the man who'd brought her here confirmed it. Jason was glaring at his mother, his mouth a flat line.

Nate said, "Meggie May." It was a warning.

And apparently, Meggie knew she'd gone too far. "Yes," she replied and then murmured, "I hear you. I'm sorry…"

Piper had had enough. "I don't know quite how to ask this, but…"

Jason caught her hand again.

She turned and looked straight at him. "What?"

"It's okay," he said. "Really, it's fine."

"No, it's not. Jason, I'm not blind." Meggie didn't want her here and that was very far from fine. As for Piper, she felt a tightness in her throat and feared she might actually burst into tears right there at Meggie Bravo's dining room table.

Instead, she drew back her shoulders and met Meggie's dark eyes squarely. "Just answer me truthfully. Do you have a problem with Jason and me as a couple?"

"Piper," insisted Jason. "Come on. Let it go. It's okay."

She jerked her hand from his. "No. No, it's not. It's not in the least okay— Meggie?"

Meggie's lips trembled. For a moment, Piper was certain she would backpedal frantically and insist that she had no problem at all with the idea of Piper and Jason together.

But then Meggie shut her eyes and drew a slow breath. When she looked at Piper again, she nodded. "The truth is I think very highly of you, Piper. I honestly do. But you're not a good fit for Jason. I mean, he's so much younger. He should be with someone his own age, don't you think?"

"That's enough." Jason shoved back his chair and threw his napkin on the table. "We are done here."

"Jason, wait." Piper needed to hear the rest. She put her hand on his rock-hard forearm. "Let your mom finish. Please?"

He gave her a long, hard look. "Have it your way," he muttered as he dropped back into his chair.

"I have something to say first." Nate's voice was measured, calm. "I just want to make it clear that *I* think our son should be with the one who's right for him. And only he can decide who that woman is."

Piper's gaze slid to Meggie, whose eyes shone with un-shed tears.

"I'm sorry, Nate," Meggie said. "And, Jason, I know I promised you that I would welcome Piper—and I do, except... Well, I just don't see you two being right for each other. When you turn fifty, Piper will already be in her sixties. Plus, what about children?"

Jason stared at Meggie as though he wondered who she was and what she'd done with his real mom. "What about them?" he sneered.

"Well, Jay. It's a hard, sad fact that a woman's fertility declines sharply after forty."

Jason shot Piper a questioning glance. She just knew he was going to blurt out the news of the baby. She gave a small, negative shake of her head. Her fertility was only part of the main issue here and she refused to let Jason use the new life inside her to one-up his mom.

Jason shifted his angry gaze back to Meggie. Piper held her breath, certain he was going to break the agreement they'd made and bring up the baby, after all.

But he didn't. "This isn't like you," he said to his mother. "It's narrow-minded, Mom. Piper and I have every right to be together and I think you know that."

Meggie looked miserable. Piper actually felt kind of sorry for her. "You're right on every count," Meggie said. "And I'm sorry. I feel awful about this. I'm not proud that I can't get past the age difference between you two, I'm truly not. But, Jay, it's honestly how I feel. And I couldn't just sit here and pretend that it's all okay when I have so many doubts."

"Well, I don't have doubts, Mom. I have none. Zero.

And it's what *I* think and what Piper thinks that matters here."

Piper couldn't take it anymore. "What I think is that this, tonight, was a bad idea." She felt sick to her stomach from sheer embarrassment. Life was too short. She had no desire to sit here in this charming old dining room and be judged as not good enough for Meggie Bravo's precious son—no. Uh-uh. She refused to stay in this house one minute longer. "Jason, please take me home now."

At least he didn't argue. He only asked, "Are you sure?"

She nodded. "Take me home."

Chapter Seven

Five minutes later, they were back in Jason's shiny-clean pickup driving away from the ranch house.

Neither of them spoke. Piper watched the drift fences flying past and the evening shadows growing longer.

When they finally got to her place, he said, "Let me come in."

"Jason, please. No. I'm tired."

"When can we talk?"

"I don't know right now. That was horrible. I'm going to need some time."

"Time for what?" he demanded.

His curt tone flat out pissed her off. "You set me up."

He flinched. "No. Piper, I—"

"You knew that your mom wasn't on board with the idea of you and me together."

"She promised she would welcome you. She said she wouldn't make any trouble."

"And that would have been *after* she said that she thought I was too old for you, am I right?"

He had no viable comeback for that, and both of them knew it. "Listen. I'm sorry, okay? I wanted you to get to know them. I was sure my mom would change her mind about us as a couple as soon as she saw us together. I knew she would only need to spend a little time with you to realize how wrong she was."

"Seems to me like you're the one who got it wrong."

"Yeah. I pushed too fast. But it will be all right, you'll see. It's just going to take her a little longer than I thought it would to see how great you and I are together."

Piper longed to start shrieking at him in sheer frustration. But she was a mature adult, after all—*too* mature if you asked Meggie Bravo. "There are so many ways you are off base here." It took effort, but she managed to speak in a level, reasonable tone. "First, we are not a couple."

"But we agreed—"

"I'm not finished." She gathered her thoughts again. "Second, I don't care what you assumed about how your mom would react when she saw us together, you had a responsibility to clue me in that she was against the idea of you and me as a couple. You needed to tell me how she felt. Instead, I ended up blindsided. It was awful and I had no idea that any of that would happen because you didn't warn me."

He swiped off his hat and sank back against the seat. "You're right. And I am truly sorry. I know I blew it. I just wanted it so bad—for them to get to know you and admire you, for you to like them and want to be around them. I was afraid if you knew my mom had doubts, you would refuse to meet them tonight."

"And how is what just happened better than your being honest with me about Meggie's reservations and my deciding I wasn't ready to go there right now?"

He tipped his head up and stared at the headliner as though seeking answers from above. "I see your point," he answered wearily. "It was a major screwup on my part.

I was way too eager and all I've got now is how damn sorry I am."

She studied his profile—the strong, proud nose, the sculpted jaw. He was one handsome specimen of a man.

And at least he'd admitted that he'd messed up. Unlike Brandon, who flat out never owned up to being in the wrong about anything—and Walter, who always had some long-winded explanation of how he might have made a mistake, but it wasn't really his fault.

"You're forgiven," she said.

He looked at her then. "Just like that?"

"Yeah. As long as you promise not to pull that kind of crap again."

He put his hand over heart. "Swear to God, Piper. Never again."

"Okay, then. We're good. But I'm still going to need some time. This is all moving way too fast and I'm putting the brakes on as of now."

His beautiful smile faded to a watchful frown. "Putting the brakes on, how?"

"I need a little space, that's all."

"For how long?"

"Please. Now you want to put me on a schedule for getting over what happened tonight?"

"I didn't say that."

"Good. Because I don't know how long it will take me to get past this. A few weeks, at least."

"A few weeks…" He draped his arm on the steering wheel and stared out the windshield as though bad stuff was going on out there. "A few weeks is too long."

Something tightened in her chest. It felt like yearning,

the deep-down kind that aches so bad and won't go away. Or maybe it was just desire, pure and simple.

Because even after the disaster of this evening, she still felt so powerfully drawn to him. Her good sense kept saying no. But the rest of her just wanted more of him.

He turned his head to meet her eyes. "I mean it, Piper. I don't want to go weeks without seeing you."

"You'll see me at the first ultrasound. It's not that far away, the second Monday in June."

"That's more than three weeks."

She held his gaze without wavering. "I'll say it again. Time, Jason. I do need some time."

"We agreed we were supposed to be dating, remember?"

She couldn't help but chuckle. "It's unnecessary. I think you know that. We spent a night together, the contraception failed and now we're having a baby. That's the truth and I'm comfortable with it. It's our business how we handle this, and after tonight, I'm kind of over trying to get ahead of people's judgments."

He slid her a glance. "You're saying you're bowing out of fake dating me?"

"Yes, I am."

He laughed then, though the sound had very little humor in it. "The truth is, I was just trying to get more time with you."

Her heart did that foolish yearning thing again. He was such a good guy and there was all that sizzling-hot chemistry between them...

But no. She couldn't afford to get swept up into an affair with him. She could so easily lose her head over him—not to mention, her heart.

The baby. The baby was what mattered.

She anchored her purse more firmly on her shoulder. "I'll see you at the ultrasound up in Sheridan."

"Piper…"

She pulled on the handle and the door swung open. "Good night, Jason." She jumped out before he could say something to make her stay.

"I'll go with you if that's what it will take," Emmaline said. It was Friday night, almost a week since she'd told Jason she needed some space.

Piper missed him.

A lot.

And she spent way too much time trying not to think about him and his beautiful smile and the look in his eyes that said he only wanted to be with her, that she was someone special to him.

"Think about it seriously, please," Emmaline said.

They sat at the table in the kitchen of the house where both of them had grown up, Emmaline from birth, the only child of middle-aged parents—and Piper starting at the age of nine when they moved home to take care of her grandma after her grandfather died. It was a simple two-story clapboard house built back in the 1920s.

Piper pushed the vegan stir-fry around on her plate. "I've got a lot going on now, Mom. I can't just head off to Southern California to meet my long-lost father and his family."

Emmaline wasn't buying her excuses. "You've always got a lot going on. And it will only get worse once you're past the first trimester. That baby's going to take up every spare second in your day and a lot of time you can't spare, just you wait—and don't try to tell me you can't get away from the library. You've mentioned more than once that you can't roll over your vacation time. You didn't even get a vacation last year, did you?"

"No, but I—"

"Just take some time off, my love. Go meet your father and his family."

"Look. I'll think about it."

"Less thinking, more action."

"Let it be, Mom."

Emmaline dropped her chopsticks and put up both hands. "Okay, okay."

They left it at that.

When Piper checked her email later that night, she had another note from the father she'd yet to meet. Simon Walsh was married with three children, two daughters and a son. His wife's name was Nia. Piper's half siblings were in their late twenties and early thirties. Her two half sisters had husbands and kids.

Simon seemed like a very nice man. Again, he invited her to come for a visit.

Just say when, he wrote. We can make it happen. Or if you would rather we came up there to Wyoming, we can do that instead. Just tell me what works for you, and we'll see what we can do.

She wrote back that she would love to come visit him, and she would let him know as soon as she could get the time away from work. It was a dodge. She could get the time if she really wanted it.

A week later, on Friday, the last day of May, Simon sent her another long, chatty email. At the end he wrote that he and her stepmom could come up to Wyoming to see her anytime over the summer, whatever worked for her.

Piper felt awful when she read that. Because Simon Walsh really did seem like a sweetheart, a sweetheart who very much wanted to meet her. Piper knew she had to quit jerking him around.

That Monday morning was the third of June. First thing that day, she checked in with Libby, who had the thankless job of managing the schedule this year. Libby took half an hour to juggle things around and then offered Piper two weeks of vacation at the end of the month.

Piper sat right down at her desk and composed an email to her father letting him know that she would love to come to visit him and the family—a short visit, for this first time.

I was thinking I would fly in for a weekend, if that works for you, she wrote, and named the dates.

He got back to her that same night. Piper, this is wonderful news. I'm so glad. And so is Nia. We will see you soon. I will be counting the days till then. There was more, about how he'd already made some calls and her half siblings would be there to meet her, too. She should stay as long as she possibly could, he wrote. And bring a friend if you'd like, he added. We have plenty of room...

Bring a friend. She would love to bring Starr. But the usual issues applied. Starr had a husband, a toddler and a business to take care of. Piper just didn't want to ask her to drop everything and hold Piper's hand while she met her father for the first time.

And she felt uncomfortable about bringing her mom along with her. At least not for this first visit.

It could end up feeling awkward with Emmaline there.

After all, Emmaline and Simon had spent a wild weekend of sex, drugs and rock and roll at the US Music Festival in the San Bernardino Mountains a little over forty years ago. Nia might be fine with all that. But Piper wanted to know her dad's wife better before springing Emmaline on her.

The week crawled by. She thought of Jason way too often, wondered what he was doing, wanted to reach out to him. But she didn't. Because they had their separate lives and they both needed to remember that.

Friday morning, she texted him a reminder that the ultrasound was set for 8:00 a.m. on Monday up in Sheridan, adding, Meet you at the front entrance at 7:45.

Four hours later, he still hadn't replied. She tried not to wonder why he hadn't gotten back. Up till now in their… whatever this thing was between them. Relationship? Friendship? Future co-parents-ship? Whatever they had going on together here, he'd always been right there, ready and waiting whenever she'd reached out to him.

Not this time.

Okay, true, she'd asked him not to contact her, so the fact that he hadn't gotten in touch the past few weeks was on her. But if being there for the ultrasound was so important to him, couldn't he hurry up and confirm that he was coming?

She promised herself she wouldn't think about him or worry about why he wasn't getting back. If he showed up, fine.

Two hours later, he did get back. Sorry. Moving cattle. Out of cell range until just now. Will be there Monday morning. Hospital front entrance. 7:45.

And that was all.

Not that she expected anything more—what else was

there to expect? He'd done what she'd asked and waited for her to contact him. As for the ultrasound, he would be there, no problem.

She tried, as she'd tried for the past three weeks, to put him from her mind. She failed. Completely. Because he was there, in her head, in her heart. In all the secret, private parts of her.

She missed him. Way too much.

Monday, he was waiting for her at the main hospital entrance looking like everybody's fantasy of a hot cowboy in clean jeans, rawhide boots, a Western shirt and a jean jacket. He swiped off his hat with a big smile as she came walking across the parking lot toward him. His hair shone black as a crow's wing in the morning sun.

Her heart just… Well, it lifted at the sight of him. There was no other word for it. Her heart went airborne the moment she saw his handsome face again. Her feet seemed to float right up off the ground.

She wanted to run to him, to throw her arms around him, show him how glad she was to see him again.

But she didn't. She walked at a steady pace and when she reached him she kept her arms to her sides. "Ready?"

"Oh, yeah. Let's get after it. I'm excited."

That just made her smile like a fool. "Me, too—and nervous. Very nervous."

His expression grew more serious. "Any problems? You feeling okay?"

"No problems, none. I feel great. It's just…a big moment. And I hope everything's okay."

He took her hand then, his rough fingers sliding between hers, grounding her somehow, easing her fears. "It's going to be fine."

"Thanks." The word came out in a breathless whisper. "That's what I needed to hear."

They went in.

After check-in, they waited until a woman in scrubs came for them. She introduced herself as the sonographer's assistant and led them into a regular exam room. Jason took a chair in the corner and Piper sat on the exam table. The woman took Piper's vitals and explained that the procedure would be transvaginal. At six weeks, the baby was so small that a traditional abdominal ultrasound might not pick up the necessary information.

The woman left long enough for Piper to take off her jeans, sneakers and panties, and cover herself with a sheet. When the assistant returned, the sonographer came, too. Piper settled her feet in the stirrups.

"This may be a little uncomfortable," said the sonographer, as she eased the long, wand-like device up under the sheet. "But there shouldn't be any pain."

Piper drew a slow, careful breath. "Jason?" She glanced his way and he rose from the chair.

When she held out her hand, he took it. It helped, the warmth of him right there beside her, the press of his palm to hers.

The wand went in. On the monitor beside her, a flickering gray image filled the screen.

"There's the sac," said the sonographer, indicating a curving black space within the flickering gray. "And... We have a heartbeat." The image zoomed in and there in the black space was a pulsing speck of...something. The sonographer fiddled with the controls and the speck became more defined. The pulsing was in the center of it.

"Is that the baby?" Jason asked.

"Oh, yes it is," replied the sonographer. "The heart is what's pulsing. It's very early days, but everything looks good at this point."

"Just one, right?" Piper asked.

"One baby, yes," the sonographer replied.

Fifteen minutes later, Piper had a flash drive of pictures in her purse and Jason at her side as they walked out into the morning sunlight.

He asked, "Do you have to get to work?"

"Not till afternoon. I took the morning off."

"Did you get breakfast?"

"I couldn't."

"Me neither. Let's get some food. It's a nice day. How about takeout? Maybe a picnic. I know a great spot by Crystal Creek."

"The same spot you mentioned when you were trying to get me to go out with you?"

He nodded. "That's the one. What do you say?"

She felt…drugged, somehow. High on his presence. Happier than she'd been in weeks. "Yes, all right. Food would be good."

He called ahead to Henry's. She followed him back down to Medicine Creek. Jason went in to pick up the food. Piper left her car around the corner from the diner and climbed up into his pickup with him.

A few miles out of town, he turned off onto a gravel side road. They rumbled along for a couple of hundred yards and then he pulled over and parked.

She took one bag. He took the other, along with a blanket from the storage box in the pickup bed. He led the way along a winding path to the creek's edge and a nice grassy spot beneath a willow tree. Five feet down the bank, the clear water raced by, glittering in the sun as it tumbled over the rocks below.

It really was a pretty spot. And right now, they had it all to themselves.

He spread the blanket and they ate breakfast—egg-and-ham sandwiches on English muffins and the best hash browns ever. She drank her orange juice and enjoyed her once-daily cup of coffee.

"I missed you," he said, his eyes on the far bank.

"You didn't call," she replied, which she knew very well was totally unfair given that she'd asked him not to.

"Come on, Piper." He stared straight ahead, toward the opposite bank. "You said you needed time."

"Yes, I did. Let me rephrase my last remark. Thank you for respecting my request."

"You're welcome." He slid her a glance then.

She gave him a smile and bumped his shoulder with hers. It felt so good that he was here, beside her, on this sunny almost-summer morning. It filled her with happiness that he'd been there to see that tiny, pulsing speck of a heart on the ultrasound monitor. The sight had made it all the more real to her that she just might become a mother, after all—so real that her throat clutched and her view of the pretty creek burbling along below them grew misty.

"Hey," he said. "What's wrong?"

She swiped away a tear as it slid down her cheek and sniffed back the next one before it could fall. "Just hormones."

"Piper…"

She swayed against him. He wrapped an arm around her. His lips touched her hair. "Is this about what happened with my mother? Please don't worry," he whispered.

"She'll come around. Plus, when she finds out about the baby, the news really will be less of a…" He seemed to have trouble choosing the right word.

She couldn't hold back a chuckle. "I think *shock* is what you're going for here."

"Hmm. More like *surprise*."

"Yeah, right." She settled her head on his shoulder. A breeze ruffled the leaves of the willow overhead. "Think of it," she said dreamily. "You're going to be a dad."

"I do think of it." She felt his lips in her hair again, and the warmth of his breath on her skin. "I think of it all the time."

It felt really good to lean on him, so she kept doing it as she continued to marvel that she was having a baby and he would be her baby's dad, a dad who insisted he would be there to see their baby grow up. She thought of her own dad and how much he seemed to want to get to get to know her. "Did you know I've never met my own dad?"

He rubbed her arm with his big hand, slowly, soothingly. "No. I noticed you never mentioned him, but sometimes people's dads just kind of drift away."

"Yeah. That's sad, but also true. I think most people assume that he must have been a deadbeat—or that my mom never even knew who he was, which is a little bit closer to the truth. We *didn't* know much about him until recently. I found him through 23andMe."

"Wow. I had no idea."

"I've been thinking it over, working my way toward the big step of meeting him in person."

Jason just went on holding her. Across the creek, a pair of bobolinks chirped at each other from the branches of a hackberry tree.

"My mom never knew his last name," she said. "She met him at a rock festival in the San Bernardino Mountains. They smoked a lot of weed, had a great time together and said goodbye when the festival was over without exchanging any information that would have helped her track him down when she found out that I was on the way. I grew up knowing virtually nothing about him, wanting desperately to find him, having no way to do that."

"That would be hard. A lifetime of wondering if you would ever get to meet him."

"I did wonder. As a little girl, I used to dream of meeting him. When we lived in my mom's Volkswagen bus, I just knew that any day, he would find us somehow. He'd appear at our campsite or show up at some outdoor art show where Mom had her paintings for sale. He would stop at our booth, and I would look up. Our eyes would meet. I would know instantly that he was my dad. I would run to his arms, and he'd scoop me up and twirl me around and whisper, *There you are, Piper. I've been looking for you.*"

Jason stroked her hair with a slow hand. "Didn't happen, though, huh?"

She shook her head. "He never appeared. Then we moved to Medicine Creek to live with my grandmother. He never knocked on our door. By the time I was fourteen or so, it started to seem pointless to keep waiting, keep hoping."

"You gave up?"

"I did, yeah. My mom knew I was losing faith that I would ever meet him. She hired a private investigator to search for him. It cost money she didn't have, and the so-called investigation went nowhere. I was seventeen or so when I finally admitted to myself that I was never going to know him. From then on, I put him behind me. I honestly wouldn't even have tried 23andMe if Mom hadn't nagged at me until I finally signed up and sent in my DNA sample."

"And now?"

"I've agreed to go meet him and his family. They live in San Diego. It'll be a short visit, just for a weekend. But I did get some time off. Two weeks starting on the fifteenth. I'll fly down there for two or three days then."

"Alone?"

"Looks like it, yes. My friends are all busy with their own lives. My mom would go, but my father is married with grown children and, well, it probably wouldn't be awkward, but you never know. For this first visit, I don't want to take any chances."

"I'll go with you."

She pulled away, but only so that she could meet his eyes. It surprised her how much his offer meant. "You would? Really?"

"I will, yeah."

She gulped down the lump in her throat. "Just as... friends, right? And as co-parents. I mean, it would be good, don't you think? For us to spend some time together before the baby's born, see how we do as a team?"

"However you want it, Piper. Two weeks starting on the fifteenth, you said?"

"No. The trip to San Diego will only be one weekend, Friday or Saturday through Sunday—or Monday at the latest. We'll fly down there and back."

"But you said you have two weeks of vacation time."

"Yes." She could see by the look on his gorgeous face that he was planning something more than just a weekend in San Diego. Whatever it was, she should put the brakes on.

Except that she did have two whole weeks of freedom coming and wouldn't it be fun to have a real vacation for once? Her mom was right. The baby would change everything. Her schedule would only get tighter. Soon enough, any getaway she managed to find the time for would include an infant and an endless array of baby gear.

"Why not make it a road trip?" he suggested. "We'll take a few days driving down there, and then map out a different route coming back. We could stop in Las Vegas on the way south and drive up the Coast Highway coming home. Remember I mentioned that my grandmother Sharilyn lives in Los Angeles?"

"I do, yes."

"If you're willing, we can stop for a visit with her and her husband, Hector. The two of them came up to the ranch for a week during the summer a few years back, but I haven't seen them since then and they are not getting any younger."

A road trip, just the two of us? She started to run a mental inventory of all the reasons she couldn't say yes.

But her mind simply refused to cooperate.

Because his suggestion sounded great. Aside from a couple of work-related conferences, she hadn't been anywhere but down to Buffalo or up to Sheridan for the past two years. This was her chance to get away for a while. And all her very good reasons not to do that just made her feel sad. For once, she wanted to do the fun thing rather than the practical one.

"Think about it, Piper. It'll be good, just you and me

on our own schedule, taking life as it comes. It'll be an adventure."

She waffled. "Are you sure you can get away?"

"Yes. Let's do it."

"I don't know…"

"Sure you do. It's a great idea. We're having a baby together. It'll be good for us, two weeks on the road, just us, alone."

When he put it like that, she should definitely say no. Shouldn't she?

But she'd missed him so much since she'd asked him to stay away. It was starting to seem nothing short of foolish to keep rejecting him.

For once, she wanted to forget what she *should* do. She wanted to be with him far away from their everyday lives. She wanted to know him better. Because he was right. Whatever went on between the two of them personally, their baby would connect them for the rest of their lives.

"Okay, Jason. Let's do it."

He leaned closer. "What was that? I didn't quite hear what you said."

She laughed. "You heard me. The road trip. Let's do it."

"You sure?"

"Yes, I am."

"That's what I wanted to hear." And then he caught her hand, jumped to his feet and pulled her up with him.

"What is it? What's going on? I don't trust that evil gleam in your eye."

Turned out she was right to be suspicious. Because with no warning whatsoever, he dipped and then scooped her high against his broad chest. "How about a swim?"

She manacled her arms around his neck. "Don't you dare."

He threw back his head with a deep, happy laugh and his hat fell off.

"Your hat!" She tried to catch it as it tumbled to the blanket.

"Don't worry about my hat. It's not going anywhere. It'll be right there when we get back."

"I have no idea what you're talking about. Back from where?"

"Our swim." He started walking down the bank.

And she almost demanded he set her down this minute. But the light in his eyes—it was beautiful. And a swim?

Not a bad idea at all.

He walked right into the icy stream. Not far from the bank, he bent at the knees and lowered them both into the freezing current. Wet from her sneakers to her butt, she laughed as he plopped down to sit on the rocky streambed.

The water reached her shoulders. It wasn't very deep, but it was cold, and it was swift. "Oh, you are going to pay for this!" she vowed gleefully. And then she took her hands from around his neck and stacked them on top of his head.

"What do you think you're doing?" He laughed at her.

"Dunking you." She pushed.

"Good luck with that." He hardly budged.

So she settled for splashing him—and herself at the same time as he just sat there in the knee-deep water, laughing at her efforts to push him under.

But then his eyes narrowed. "You're shivering," he said. He wasn't laughing anymore.

"I'm fine," she replied.

"This was a bad idea."

"Uh-uh. It was a great idea." She splashed him some more. But he just got his boots under him again and rose to his height. Water streamed off them as he carried her to the shore and up the bank to the waiting blanket.

Carefully, he set her on her feet. "There you go."

"That was so refreshing," she said brightly as her teeth knocked together.

"Yeah?"

"Oh, yeah."

"It seemed like a good idea at the time—but look at you. You're dripping wet and shaking like a leaf."

"I'm fine, Jason."

Stooping, he grabbed the blanket and shook it out, scattering the remains of their breakfast and sending his hat tumbling a few feet away in the process. He wrapped the blanket around her shoulders.

"Thank you," she said between shivers. "I might be just a tad chilly, after all."

Using the sides of the blanket, he pulled her close to him. "You sure you're okay?"

She beamed up at him. "I am, definitely."

Those blue eyes glittered down at her. "You look like a drowned rat. A really cute redheaded rat."

"You are just asking for trouble," she sneered, thinking that she was having a whole lot of fun and maybe there hadn't been enough of that in her life—not that she planned to admit it to him.

He stared down at her.

She grinned right back at him.

And everything changed. Suddenly, her heart was beating hard and deep, and her breath had gotten all snarled up inside her chest.

He said in a growl, "Tell me no. Say it now."

She blinked up at him. "Or what?"

"You know what."

She swallowed hard and tried to make that *no* take form. It didn't. And now she was biting her lip, whispering, "Jason...?" It came out like a question, like she was asking him for something.

Because she was. How could she help it?

She hadn't kissed him in four weeks. Not since the day Dr. Hayes confirmed her pregnancy.

Yes, she ought to be ashamed of herself for not stopping him now.

But all she could think about was the press of his lips to hers, the longing for him that would not go away no matter how many times she told herself to get over him—*and* their one unforgettable night together.

"Jason..."

"Piper." He said her name in the sweetest, roughest whisper.

And then that wonderful mouth came down to cover hers.

Chapter Eight

Jason just might have been the happiest man on the planet at that moment—and with very good reason. He had Piper in his arms and his mouth on hers, and so far she hadn't pushed him away.

On the contrary, she let go of the blanket. It plopped down around their feet. Her hands slid up his chest to encircle his neck. The move brought her right where he wanted her—even closer. Her soft breasts pressed against him. As for that perfect, plump, supple mouth of hers, it was *his* right now.

He took shameless advantage of her sudden willingness. Dipping his tongue into the heat beyond her parted lips, he stroked it slowly over hers.

She moaned. The sound echoed in his head and in an instant, he was hard. It was almost painful, how much he wanted her. How much he longed to rip off that soaking-wet camp shirt she was wearing, to shove down her dripping jeans and her panties along with them. He burned to strip her bare right there at the side of the creek.

But even if she let him, the chances were far too high that she would regret that choice later. She could too easily come down with a serious case of buyer's remorse for allowing herself to get carried away with him. If he didn't keep a rein on his eagerness to get up close and personal with her again, she just might change her mind about letting him go with her to meet her father.

That couldn't happen. He needed the time with her on the road, just the two of them. Time to be together, to grow closer, with none of their usual everyday concerns to drive a wedge between them. He couldn't wait to be on the way.

And he wasn't going to mess this up, not even for the chance to hold her sweet, naked body in his arms again after so damn long.

With a last, slow brush of his lips across hers, he lifted his head. She opened those leaf-green eyes and stared up at him, dazed.

He gave her a smile. "You're still shivering."

She blinked and instantly she was her usual, brisk, commanding self. "Probably because somebody dunked me in the creek."

He rubbed his hands up and down her chilled, wet arms. "Some people are just plain rude."

"Humph. Tell me about it—I can't believe I just kissed you. We can't be letting that happen again."

Oh, yes they could. If things went the way he wanted them to, she'd be doing a lot more than just kissing him. But right now, she wasn't ready for any of that, and he needed to respect her wishes. "I should get you home, huh?"

Did he see the shadow of disappointment in her eyes because she wasn't ready to go home yet? He sure hoped so. She drew a deep breath and aimed her pretty chin high. "Yes, I suppose you should. I need to clean up for work this afternoon." She was maybe five foot three in her soaking-wet Vans, yet somehow she had the ability to seem tall and commanding even when she was looking up.

"All right, then." He bent, picked up his hat and plunked it on his head. Then he gathered the scattered remains of their breakfast and stuffed it all back in the to-go bags. "Hold these." He held out the bags. When she took them, he grabbed the blanket, shook it once more and quickly folded it so he could drape it over his shoulder. "Ready?"

She nodded and started to turn.

"Wait a minute." He caught her free hand.

She glanced back at him. "What?" In response, he guided her captured hand around his neck and lifted her high into his arms again. "Well," she said, clearly trying not to grin. "Now you've got hold of me again, what next?"

He let his feet do the talking. His waterlogged boots made squishy noises as he carried her up to the truck, where he set her down in order to open her door. "I'll get water all over the seat," she warned.

"No problem. Up you go…"

Too soon, he was parking his pickup around the corner from Henry's in the empty space behind her SUV.

Turning in his seat to face her, he asked, "What day are we leaving?"

"My vacation starts this Saturday. I'm expected at my father's house the following weekend."

"So we can take our time getting there. I used to drive back and forth to Los Angeles when I was going to school. If we take the route down through Utah and Nevada, it's about twenty hours driving time from here to San Diego. You want to leave on Saturday? We can stop at Yellowstone, Palm Springs, Bryce Canyon, Las Vegas—and there's more. Think about it. We should get going now on the hotel reservations along the way—unless you're in the mood for camping."

"Maybe a little of both?"

That she didn't balk at the idea of camping pleased him. He liked sleeping outside. "A little of both, that works."

"And I would like to leave Monday, give myself a day to pack and get ready."

"Monday, it is."

She took hold of the door handle. "I need to get moving—to clean up and go to work. But I keep thinking that two weeks is a long time. Are you sure you can get away for that long?"

"Yeah, I'm sure." There was always too much to do on the Double-K during the summer. But too bad. He more than carried his weight as a rule. They would have to manage without him for a little while. And he had a project to carve on-site—a farmer in Clear Creek wanted a bald eagle from a lodgepole pine stump that was still in the ground not far from his back door. Jason felt confident he could get that finished before the time to go.

Piper gave him a look from under her eyelashes. It was a sweet look, almost shy, and it made his chest ache in a good way. He had that feeling that finally they were getting somewhere, the two of them. That her considerable defenses against him were weakening at last.

"You could come to my house for dinner, say on Wednesday?" she suggested. "Bring your ideas, places you want to visit. I'll think about where I'd like to go. We'll put our heads together." She sounded excited, to be planning her road trip adventure—with him.

He kind of wanted to let out a whoop of triumph, that she really must have missed him after she sent him away, that by some minor miracle, they were running off together for two weeks on the road. "Wednesday," he repeated. "I'll be there."

"All right, then—and thank you," she said, her face flushing the prettiest pink. "For today at the hospital. It was good, having you there."

He kept his butt in his seat and his hands to himself, though doing so required considerable effort. "I wanted to be there."

With a quick nod, she grabbed the door handle again.

Too soon, she was gone. He watched her get into her car and waved as she drove off.

At home, he changed into dry work clothes. With Kenzo in the front seat beside him, he headed for the corrals and the pastures farther out, to help with whatever needed doing.

That night, he skipped dinner with the family. Instead, he made himself a couple of roast beef sandwiches, sat at his kitchen table with the food and his laptop, and began planning his dream route to and from San Diego. He'd finished the food and was checking into the lodging options in and near Yellowstone when there was a knock on the front door.

It was his mother, her hands in the pockets of her faded jeans. "Jay." She smiled kind of nervously. "We missed you at dinner."

Now was as good a time as any to let her in on his plans. "I'm glad you came over. I need to talk to you." Now she looked worried. He asked, "Want some coffee?"

She managed a smile. "I would love some."

In the kitchen, he put a pod in the machine. "Have a seat."

She sat at the table. Neither of them spoke until he

set her coffee in front of her. She sipped it. "It's good. Thanks."

He took his own chair again, shut his laptop and pushed it aside. "What I wanted to talk to you about is that I'm going away for a couple of weeks starting next Monday, so if there's anything you really need me for, we should try to get on it this week. Also, I'll be staying at a lot of different places while I'm gone. Some of them likely won't take pets, so I'm hoping you'll look after Kenzo for me?" At his feet, the dog let out a whine. He leaned down to give the guy a reassuring scratch between the ears. "It's okay, boy…"

"Of course we'll look after Kenzo," she said. "But you're going away where…?" Her voice was too soft, too careful—because she knew damn well he was having trouble getting over the way she'd disrespected Piper. He loved his mother, and he didn't want to give himself any opportunities to say things he would later regret, so he'd been avoiding her lately.

"Piper and I are driving to San Diego to visit her father and his family. We're also stopping to see Grandma and Hector. The rest of the trip is kind of open-ended. We'll be taking our time, driving down through Las Vegas, then coming back up along the Coast Highway—at least that's the plan as of now. We just started figuring out the route."

"Ah. So, then you *are* still seeing her?"

"Not exactly. She wanted some time away from me after you ambushed her during dinner last month." Was that too harsh? Probably. But he felt zero desire to take the words back.

"You're *not exactly* seeing her, but you're leaving on a two-week trip with her?"

"That's right."

Meggie's eyes filled with tears. She blinked the wetness away and set her cup down with great care. "I understand that you're angry with me. But I honestly only want the best for you."

"I think I'm the one who gets to decide what's best for me, Mom."

She met his eyes squarely. "You're in love with her."

Love. That was between him and Piper, and they hadn't come anywhere near saying that word to each other. Damned if he would be discussing it with his mother first. "If I want to talk about Piper with you, Mom, I'll let you know."

Her mouth twisted. "I'm sorry, Jay." It came out in a ragged little whisper. "Your father says I've really put my foot in it. And I suppose I have. I never thought of myself as a person with prejudices."

"Oh, come on, Mom. We all have them. Face it."

"I'm sitting here looking at you and I see in your eyes that you are disappointed in me. And that breaks my heart. At the same time, I still feel that you would be happier with someone your own age."

"I'll say it again. It's up to me to decide who I'll be happy with. It's your job to back me up."

"Not if you're making a big mistake."

"A big mistake according to you, Mom. Think about it. Piper is a good person. She's smart and beautiful, with a big heart. She's also a lot of fun. She's someone you can count on to always hold up her end—and she works for a living at a job that really matters. I will never do better than Piper. I have a hard time believing that you can't see that. Piper and I are both adults. At this point in our lives, the years between us don't matter all that much, not the way I see it."

"But—"

He put up a hand. "But nothing. I could get hit by a truck tomorrow, or thrown from a horse. I could slip up with a chain saw, cut my femoral artery and bleed out before anyone knew I was dying. And then Piper could live on for fifty more years. Because we don't get to know how it's all going to shake out, how much time we'll be given. The best we can do is to choose someone extraordinary to stand up beside us and pray that our chosen one chooses us right back."

His mother looked down at her folded hands. When she lifted her head again, she gulped. "I know I already said this and that it offended you horribly, but what if you can never have children with her?"

He thought of the pulsing heart on the monitor that morning. That tiny life mattered to him. A lot. But that life was not the reason that he wanted Piper. "There are children in the world who need parents. That would be an option. And some couples never have kids, Mom—they never have kids and yet they have a great life together anyway."

Meggie picked up her empty cup and went to the counter. She rinsed it out and set it on the rack to dry. Finally, she turned and folded her arms across her middle. "I'll go to her. I'll apologize."

He shook his head. "Mom."

"What?"

"Just leave it alone for now."

"But I want to—"

"Don't. Leave it be."

She let out a frustrated sound. "Are you going to forgive me?"

"Of course."

She studied his face. "But...?"

"Please don't mess things up any more than you already have."

"I have a question," Piper said.

"Shoot."

"Would you consider just climbing in your pickup and winging it?"

It was almost nine on Wednesday night. After the terrific slow-cooker chicken cacciatore dinner she'd served him, they'd cleared off the table, opened their laptops and started planning their route to and from San Diego. So far, they'd discussed Yellowstone and Grand Teton, Salt Lake City and Las Vegas.

But campsites in Yellowstone were booked up months—even years—ahead. The hotels near the park were mostly booked, too. In Grand Teton, you couldn't book a campsite in advance. They would need to get there early in the morning or after four at night to have a chance at a spot. There was always a hotel room available in Vegas, but by the time they moved on to planning that part of the trip, Piper seemed pretty tense.

He put his hand over hers. "If you want to wing it, we'll wing it."

"You mean that?"

"Sure. But you know, if we don't book ahead, there might be nights when we can't get a room or a campsite. We could end up sleeping in the truck."

"One night in a truck isn't going to kill me—especially if it's that roomy GMC Sierra Denali of yours."

He wanted to kiss her. But then, he always wanted to kiss her. "Piper, we have to face facts."

"What facts, exactly?"

"You're pregnant. You sure that you want to sleep in the back of my truck?"

"Please. I'm perfectly healthy and not even showing yet. A night on a blow-up mattress or one of those foam pads is not going to kill me. My mom slept in the back of a VW bus through all but the last two months she was pregnant with me with no ill effects whatsoever."

"You're sure about this?"

"I am positive."

"Alrighty, then. We'll wing it."

She pushed her laptop away with a sigh. "Can you guess I have issues around planning trips? I really thought I was over that. But apparently not."

He still had hold of her other hand, so he gave it a squeeze. "What kind of issues?"

There was more sighing. She flipped a long swatch of that cinnamon-red hair back over her shoulder. "I really hate to criticize a man who can't defend himself."

This was getting more interesting by the minute. "You must mean Walter, am I right?"

"I do, yes. He planned every vacation we took together. He planned them meticulously, getting the best deals, locking us into a schedule we weren't allowed to vary from. He planned what time we would get up and what time we had to be in bed to get eight hours of sleep every night. He planned what restaurants we would go to. And he invariably tried to find a hotel with a free breakfast that we would eat in the hour he had reserved for breakfast on any given day.

"Every moment of every day was on the schedule. If anything ever messed up the schedule, he was a nervous wreck. He was driven to get things back to the plan. He meant well, you know? He really did. He wanted things to go smoothly. But by the last vacation we took together the year before he died, I didn't want to go. We had one of our few serious arguments that year. I laid it on the line that I wasn't going on a trip with him again until he could get a handle on his obsession with scheduling. He very gently suggested that I was making a big deal out of nothing. We left it at that. He died eight months later."

"Hey…"

She made a pouty face at him. "Now I feel terrible, saying bad things about Walter. He was a good man."

"Yes, he was."

"We had a good life, overall." What was it in her voice? Sadness? Yearning?

"Come here." He wrapped his arm around her and felt a surge of satisfaction when she didn't duck away.

And then she rested her head on his shoulder. Suddenly, life was nothing short of perfect. "Walter's been gone for four years," she said. "I really thought I could plan a trip without having a flashback over his obsession with scheduling…"

He stroked her arm and breathed in the apple scent of her shampoo. "So, then. What you're saying is that you need to get in the truck and hit the road. As for planning, you want to start looking for a place to eat whenever we get hungry. You want to find a motel when we need one and if one's not available, we'll camp out or sleep in the truck."

"That sounds so good."

"All right. I'll put on the camper shell. It's going to be downright cozy."

She laughed. The husky sound made him smile. "Yes. Please. I don't want a damn plan. I want to spend a weekend at my dad's place and then go see your grandmother from there. The rest can take care of itself."

"You're just lucky I've got a decent tent and sleeping bags. Bring hiking boots."

"I will, don't worry. Oh, Jason, a camper shell, a nice, big comfy truck, a tent and two sleeping bags. That's all the planning we need."

They left Medicine Creek behind at 8:00 a.m. on Monday morning. The sun was up, the sky a wide, baby blue bowl overhead with a few clouds snagged on the crests of the Bighorns to the west.

Jason felt like a million bucks, heading off for two weeks with Piper. Did it get any better than this?

Doubtful.

"What about Kenzo?" she asked, as the Welcome to Medicine Creek sign got smaller in the rearview. "I just assumed that you would bring him."

"He's a big guy and he needs space to roam. Plus, having him along would make it even harder to get a room at the last minute."

"Will he be all right without you there?"

"Oh, yeah. My mom loves him. He follows my dad around. And Kenzo loves his Frisbee. Joe is always willing to throw it for him."

They stopped at the Henry's Diner in Buffalo for breakfast and got right back on the road. The rolling land was still green, the prairie grasses waving in the wind, stretching out forever to the east, meeting the mountains in the west.

Piper said, "We could spend a little time in Red Lodge or Sweetwater, visit the county museums."

"I can't believe we're skipping both Yellowstone and Grand Teton."

"It's okay. I like this route better. And right now, I'm just not in the mood for driving around trying to get a good shot of a bear or maybe a buffalo so I can post it to Instagram. But I do love that we're taking our time getting there. It feels less pressured than jumping on a plane and showing up at my long-lost father's house that same day."

He stole another look at her. She had her head tipped back, her eyes closed, and she'd opened her window a crack. Her hair was gathered up in a fat knot, but bits of it had escaped. The wind blew the shiny strands against her cheek. She kept brushing them away from those soft lips of hers.

"This is wonderful," she said kind of drowsily. "You know, the open road? Just you and me heading on toward the far horizon."

"I like it, too." A lot. "Are you nervous about meeting your dad?"

She slid him a look then. "I am, yes. But that won't be till next weekend. I'm going to try not to get too worked up about it ahead of time."

"Good idea. Are we telling him that he's going to be a grandfather?"

She made a little humming sound. It was soft and husky at the same time. It reminded him of their one night together, of her lips on his skin, of all the things he'd done to her, and also the ones he hadn't done. Yet. "I haven't decided if I'm ready to tell him," she said. "I don't even know him, Jason. And I'm still in the first trimester. We had kind of decided to wait until the twelve-week mark, hadn't we?"

"Yeah. You'll be nine weeks along on the day we arrive at your dad's."

"I am aware." She pressed a palm to her flat belly. "The day I meet my father, our baby will be the size of a Hershey's Kiss."

Our baby. He loved the sound of that even more than he had hearing her say she liked being out on the open road with him.

The rest of the morning went by mostly in silence. He drove. She read one of the books she'd brought and snoozed on and off. He played country and soft rock, nothing too exciting, the kind of music that didn't interfere with conversation—or with her dropping off to sleep now and then.

They stopped in Rawlins for a quick lunch.

Back in the car, she rolled up her window. He heard her soft sigh as she tucked her small pillow against the glass and rested her head on it.

They rode in silence for a while. It didn't take long for her to fall asleep again. She looked peaceful, he thought, as he turned his gaze back to the road.

Piper woke with a groan. Her belly churned. "Oh, no! Not now…"

"What is it? What's wrong?" Jason shot her a worried glance from behind the wheel. "Are you sick?"

"I'm about to throw up. Pull over, please."

The road went on forever, the land stretching out end-lessly to either side, mesas and buttes rising in the distance, red and gold against the endless sky. Charming, wispy clouds drifted in the giant bowl of the sky. There was an 18-wheeler in front of them and another big rig coming up fast in her side-view mirror.

Again, her stomach lurched. "I'm sorry, Jason. I'm about to…"

"It's okay, we're stopping." He was already pulling to the shoulder. The semitruck behind them blew on by.

Not that she cared about anything but getting out of that vehicle before she ejected the contents of her stomach all over the dashboard.

She yanked the handle and the door swung open as she more or less fell out onto the graveled shoulder, getting her feet under her just in time to keep from ending up flat on her face. Vaguely, she heard the sound of the driver's door slamming shut.

A dry, narrow ditch waited about ten inches from her Nikes. All she had to do was lean over it and let nature take its course.

It was convenient, but not pretty. By then, Jason had rounded the front of the crew cab. He skidded to a halt beside her as the remains of the burger and fries she'd gobbled back in Rawlins made a truly unattractive reap-pearance.

She coughed and sputtered.

Hey, at least she had her hair anchored in a bun and out of the way.

"Oh, sweetheart…" *Sweetheart.* He'd never called her that before. It sounded way too wonderful in that deep, serious voice of his. He rubbed her back, his big, warm hand stroking between her shoulder blades. His touch felt so right, so soothing and good.

Or it did until she started heaving again. Every last thing in her stomach came up. There was nothing left in there but a weird, gurgling sound.

"Oh, my dear Lord," she moaned.

"That's right," he said, his voice so calm and in control, reminding her sharply of the night in April when she'd been bold and free and naked in his big arms. "That's right," he soothed again. "Better...?"

"Ugh. Well, it seems to be over, so that's something."

"Here." He took her hand and put a bottled water in her palm. He must have grabbed it from the cooler in the back seat before racing to her side.

"You read my mind." Screwing off the cap, she took a big sip and used it to rinse the awful taste from her mouth by gargling and spitting right there in front of him. Once that was done, she took a long, much-needed drink. "Oh, Jason. Thank you."

He kept rubbing her back. It felt really good. "Be honest with me. Are you okay?"

She sipped more water and then took a few slow, deep breaths. "I am now."

"Should we find a doctor?" Beneath the shadow of his hat, his face was drawn with concern.

"A doctor? It's just morning sickness."

He blinked at her. "You never said you had morning sickness."

"You're right. I didn't. It never, uh, came up." She stuck out her tongue and pretended to gag.

He groaned. "Oh, now you're a comedian." Another

semitruck flew past, loud and fast. The pickup behind them swayed in its wake.

"We should get back on the road," she said, "before one of those big rigs mows us down."

He didn't reply, just backed up and held the door wide as she climbed into her seat. Two minutes later, they were on their way again.

She drank the last of her water and slipped the empty bottle down by her feet to deal with later. The cab seemed too quiet. At some point, he'd turned the music off.

"How about if we stop in Green River?" he asked. "We can look around there for a place to spend the night."

"It's early," she said. "It hasn't even been seven hours since we left home."

"It's not a race," he offered quietly. "We have days to get there."

She glanced his way, saw how serious he looked and dropped the teasing attitude. "You're worried about me."

"Well, Piper. You're pregnant. You just threw up everything you've eaten today."

"I'm okay, I promise you. Throwing up is what pregnant ladies do—at least during the first few months." She kept her voice light and teasing.

He still looked grim. "Are you sick every morning?"

"No."

"How often?"

She thought about that. "Two or three times a week. And not always in the morning. Sometimes, like today, it happens in the afternoon. Sometimes in the evening."

"Have you lost weight?"

"Stop worrying. This is normal. Just ask Dr. Hayes. All the pregnancy and childbirth books say so, too."

"But have you lost weight?"

"A few pounds, which is also normal. Don't worry. I'll put it back on and a lot more before this baby makes her appearance in the big, wide world."

"You think it's a girl?" Was he almost smiling now? Definitely.

"Not sure," she said. "Sometimes I do. Sometimes I'm a hundred percent positive it's a strong, handsome boy. Then a day or two later, I'm absolutely certain it's a beautiful little girl all over again."

"It's just that I had no idea." He was so solemn, so serious again. "You should have told me."

"I'm lost. I should have told you what?"

"The morning sickness. Has it been bad?"

"No. I mean, it's no fun, but I really am healthy and feeling great overall. Plus, I read that some experts believe that women who have morning sickness during the first trimester have a lower risk of miscarriage than women who don't."

"You think that's true?"

"I have no idea, but every time I run to the bathroom to lose my lunch, I remind myself that hugging the toilet is a good thing because it's proof that the baby is doing just fine."

"Well, all right, then." He took off his hat and plunked it on her head.

Grinning, she flipped down the visor to admire her look in the mirror there. "I've always loved this hat. Unfortunately, it's too big for me." She had to push it back off her forehead or it covered her eyes. "Here you go." Plucking it off, she reached across the console and put it back on his head. "And stop worrying about the morning sickness. I'm the expert and I'm telling you it's perfectly natural."

He tipped the brim to his liking. "Got it all figured out, huh?"

"No. But I'm faking it for all I'm worth."

At the Green River Hampton Inn and Suites, they could have had adjoining rooms. But they agreed that one room with two queen beds would do just fine. Sharing a room saved money. Plus, Piper didn't want to be apart from him—and no, she would not be sharing his queen bed with him. But it was so great, just the two of them, off on their big adventure, future co-parents getting to know each other better. It seemed so natural to stay in the same room.

The room was inviting and comfortable. It even had a view of the Green River Buttes, a beautiful, layered shale formation rising up out of the desert hills behind the hotel.

"Maybe an early dinner?" he asked as soon as they'd each claimed a bed and put their toiletries in the bathroom.

"Absolutely. I need to eat. And soon."

They went to the Hitching Post, a rustic place on the main drag a few miles from the hotel. Their server was friendly and fast. Piper ate all of her salad and then gobbled down her chicken fried steak and fries—and some of Jason's, too.

He sipped his beer and watched her eat. "So, then, I guess you're feeling better?"

"Pass the hot sauce. Yes, I am."

After dinner, they returned to the hotel. Jason toed off his boots, grabbed the remote and dropped to the end of his bed.

Piper removed her shoes, too, and stretched out on her

bed. Her stomach was full, and she felt good—tired, but satisfied. And completely relaxed, too. She'd left all her everyday concerns back home in Medicine Creek. She stared up at the ceiling as she slowly wound a swatch of her hair around her index finger.

"Deep thoughts?" Jason asked.

She glanced his way and saw he'd hitched a knee up on his bed and turned to watch her. "Not really," she said. "Just thinking that until I was nine years old, all I wanted in the world was to get out of my mom's Volkswagen bus and go live in Medicine Creek like a regular girl. And yet, here I am, finally back on the road thirty-one years later, headed off to meet my bio-dad for the first time. And so far, I'm loving every minute of it."

"You are, huh?"

"Yeah."

"Well, good." His eyes still locked with hers, he pointed the remote at the TV, muting the sound.

They shared a smile that went on for a long time. Finally, she covered her mouth with the back of her hand as she yawned. "I'm just going to close my eyes for a minute."

"Go for it. Sleep as long as you want."

She yawned again and let her eyes drift shut. "Not sleeping, only...resting."

For a while, Jason just sat there at the end of his bed watching her sleep. She was really out. He could see her eyes moving behind the delicate screens of her eyelids. She must be dreaming.

He looked down at his stocking feet and grinned. Because hey, it was just him and Piper and life was good.

Couldn't get any better—unless at some point they only needed one bed.

That would be about as perfect as it gets.

He crawled up the mattress, tucked a pillow under his head and pointed the remote at the TV one more time to turn it off. And then he shut his eyes.

Might as well nap while she was napping.

The next thing he knew, Piper was standing over him, wearing a red swimsuit that clung to every beautiful curve. "Wake up, sleepyhead."

"Huh?" he asked stupidly, enraptured by the view. She had a happy gleam in her eyes and constellations of freckles on her shoulders and down her pale arms. He hadn't seen most of those freckles since that night in April.

"They have an indoor pool here," she said. "I want to try it. Come with me. Put on your swim trunks and let's go."

How could he say no to Piper in a red swimsuit?

He dug his board shorts from his duffel and changed in the bathroom like the future co-parent and good friend he'd agreed to be.

The pool was pretty basic. The only people there were kids and enough parents to keep an eye on them. Still, he and Piper got in and swam around a bit. They acted like kids themselves, dunking each other and splashing around.

Eventually, they got out, toweled off and went back to the room, where they took turns in the shower. At her urging, he went first. Took him fifteen minutes to shower, brush his teeth and get dressed for bed in an old pair of gray sweatpants. He flopped down on his bed.

"My turn," she said, and disappeared into the bathroom, where she took her time. When she came out into the main room again, she had on a big T-shirt printed with an image of a flying female superhero holding a thick book high beneath the caption *Librarian. The original search engine.*

"Lookin' good," he remarked.

"Why, thank you." She gave him a game little grin and moved in between their two beds. As she climbed into her bed, he got a whiff of apple-scented shampoo and minty toothpaste.

"Want to try a movie?" he asked.

She turned to lie on her side facing him. Plumping her pillow, she tucked it under her cheek. "Go for it. Choose whatever you like." Her eyes were already drifting closed.

"Never mind," he said. "We can watch a movie some other time."

"Okay, then…" She smiled but didn't open her eyes.

He got up to get his sketch pad from his duffel bag. Back in bed, he fiddled around drawing the buttes that rose up behind the hotel. The curtains were shut and he couldn't actually see them, so he faked it from memory. When that got old, he put the sketch pad aside and turned off the lamp between their beds.

His eyes adjusted to the gloom. There was just enough light bleeding through from outside that he could he indulge himself watching Piper sleep. She didn't move at all. Her breath came shallow and even. The pale curve of her cheek enthralled him.

"Jason?" she asked sleepily.

"Yeah?"

"You're staring at me."

He laughed. "Call me a creeper. I thought you were out for the night."

"Actually, I *was* asleep. For a few minutes anyway." She rolled to her back and put her hands behind her head.

"You know, you've listened to me blather on about Walter and my childhood. I think you should tell me about you."

"What? So we can be better co-parents?" He said the dreaded word and waited for the irritation to rise. But strangely enough, right now, with her nice and close in the other bed, saying *co-parent* out loud didn't piss him off as much as usual.

"No," she replied. "You should tell me more about you so that we can be better friends."

Friends. Another word he didn't like all that much since she started using it to define the distance between them. But fair enough. She wanted him to talk about himself. He would talk. "Relationships with women, you mean?"

"Sure."

"I told you about Jenny Rosario."

"You did. Now tell me more."

"What, specifically?"

"You said that you told her you loved her."

"I did, yes."

"So, then, what happened? How did it end with her?"

"We found out we wanted different things."

"Like...?"

"I realized I wanted to go away to college for a couple of years. She didn't want me to go."

"When did you decide to go away to college?"

"The summer after junior year. I went off to California to visit my grandma Sharilyn. My grandmother saw that I'd started carrying a sketchbook around with me. I would draw all the time, doodles mostly, but also sketches of things I saw or imagined. Grandma Sharilyn took me to art shows, and I loved it."

"And you decided you wanted to go away to college?"

"That's right. I came back to Wyoming excited over the idea of spending a couple of years in California, studying art. I told Jenny all about it, reassuring her that it wouldn't be forever, that I would come home to live, help run the ranch as I'd grown up knowing I would. We would get married in a few years, as we'd planned. But I wanted more, too. I wanted to find a way to get lost in making something beautiful, something special. I said I would love it if she wanted to come with me. Or that if she chose to stay home, we would make it work long-distance. After all, I would be home in the summers and back at the ranch for good within two years."

"How did she react?"

"She asked me why I couldn't just draw my pictures right here in Wyoming, maybe go to Wyoming State if I just *had* to go to college. Her idea was that I could take a few art classes and study ranch management, too. She pretty much had our future mapped out. But I wasn't on board with her plan anymore, and it just kind of fell apart between us. We broke up before Christmas that year." It still hurt to remember how it had ended with Jenny. She'd cried and said he'd ruined everything, that he'd changed, and she hardly knew him anymore.

And he *had* changed. He'd flown to California to see his grandmother and returned wanting something he hadn't realized he needed.

Piper lifted up on an elbow. "Are you okay? You seem kind of down all of a sudden." She turned on the light.

He blinked against the sudden brightness. And then he shook his head. "When I look back on that time, I'm disappointed. In myself, mostly. I hurt Jenny. When we broke up, she said that I'd lied to her, that I'd said I wanted our life together just the way she had it all planned—and then suddenly I decided I needed to move halfway across the country for two years."

"But Jason, you were in high school. You were just learning what you wanted from life. It turned out that what you wanted didn't mesh with Jenny's goals. That seems like a natural progression to me. And by that I mean, people do fall in love in high school all the time—and then most of them change. They grow apart. It doesn't last."

"Yeah, that is exactly what happened. But I'd had it in my head that Jenny and I were going to be the rare exception. We were going to be forever—and we didn't even make it till graduation. I'd believed we had everything in common. I'd considered her my everything and then all of a sudden she was walking away. And I let her go. I wanted those two years at college in LA more than I wanted a lifetime with Jenny."

"Look on the bright side. You didn't let what happened with Jenny make you cynical about love. You said you did try again…"

"Right. I wasn't giving up. I met Eloise Delaney at Santa Monica College. She was studying graphic design. Eloise and I lasted until I was ready to come home. She made it crystal clear that she had no interest in moving to Wyoming. And I realized I wasn't willing to stay in California for her. I came home alone. For a while, I tried just being single, hooking up now and then, keeping it casual. But then, two years after Eloise and I called it quits, I started going out with Caroline Frost."

"I think I've met her. She's a teacher, right?"

"Yep. Caroline teaches first grade at Medicine Creek Elementary. I was settled at the ranch by then, building my house, planning to add my workshop in back. Caroline's a good woman. She's sweet and she's giving. She was willing to move in with me, but…"

"What?"

"It just wasn't right between us. There was something missing. I don't even know what to call it. I mean, I did love her, but the word *love* covers a whole lot of ground. What I've been looking for is more specific."

"Specific, how?"

He leveled his best tough-guy glare at her. "Don't laugh."

"I won't. I swear it," she vowed. His heart ached at the fierce determination on her face. She looked so young right then. He could almost picture what she must have been like as a child. Quiet. Curious. Observant. Passionate about the things that mattered to her. No doubt an avid reader with a big vocabulary.

He wanted to get up, join her in her bed, take her in his arms. But he doubted she would go for that—not right now anyway—so he stayed where he was and said, "It's my parents."

"What do you mean, what about them?"

"It's…what they have together. Who they are to each other. My dad can be too tough for his own good and my mom can be infuriatingly overprotective of me and my brother and sister. But together, they have what I'm talking about. They have that…connection. I grew up seeing that every day. Feeling the strength in it, the power of knowing you're with someone who thrills you, someone who's with you in the deepest ways. Someone you can count on who knows she can depend on you right back."

Those green eyes were enormous now. "Jason, what you just said…"

"What about it?"

"It's beautiful."

"You think so?" He didn't know what he felt now. Embarrassed to have said so much? Thrilled that she seemed to get it?

"Yes, I do think so," she answered him in a near whisper. And then she sighed. It wasn't a happy sound.

He tried to lighten the mood by teasing, "I didn't talk your ear off just to make you feel sad."

"Sometimes life is sad, that's all."

He should let it go. He knew it. Enough had been said for one night—and way too much of it by him. But he wanted to know about her life, about the events and choices that made her who she was. "Why did you marry Walter Wallace? I mean, you told me you shouldn't have married him, but that he made you feel safe. So is that it? You married him because you needed to feel safe?"

She said nothing.

He had no idea what was happening in that sharp mind of hers. And after several painful seconds ticked by in silence, he knew he'd pushed her further than she was willing to go. "You're not going to tell me, are you?"

She shook her head. "Not tonight."

"Fair enough." He tamped down his impatience with her and kept his voice neutral. Yeah, he wanted her to let him in on her secrets. He wanted that a lot. But only when she was ready to share them with him. "Good night, Piper." He turned out the light.

Chapter Nine

Piper didn't sleep well that night.

And not because she was in a strange bed.

She felt guilty that she hadn't made herself answer Jason when he'd asked her why she'd married Walter. After all, the man had answered every question she'd thrown at him about Jenny and Eloise and Caroline. About his take on love in general and how his parents' relationship had shaped his beliefs about life. Whatever she'd asked, he'd answered frankly and directly. And before that, in the afternoon, he'd rubbed her back while she chucked up her lunch on the side of the road.

Jason Bravo was a good man with an honest heart. And yet, she couldn't bring herself to explain to him why she'd said yes when Walter Wallace asked her to be his wife. To explain that she would have to talk about Brandon McAdams.

Piper hated to get into the catastrophe of Brandon. It was an ugly story. One best left unshared.

In the morning, she expected Jason to be unhappy with her—either curt and sarcastic or distant and reproachful. In her intimate experience with the male of the species, she'd found that neither Brandon nor Walter could just let an issue go. If they didn't get their way, they seemed driven to make their displeasure painfully clear, Brandon aggressively and Walter with silence and wounded looks.

But not Jason.

He woke with a smile. "Mornin'. Are you starving or is it just me?" Sitting up, he stretched and yawned, his strong arms flexing, those beautiful back muscles bunching in the most tempting way under all that smooth, tanned skin—and then he caught her watching him. He winked.

She laughed and threw her pillow at him.

He caught it. "So, then. Breakfast here at the hotel?"

"Yes. And let's get going on that. I'm starving."

After they left the hotel, they paid a visit to the Sweetwater County Historical Museum right there in Green River. It was a quick tour. They viewed several fine examples of Native American art and learned about coal mining in Sweetwater County.

By ten, they were back on the road. She used a little of the drive time to book them a nice room at the Hyatt in Lehi for that night.

"Separate rooms?" she asked. "We can get them adjoining…"

He shot her a look—half amused, half watchful—and then dumped the question right back in her lap. "What do *you* think?"

"Well, there's a separate sitting area in each room anyway. Why waste our money? I'll just get us one room with two queens. Last night, it worked out fine, I thought."

"Sounds great to me."

Three hours after leaving Green River, they reached the Great Salt Lake at Saltair, a former resort area where they could walk out across the endless hard, white sand to the edge of what was left of the lake.

It was beautiful and somewhat haunting, the whiteness of all that sand, the diminishing lake gray in the shallows, cool blue farther out. The wind tossed her hair and Jason took her hand.

She was glad just to be there, to have his fingers twined with hers.

And she didn't throw up until they were headed east toward the junction of I-80 and I-15. Once again, he rubbed her back as she lost the contents of her stomach on the side of the road. At least she'd had the good sense to pull her hair back again, so he didn't have to choose between holding it out of the way and giving her that gentle, soothing back rub that made puking a lot easier to bear.

Afterward, he gave her a bottle of water just like the day before. She took it gratefully.

When they got back in the car, she burst into tears for no real reason that she could come up with. He popped open the glove box and handed her a packet of tissues.

After she blew her nose and dabbed at her eyes, she sniffled and admitted, "I honestly have no idea why I'm crying."

"You're allowed." He reached out an arm and wrapped his fingers around the back of her neck.

She sagged across the console to rest her head on his shoulder. "My life as I have known it is gone."

He stroked her pulled-back hair. "A lot of things will stay the same."

"Uh-uh. Everything's changing. I love it."

He kissed the top of her head, and she liked it too much to remind him that they were friends and future co-parents and that was all. Then he asked, "You love that everything's changing and that makes you cry?"

She glanced up at his granite-firm jaw and those lips she thought way too often about kissing again. "Actually, it's the terror that makes me cry."

"The terror of...?"

"Childbirth, stretch marks, not being any good at nursing, doing everything wrong and traumatizing an innocent child. Being torn between my work and my baby. Never getting a single night of decent sleep for... I don't know, two or three years, at least."

"It's not going to be that bad."

"Easy for you to say."

"Yeah, because I intend to hold up my end. You won't be doing this alone."

She dabbed at her eyes again. "Thank you. I needed to hear that."

"Well, it's true. As for the rest of your concerns, you're going to be a wonderful mother and our kid will be a happy kid. You're amazing at your job and you'll work out a good balance. They have drugs to help you through labor if you need them. And I'm happy to look after the baby whenever you're short on sleep."

"Hmph. I notice you failed to address stretch marks or nursing."

He gave her that irresistible half grin of his. "Keeping track, were you?"

"Well, they are my worries. Of course I was keeping track—and we should probably get off the shoulder before a state trooper stops to ask us what's going on."

"Good idea."

She peeled herself off him and he started up the truck.

At the Hyatt Place in Lehi, their sleek, modern room had a view of Traverse Mountain.

"See?" she said only half-jokingly. "We always get the terrific mountain views in our hotels—and okay, the butte in Green River isn't quite a mountain. But close…"

"The mountain looks great," he agreed.

"And there's an outside pool. The weather's good. We can swim."

"But first…"

"Food," she finished for him. "Absolutely."

They left their suitcases in the middle of the floor and went to search out a good place to eat.

It was late afternoon when they returned to the Hyatt. She had a nap. When she woke, Jason was drawing something in his sketchbook, and it was still daylight.

"Swim?" she asked.

He tossed his sketchbook aside. "Sure."

In the pool, they acted like a couple of rowdy fools. She made him let her get up on his shoulders and then had him walk around in the water with her that way while she laughed and waved her arms and then had to grab his head with both hands so she wouldn't fall off. He ended up dunking her. She squealed like a six-year-old as she went under. It was so much fun.

How long had it been, really, since she'd laughed with a man and acted silly and young? Forever, it felt like— and just possibly never. Walter was always so serious. As for Brandon, well, she'd been head over heels for him, but he'd never been the type to goof around. Far from it. Brandon approached every activity as an opportunity to win.

When it started to get dark, they went back to the room. She had a shower, put on her sleep shirt and sat on her bed with her iPad to check messages. There was an email from Starr asking where she'd run off to.

I stopped in at the library today. Libby at the circulation desk says you're away on a two-week vacation. Good for you—and where to? I will need details.

Piper started to compose a fluffy response about driving to San Diego just for the fun of it, implying that she was all on her own. But no way Starr would buy that story. And why keep the truth about the trip a secret anyway? Starr was her friend and friends deserved the truth—no, not about the baby. Yet. But everything else, definitely.

She wrote a long, chatty email explaining that she was on the road with Jason to meet her bio-dad and visit his grandmother in LA.

Starr zipped back a short response. You're on a road trip with my cousin to meet your long-lost father? I am smiling ear to ear. Send my love to Jason and have a fabulous time. I will want to know all on our next coffee date.

On the other bed, Jason looked up from his sketchbook. "Good news?"

She realized she'd chuckled over Starr's note. "Just an email from Starr. She sends you her love."

"So Starr knows…?"

"…that we're on our way to meet my dad and see your grandmother."

He gave her a slow nod and a smile to match. Then he tossed his sketchbook aside. "How about a movie?"

They chose one together. She fell asleep before the end without getting under the covers.

When she woke at four the next morning, she had the extra blanket from the closet tucked in close around her. In the other bed, Jason was fast asleep. With a happy sigh, she closed her eyes and drifted off again.

* * *

Jason woke suddenly. The sun was up, light bleeding into the room around the edges of the still-shut blinds. He stretched out a hand for his phone to check the time.

"It's a little after eight," Piper informed him from the other bed. "I brought you coffee. It's right there on the nightstand, next to your phone."

"Uh, thanks." Blinking away the last remnants of sleep, he dragged himself to a sitting position and grabbed the coffee. It was perfect, hot and black. "So good," he said.

Piper was sitting up against the headboard with her iPad. She still wore her big shirt, but she'd pulled on a pair of jeans, too. "I have a plan." She slid him a grin.

He took another sip of coffee. "Tell me."

"We haven't camped. You brought a tent and sleeping bags. I say we skip Vegas and camp at Zion National Park."

Gently, he reminded her, "We'll never get a campsite."

"Never say never. I was up and online at six. Somebody canceled. It's at Watchman Campground. I read a bunch of reviews. It's kind of crowded, not a lot of shade. But there's parking right there in the campground. No showers, but water and nice restrooms. It's a good place to hike from and the views are spectacular." She looked at him hopefully.

"Tell me you already booked it."

"Well, yeah. I did."

"Terrific. Otherwise it would be gone by now."

She grinned. "I kind of figured that, so I made my move."

"Smart girl."

She dropped her iPad to the mattress, jumped up and plopped down next to him on his bed. Her hair hung in a braid down her back and her face was scrubbed clean of makeup. She looked so young—young and carefree, ready for anything. "Is that a yes to camping at Zion National Park?"

He dared to reach out and tug on that red braid. "You bet."

"Yes!" And she threw those soft arms around him.

What could he do but wrap her up in a hug? He breathed in her sweetness and reveled in the feel of her soft cheek against his scruffy one.

Too soon, she was pulling away. Taking him by the shoulders, she announced, "It's a three-and-a-half-hour drive to the park. I booked tonight and tomorrow night. I was thinking we'd get up early Friday, drive to San Diego and get a room for that night. And then we can go on to my dad's house Saturday morning."

"Well, all right. We'll need to stop for food and a few supplies. Let's get some breakfast and get a move on."

The Watchman Campground was pretty much what he'd expected—endless loops of camping slots, lots of people, kind of noisy.

And gorgeous, with the giant sandstone bluffs known as monoliths all around. Deer that had no fear of noise or giant RVs wandered freely among the campsites, nipping at the grass.

Piper had reserved a spot midway between the creek and the road. Their camp was out of sight of the parking area, so that was pretty nice. They set up the tent and walked past the visitor center and right into the town of Springdale to eat.

That night, he built a campfire. They roasted marshmallows and laughed together at the stuff the people camping nearby said and did. There was trash talk and even a little yelling and at one point, someone played "Hey, Soul Sister" on the ukulele. It was noisy, no doubt about it.

Around ten thirty they crawled into the tent. They were lying close, their sleeping bags touching. He didn't mind that at all. A couple nearby argued over whether or not they were stopping in Palm Springs to visit her mother.

Piper whispered, "Don't you just love the wilderness?"

"I do," he agreed. "Or I would, if there was anything left of it around here."

Sometime after midnight, he finally fell asleep.

When he woke up later in the night, Piper was even closer than before. Much closer. She'd turned on her side with her back to him and scooted his way until they were smashed together, spoon-style, separated only by their sleeping bags. For about half a second, he felt guilty that he was in her space, cradling her round bottom on his thighs—but she was out cold, completely unbothered by the fact that she was essentially perched in his lap. He wrapped an arm around her, pulled her closer still, buried his face in her apple-scented hair and went back to sleep.

Near daylight, he woke again, smiling before he opened his eyes because he still held her in his arms, though she'd turned over at some point. Now they were face-to-face. Through the layers of their sleeping bags, he could feel the curve of her waist, the round softness of her breasts.

"Jason…"

He let his eyelids drift open and found himself looking directly into her green eyes. "Mornin'," he said. She brought her hands up between them and pressed them to his chest. He grumbled, "I suppose I'm going to have to let you go."

She nodded but made no move to escape. "I was thinking we could get up, grab a couple of protein bars and bottles of water and take the Watchman Trail. The trailhead is here, by the visitor center. From what I read about it, the hike is pretty easy, the trail smooth and clear, about three miles round trip, and the views are supposed to be spectacular."

"You want it, we'll do it."

Twenty minutes later, they were on their way.

As she'd predicted, the trail was easy and well marked, scattered with pretty patches of wildflowers. They weren't alone. Others walked ahead and behind them.

At the lookout, they got a panoramic view of Zion National Park, including more than one of the spectacular sandstone monoliths. As a bonus, they could see the town of Springdale tucked beneath the cliffs below.

Piper had her hair corralled in that big braid, but bits of it were loose, blowing against her cheeks. She would brush them away and they would blow right back again. He got out his phone and took some pictures of her gazing out over the town below.

The rest of the day went by too fast. They took the shuttle to the trailhead and hiked the West Bank of the Virgin River. Then they explored the Emerald Pools Trails, where there were waterfalls tumbling into small green pools and gorgeous views of stunning cliffs in all directions.

As dinnertime approached, they took the shuttle back to camp, washed up in the campground restroom and then went to Springdale for burgers. They turned in early with plans to get going before dawn for the long drive to San Diego.

"Today was amazing," she said, when they were bedded down in the tent, facing each other in their separate sleeping bags. "I'm glad you got pictures."

"Me, too." He'd taken a bunch of them, the majority with Piper in the foreground. It had been a great day and he hated to see it end. He was smiling to himself, feeling good about this trip, happy about his growing closeness with Piper. Everything seemed to be going so well.

And then, with zero warning, Piper said, "I feel kind of sick to my stomach."

Alarm skittered through him. Vomit in sleeping bags was never pretty. "Let's get you outside."

He was crawling out of his bag when she put her hand on his arm. "It's okay. I'm not actually going to throw up this time."

How could she know that? "You're sure?"

"Yeah. I'm not *that* kind of sick."

"Okay." He was all the way out of his sleeping bag and staying there in case quick action might still be called for. "What kind of sick are we talking about, then?" Sitting cross-legged in the fleece shorts he'd worn to sleep in, he turned on his lantern and waited for her to explain.

Meanwhile, from the next camp over, a woman started singing "Someone Like You." She sounded drunk.

Piper laughed. "I'm pretty sure that's not Adele."

"I'm pretty sure you're right—tell me what's wrong."

The woman kept on singing. Piper clutched her middle and laughed even harder. And then, in an instant, she was sobbing.

"Ah, sweetheart..." He reached for her.

With a little moan, she scrambled from her sleeping bag and crawled into his lap.

He held her close, rubbed her back and whispered soothing, meaningless things. It was heaven, the feel of her in his arms. He enjoyed the moment far too much, given that she was clearly miserable, and he had no real idea how to help. At least his duffel was in reach. He took a travel pack of tissues from the front pocket and handed them over.

She laughed through her tears. "At this rate, I'm going to use up all your Kleenex."

He stroked her hair. "It's not a problem. I know where they sell them."

She sniffled and blew her nose as the woman at the other campsite finished the song.

There was clapping from more than one direction.

The drunken singer shouted, "Thank you, thank you! I love you all!"

"No more, damn it!" a gruff voice bellowed from the opposite direction. "No more, I'm begging you!"

Not too far away, someone burst into laughter.

By then, Piper's tears had stopped. She looked up at him through misty eyes. Her nose was red. He wanted to kiss her so bad it hurt.

But right now, kissing was not what she needed. "Talk to me," he said.

She sniffed. "I'm meeting my father the day after to-morrow. It's really going to happen. And I can't stop thinking, what if I hate him? What if his wife resents me? And what about their kids—who aren't actually kids anymore? What if my half sisters and brother want nothing to do with me?"

"You liked him from his emails and texts, remember? You said you thought he was a very nice man."

"You're right, I did." She swiped at her eyes with the tissue again. "But what if I was wrong? What if...?" She stopped in midsentence and let out a long sigh. "I'm being ridiculous."

"Uh-uh. You're being human. You're going to meet your father for the first time. That's big. So big. It's only natural for you to have all kinds of questions that can't be answered until you get to know him a little. Of course you feel anxious and uneasy..."

"Is it only natural to crawl into your lap and cry like a baby?"

"What are you talking about? You didn't cry like a baby."

She scoffed. "Jason, we both know I did."

"No. You cried like a woman—for a totally understandable reason. It's a whole different thing."

That brought a sniffly laugh from her. "Well. I feel so much better about bawling all over you now." Biting that tender lower lip of hers, she patted his chest. "You're a rock. Thank you."

"You can bawl all over me anytime."

"Yeah, well..." Now her cheeks were as red as her nose. She chose that moment to retreat. Scrambling out of his lap, she wriggled back into her sleeping bag. "We should probably try to get some sleep."

"Good idea," he lied. He would rather she crawled back into his lap so that he could sit there, grinning like a fool, holding her all night long.

But that wasn't going to happen, so he turned off the lantern and climbed into his own bag.

It took him quite a while to get to sleep. When he did, it wasn't for all that long.

He woke again to the feel of Piper, sound asleep and plastered right up against him the way she'd done the night before. He eased onto his side. Pulling her closer still, he buried his face in her hair.

Piper woke to the gray light of dawn bleeding in through the tent flap, which was no longer zipped. She glanced over her shoulder to find Jason's sleeping bag neatly rolled and ready for their imminent departure.

Right then, she heard the crunch of boots outside. A moment later he ducked through the flaps, looking like a hot mountain-climbing cowboy in jeans, a blue plaid flannel shirt and black Timberlands.

"You're awake." He gave her that special smile, the one that made her feel everything was right with the world. "I was thinking of getting the fire going, making coffee…"

Her eyes felt puffy from all that crying. She must look half-dead. Gulping down a soggy mishmash of feelings, she shook her head. "Let's just pack up, have breakfast in Springdale and then get on the road."

"You got it."

After quickly cleaning up in the campground washrooms, they got breakfast burritos and really great coffee in a little place called the Deep Creek Coffee Company. The service was as good as the food. Smiling, with full bellies, they were on the road by seven.

The trip through the desert to Southern California took almost eight hours. There were lots of things to see on the way, but Piper wasn't paying a whole lot of attention. The endless, dry, rolling desert fled away beneath the wheels of Jason's crew cab. She kept thinking of the stranger and his family she was rushing to meet.

It all seemed unreal.

Never leaving the highway, they blew right past Vegas and kept going till Barstow, where they stopped at a roadside diner for lunch. She barely tasted her Reuben sandwich and Jason ate most of her fries.

He didn't ask her if she was okay. She could see in his eyes that he understood her anxiety. It wasn't something she wanted to talk about. She just needed to get there and get that first meeting over with.

Too bad she had to live through the rest of the day and the night to follow before she would see her father's face for the very first time and begin to find out if he was someone she could ever feel close to.

"You in the mood to take the wheel?" Jason asked when they left the diner. He'd driven the whole way up till now and they'd both been perfectly happy with that.

She knew his game. "You're trying to distract me from this latest bout of tortured anxiety and doubt, right?"

"Is it working?"

"No. But I appreciate the effort. And sure, I'll drive for a while."

She got behind the wheel. He took her spot on the passenger side and off they went.

"We need some good music," he announced and then got busy working up a playlist. He turned the sound up loud. Everything he played was upbeat—from "Walking on Sunshine" to "Get the Party Started" to "Boot Scootin' Boogie" and "Proud Mary."

After an hour of relentlessly happy songs, she groaned.

"Okay, okay. I'm starting to feel cheerful. I promise you I am. You can turn it down a little now."

He laughed. Really, he had the greatest laugh. Rich and happy, deep and real. "I *might* be willing to turn the volume down," he hedged. "But at the first sign of moping, it's getting loud in here again."

She couldn't hold back a laugh of her own then. "You're going to make a wonderful dad." The words were out of her mouth before she knew she would say them.

Time stopped—well, not really. But it sure felt like it.

When she snuck a glance at him, he was looking straight at her. "I'm sure as hell going to give it my all," he replied.

"Yeah." Her voice was barely a whisper. "I get that. I believe that you will."

She drove the rest of the way to the Marriott Del Mar, which Jason had booked during the ride.

San Diego was gorgeous, beachy and bright. They checked into the Marriott, went to their room, stuck their bags in the corner and stared at each other.

"We made it," she said. "I want a shower so bad."

"Go ahead."

"No way. You go first. Make it fast. I'm going to be in there for a while."

He hoisted his duffel onto one of the beds, zipped it open and pulled out a fresh change of clothes.

When he vanished into the bathroom, she got out her phone to text her dad. But then she hesitated, her heart thumping against her breastbone, her face hot and her hands clammy.

Because how long was she going to avoid actually talking to him? He'd called her twice in the past couple of weeks. She'd listened to his voice mails and then texted her replies.

Somehow, being on the phone with him, hearing his voice in real time and letting him hear hers, had seemed too scary, too…real.

"Oh, just do it," she whispered to herself—because she was that nervous right now, nervous enough to give herself orders out loud.

She brought up her dad's number and hit the phone icon. He picked up on the first ring. "Is this Piper?" He sounded excited, like he'd been waiting, phone in hand, to hear from her.

"Hi, uh, Simon. Just wanted you to know that we're here—me and my friend, Jason."

"You did bring a friend. Wonderful." Simon really did sound nice… "Piper? You still with me?"

"Yes. Yes, I am. And yes, I did bring a friend. Jason's a great guy."

"We can't wait to meet him—and you, Piper. You most of all." Now he sounded choked up. "Oh, listen to me. I'm almost blubbering all over you right here on the phone. Don't be afraid. I promise to pull myself together before you arrive. When will you be here?"

"Well, it's been a long trip so we're going to get some rest and see you in the morning."

"Oh, Piper. It's so good to hear your voice at last and to know that I'll be seeing you tomorrow. Nia is as excited as I am. And Maris, Shannon and Cameron will be here, too." Those were her half siblings. Maris and Shannon were married with kids. Cameron was still single.

"I…can't wait." She knew she sounded hesitant and nervous. Because she was. "What time should we be there?"

"The earlier the better. Where are you for tonight?"

"The Marriott Del Mar."

"That's nice and close. Hold on. Let me consult with my better half."

"Sure." She tried to regulate her breathing as she waited for him to come back on the phone. He did seem like a sweetheart. He really did.

"Piper? Do you think you could come at ten for a late breakfast?"

"Yes. Ten is great. We'll be there."

"And you'll stay over tomorrow night—Sunday night, too, if that works for you. But tomorrow night, definitely?"

She agreed that she would. "So we'll see you at ten in the morning, then."

"We'll be expecting you."

Piper hung up, tossed her phone on the nearest bed and then stood there staring at a vivid seascape above the headboard. She was shaking a little just from the unreality of having an actual phone conversation with her father after she'd long stopped believing she would ever even know his name.

But aside from the trembling, she felt fine.

Good. Pleased, even.

Yes, she still worried a little that she might burst into tears, but in a happy way. He really had seemed welcoming, eager to meet her in person at last.

The bathroom door opened.

She glanced that way as Jason emerged wearing clean jeans that rode low on his lean hips. He truly was a beautiful man, strong and broad in all the right places, with just the right amount of silky dark hair trailing across his hard chest and down, leading the way to all the good stuff below.

He was rubbing his wet hair with a towel, but when he saw her staring, he stopped. "Piper?" The sound of his voice had her suddenly wanting to cry again. He asked, "Did something happen?"

She nodded. "I just called my dad. He sounds like a really nice person."

"Well, great." He still looked unsure. "So... You're okay, then?"

"Yeah. I just..." She turned and dropped to the end of the bed. "The truth is, I've been avoiding calling him, afraid of... Oh, I don't even know what I was afraid of. That I wouldn't like him, I guess. That he would seem like someone I didn't even want to know. So I've been texting and emailing him instead of calling."

"But just now, you did call?"

"Yeah. Yeah, I did. I called him. And he sounds like a lovely man. And... I just never thought I would meet him. I gave up on ever knowing him so long ago. I walled him off in my mind, in my heart. And it makes no sense, but now that I've found him, I've been afraid to let down that wall."

"Hey." He came and sat on the bed beside her. When she leaned into him, he put his arm around her. She rested her head on his bare shoulder, breathed in his just-showered scent. "You were cautious," he said. "You were protecting your heart. That's completely understandable."

"Yeah, but it wasn't his fault, not ever. He had no idea I even existed—as my mother has told me repeatedly. But I wouldn't listen to her. I blamed him for not finding me."

"You were a kid."

"True. But I didn't stop blaming him, not really—not even after I grew up."

Jason said nothing. He just sat there with his arm around her, giving her time to let go of some of the old crap in her head.

Eventually, she drew a breath and straightened her shoulders. "Well. All of a sudden, I'm thinking this might be a very nice visit."

"That's the spirit."

She nudged him with her elbow. "I really need to stop having these meltdowns around you."

"Nah. I can take it."

"But you shouldn't have to."

"Piper. I don't *have* to. I'm here because I want to be here."

She met his eyes directly. "Thank you."

"Anytime."

She nudged him again. "Your mom thinks I'm too old for you—but sometimes I wonder if it's the other way around."

Chapter Ten

The minute Simon Walsh answered the door and she saw his face for the very first time, Piper knew that everything really was going to be all right.

Her father had ruddy skin, white hair and a short beard to match. His eyes were the same green as hers. He reached for a hug, and she didn't hesitate to hug him right back.

Inside, he introduced her to his pretty wife, Nia, and to Piper's adult half siblings. Everyone seemed welcoming. There were children, five of them, aged two through thirteen. Maris had three kids, Shannon had two. Maris's two-year-old regarded her warily, but the other four children smiled and called her Aunt Piper, which felt simultaneously wonderful and disorienting.

They had breakfast at a giant, round table in the sunroom, where the arched floor-to-ceiling windows looked out on lush, subtropical landscaping and a gleaming fenced-in pool. Clearly, Simon and Nia had done well for themselves. Simon seemed happy—with his children and grandchildren. And most of all, with his wife. It was Nia who encouraged him to talk about how he'd met Piper's mom.

Simon explained that he'd been on his way to USC from

the Kansas farm where he'd grown up. He'd stopped at a music festival in the San Bernardino Mountains.

"And I met your mom," he said to Piper. "We should have exchanged phone numbers, I know that now. But I was away from the farm and out on my own, feeling free for the first time in my life, everything wide-open. No boundaries, no morning chores, nobody reminding me what to do or when to do it. Your mom and I agreed it was first names only and that made perfect sense at the time. She was going north, and I was headed south. What can I tell you? We were young and it was the eighties…"

Nia leaned close enough to Simon to brush his shoulder with hers. She gave him a small, private smile and then she said to Piper, "When he found out he had a daughter he'd never met, he went in our bedroom and didn't come out for two days."

"It was a shock," said Simon, his voice a little unsteady. "To accept how much I had missed, all the years you were growing up, your first steps, your first high school dance…"

Piper blinked away the sudden tears. "I understand completely. Believe me, I do."

"I'm just glad that you're here now," said her father. "I hope that we can keep in touch, get to know each other better, make up for at least a little of all the time we've lost."

"I would love that."

A few minutes later, Maris asked, "So, Jason. How did you and Piper meet?"

He put his arm across the back of her chair. She leaned toward him a little, realizing that she felt comfortable in her father's house. Safe. And that whatever Jason said in response to her half sister's question was all right with her.

"We met at the public library years ago," Jason explained. "I thought she was beautiful. She helped me find whatever books I needed, and I had a giant crush on her. But I was too shy to make a move—plus, I knew I didn't have a chance."

Piper added, "But lately we've become very good friends."

"Oh, we can see that," said Shannon with a sly grin.

Piper only smiled.

By then, the kids were getting rowdy. Everyone helped clear the table and they all moved out to the backyard. The children went swimming. Later, there was a big family dinner on the patio, with everyone laughing and talking over each other. It was absolutely beautiful, Piper thought. Her fantasy of a big, close, happy family come miraculously to life.

After the meal, Nia took Piper aside. "I've put you and Jason in the same room. It's a nice size, with its own bath. Does that work?"

"Absolutely." She winked at her stepmother. "As I said, we are very good friends."

And as very good friends, they got to share a queen-size bed. Which was fine. By now, Piper was accustomed to being near him at night—more than accustomed, to be strictly honest.

She liked being near him as they slept, liked waking up spooned against him with his muscular arm holding her close. She even liked feeling how much he wanted her, which happened every morning—and sometimes during the night. Neither of them ever mentioned that. She always knew when he was awake because he would groan softly, carefully remove his arm from around her and roll over onto his other side.

That night at bedtime, they took turns in the bathroom. Piper emerged in both a T-shirt and pajama shorts. Jason came out in sleep pants and a soft, short-sleeved Henley. In bed, they were careful to respect each other's space, facing each other on their separate pillows, leaving the center of the bed empty. They whispered together about how well the day had gone. He said he liked her newfound family.

She whispered back, "I like them, too."

When she faded into sleep, she was still very much on her own side of the bed. But in the middle of the night, she woke plastered close to his big, hard body, with his arm wrapped around her.

"Sorry," he mumbled a few minutes later, and pulled away.

Her side of the bed felt empty without him.

But then, in the morning, she woke with him curled around her all over again. And she thought how good it felt to be with him this way.

Until he groaned, rolled off the far side of the bed and disappeared into the bathroom.

They spent Sunday there at her father's house. It was a good day, easy and relaxed. She got a little time with each of her sisters and she and Cameron played Ping-Pong. Her half brother was very competitive. But way back in college, Piper had learned how to play from Brandon, who always played to win. Brandon had coached her as fiercely and aggressively as he did everything else. Now, all these years later, she managed to hold her own against her newfound half brother.

They said goodbye to Cameron before dinner. He lived in Denver and had a flight to catch. Her half sisters and their families lived in the San Diego area. They stayed for the evening meal but left soon after.

That night, Piper decided she'd had enough of trying to stay on her side of the bed. She scooted right over to Jason. He reached out his arm and pulled her close.

She settled in with a happy sigh. "This is nice."

He made a sound. It might have been a laugh. Or possibly a groan.

Monday morning, it was just the four of them—Jason and Piper, Simon and Nia. Piper felt right at home. They made plans. Simon and Nia accepted Piper's invitation to visit Wyoming next year for the Fourth of July. Piper felt Jason's gaze on her when Nia said they would love to come. She looked his way and knew just what he was thinking.

Next July, their baby would be six months old. And by then, her dad and her stepmom would be well aware of their new grandbaby. Piper planned to call them and tell them as soon as she made the three-month mark.

After breakfast, Simon and Nia stood in the long, curving driveway with their arms wrapped around each other waving goodbye under the bright morning sun. Piper leaned out her window and waved right back at them until Jason turned the corner.

"I miss them already." She sat back in her seat, stared out the windshield and almost considered ordering Jason to turn around and go back. Maybe they could stay on for a few days. Or longer. She laughed at the thought.

Jason sent her a quick glance and focused his eyes on the road again. "You miss them and that's funny?"

"I was just thinking that I wish we could stay longer—

and yet a couple of days ago, I was a basket case at the prospect of seeing my father's face."

"Sometimes, you put one foot in front of the other and you keep moving forward and things work themselves out."

"I get that, I do."

He shifted his gaze her way again, those blue eyes sweeping over her, warm and thrilling as a physical caress. How did he do that? The man excited her with just a look. "But…?" he asked.

"Some things are just so…difficult, that's all. Sometimes the past makes it hard to give people a chance."

He was watching the road again. "You worked through it, though."

"I did—and all of a sudden, I have a dad and a stepmom, two sisters, a brother, a couple of brothers-in-law… Oh, and I'm an auntie several times over. Miracles can happen, they really can."

A little while later, she got out her iPad. "I'll find us a place to stay in Hollywood," she said.

"No need." He sent her a quick, warm glance. "I already booked us a room."

"What hotel?"

"You'll see…"

Two and a half hours after they left her father's house, they were cruising down Hollywood Boulevard. Jason turned in at the Hollywood Roosevelt Hotel.

A valet appeared. Jason leaned out the truck window. "Two nights. The reservation is under Jason Bravo."

The valet took their bags from the back. Piper sat in the truck, watching Jason and the valet in her side-view mirror. Jason tipped the valet, who hustled right over to open her door. "Enjoy your stay, miss."

"Thank you." A bellman had emerged from the hotel. He piled their bags on a cart and wheeled the cart back inside.

Piper felt more than a little out of the loop, but she followed Jason through the glass-and-ironwork entry doors to the lobby with its coffered ceiling and Spanish archways. He checked in and they went to their room, a cabana room complete with balcony overlooking the long blue pool in a central courtyard below. The room had light oak walls, an ebony floor and midcentury modern furniture. It was as cool and bright as the lobby had been.

She sat on the end of the platform bed and smoothed the skirt of her red sleeveless sundress, waiting as the bellman delivered their luggage. When it was finally just the two of them, she fell back across the bed, arms spread wide. "Well, this is all very glamorous."

He stood over her. "This hotel is a Hollywood landmark. They held the first Oscar awards here. Marilyn Monroe used to stay in one of these cabana rooms before she made it big—oh, and the inside of the blue pool down below was painted by David Hockney. He's—"

"I know who David Hockney is. I took a few art classes in college myself—and as I said, so glamorous. And I had no idea you would book us a room here. When did you do that?"

"I booked it yesterday while you were beating your brother at Ping-Pong."

"Sneaky. I like that. And by the way, excellent choice."

"I'm glad you approve." He sat on the end of the bed. She moved her arm so that he could lie back beside her.

They turned their heads to smile at each other and he said, "I've always wanted to stay here. For sentimental reasons."

Kicking off her red wedges, she rolled to her side facing him and rested her cheek on her hand. "Okay, now I'm intrigued. What sentimental reasons?"

"My mom stayed here before I was born—before she married my dad. She'd been in love with him since they were both fourteen years old. But he'd left Wyoming and come here to LA. He'd set up shop as a private investigator."

"And your mom came after him."

"That's right."

"I'm impressed. I mean, your mom and I may have our issues to work through, but props to her, going after her man like that."

He touched her cheek, a slow, featherlight caress. Her skin warmed at his touch. "You think so?"

"I do…"

"Too bad my dad turned her down."

She laughed, the sound low. Husky to her own ears. "But wait. Let me guess. Judging by the fact that they are very much together now and have been for years, I'm guessing that in the end, he couldn't resist her."

"That's right. He couldn't." He stroked a slow finger down her bare arm, raising a lovely chain of happy shivers. "I like this dress." It had a flipped-up red collar and little buttons down the front, very '50s retro. He undid the first button and then the one after that. Her body felt lazy now, lazy and warm and so relaxed. "I would really like to take this dress off you. Does that work for you?"

"Hmm." She scooted closer as she pretended to consider his request.

"Well?"

"Yes! That works. You should definitely take this dress off me." She was looking in his eyes, thinking that she'd never felt this good, this easy and open, with anyone before. There were maybe three inches between his mouth and hers now. He closed that distance. She sighed and opened for him. "Jason…"

"Right here…" His mouth covered hers again. He shared her breath as he drew her closer, his hand stroking down her arm and lower. Fireworks exploded, bright and so hot, rolling out along her limbs.

"The way I see it," she began on a breathy sigh, "why not make the most of this time we have together? Just for now, just until we get home…"

He laughed, low and soft and somehow rough all at the same time. "You want to have sex with me until we get home?"

"Oh, yes, I do. So much. I want to have *all* the sex…"

"Well, now that's a tall order." He pressed a perfect line of kisses along the edge of her jaw.

Did he want that, too? She needed to find out. "I mean, if *you* want that, too…"

"Is that a question?"

"Well, do you?"

He pulled back enough to look down at her. Now his eyes were watchful. "Yeah, Piper. I do. But you need to be sure about it."

She swallowed. Hard. "Okay, then. We can be together. *Really* together in every way for the rest of this trip. And then, when we get home, we can go back to being—"

He cut her off. "I don't need to hear it. I get it. It's just for now."

"Yes. Just for now. While we're on our way home."

"Seven days, six nights. Today through Sunday."

"Yes, please." She couldn't help grinning.

"And one more thing…" He hesitated.

"Just say it," she coaxed. "It's okay."

"Well, other than the morning sickness, you seem perfectly healthy."

"Because I am."

"So then, no danger to the baby if we—"

"Honestly, Jason. Dr. Hayes says I'm healthy and strong. There is no danger to the baby at all."

He smiled. Finally. It was a very wicked smile, which made it all the better. "I'm glad we're taking the long way," he added, the dark glint of sexual promise in his eyes. "We'll need to make the most of every moment."

Oh, that sounded so very good good. "Yes, Jason. Exactly. That. Let's do that."

He caught her lower lip between his teeth and worried it with care. She felt that gentle bite all the way through her body. Heat bloomed in her core, and she moaned.

"It's been way too long," he growled against her throat, kissing his way downward, unbuttoning her sundress as he went. "Two damn months since that one night in April…"

"It seems like forever," she agreed, breathless now, eager to have him, to be with him in every way.

He asked, "What about condoms?"

"Do you have them?"

"I do," he said. "I wanted to be ready. Just in case."

"What do you think…?"

"Piper, it's your call. There's been no one else, I promise you."

"Well, then, never mind about them."

"Works for me." He turned his attention to her dress again. It had buttons all the way down the front. He undid them to her waist. And then, with slow care, he peeled the dress wide. "So pretty." Bending close, he pressed a line of kisses where the tops of her breasts met the lace cups of her bra. Her skin burned with each kiss. Her breasts ached so sweetly, and her breath came ragged now.

He took hold of her hand. "Come on." Rising, he pulled her up with him. "All these clothes have to go."

That sounded so good to her. "Okay…" She stood before him, deliciously dazed, as he untied the sash belt at her waist and undid a few more buttons.

The dress collapsed around her feet. When she stepped out of it, he bent, scooped it up and tossed it toward the nearest chair.

"There we go— Damn, Piper. You are fine." He pulled her into those big, hard arms and kissed her long and thoroughly. She moaned shamelessly into his mouth.

But then he tried to step away.

"Wait…" She grabbed for him.

Grinning, he caught her hand and kissed it. "Have patience." His voice was slow and sweet as honey. He got to work unbuckling his belt, undoing his jeans. Sitting just long enough to tug off his boots and socks, he rose once more and shoved down his pants. He kicked them away as he whipped his black T-shirt over his head.

Ohmygoodness. She'd forgotten how good he looked minus all his clothes. Every inch of him broad and hard and strong, his legs muscled from all that time spent on horseback, his arms corded and powerful. Just looking at him made her melt into a hot puddle of longing.

"Turn around."

She sucked in a sharp breath and did as he instructed. He took away her bra, hooked his thumbs in at the sides of her panties and slid them down to her feet.

"Step out."

She did, and then she turned to face him again. They stared at each other. Her body ached with yearning.

"Come here…" He took her arm and pulled her close.

She lifted on tiptoe, offering her mouth. He claimed it. They kissed for an endless time. She pressed herself against him, felt his desire hot and hard, poking at her belly.

It was paradise, to be in his arms this way once more.

She'd told herself so many times that this couldn't happen ever again.

Well, she'd been wrong. This was perfect. And they had days together, just the two of them.

His big hands roamed her back, stroking her, *knowing* her, straying down her sides in long, caressing sweeps and sliding in between their bodies, cupping her breasts, rolling her nipples.

Making her groan and whisper, "Yes. Like that. More…" against his hot, ardent mouth.

His palms glided downward. He grasped her waist. She let out a sharp "Oh!" of surprise as he lifted her. But then she twined her legs around him, clutched her arms even tighter around his neck and kissed him all the harder as he climbed onto the bed carrying her wrapped around him like a vine on a tree.

As soon as they were prone on the white coverlet, he rolled her beneath him. For a long, sweet string of minutes, he kissed her, his mouth playing on hers, his hands on either side of her head, fingers threading through her hair.

But then his lips wandered. They burned a searing path down the side of her neck, out along the ridge of her collarbone and back again. Detouring lower, he rained kisses across the top of her chest.

"Freckles," he whispered against her skin. She had them there, too, on her upper chest. "I love them."

She surfaced from the delicious haze of pleasure long enough to laugh. "It's good that somebody does."

"They're beautiful," he said. "*You're* beautiful."

She didn't reply, just caught his face between her hands and kissed him again, slow and deep and achingly sweet.

Until he took her wrists and pressed her hands back onto the pillow to either side of her head. "Open your eyes."

She blinked up at him, feeling like a dreamer roused from a deep and satisfying sleep. "What?"

"This."

And then he kissed her again. Endlessly. Perfectly.

She sank again beneath the sweet waves of pleasure, giving herself up to the moment, to his big hands on her tender skin. It was so good.

Better, even, than their one glorious night in April.

Because she knew him now. Knew his heart-deep goodness. Knew his kindness and his honest, helpful ways. She trusted him to treat her with understanding, to respect her wishes even when he didn't agree with them.

He took her nipple in his mouth. She moaned in delight as he swirled his tongue around it before settling in to suck slow and deep, making her lift herself eagerly up to him, making her beg him never to stop.

But he did stop—in order to kiss his way lower, his lips straying to the thin skin over her ribs. She cried out at the shiver that went through her when he scraped his teeth over her flesh, followed immediately by the warm, rough lapping of his clever tongue.

And then he was on the move again. Her belly jerked and a laugh escaped her when he stuck his tongue in her navel. "Don't!" she cried, laughing some more.

He did it again anyway.

And then he went lower, his big hands sliding under her thighs, lifting them so he could ease between them. She rested them on his shoulders, moaning as he began to kiss her in the most intimate way.

She clutched the sheets and begged him—a cascade of pleas completely at odds with each other. She demanded more, ordered him to hold it right there, then commanded him never, ever to stop...

He just went on pleasuring her until she was nothing but a hot, tightening spiral of purest sensation. She cried out at the thrilling agony of it as the scorching swirl of bliss broke wide open into the joyous pulse of completion.

She was still in the throes of that bone-melting climax when he crawled up her body, notched his thick erection at her entrance and pushed inside.

It felt so good, so right, to have him filling her, pressing her down, surrounding her completely.

"Piper..." His mouth claimed hers. He tasted of sex, of sheer, undiluted desire. He was everything carnal, all the sins of the flesh turned to something so good and true and pure.

She put her arms around him and her legs, too, hooking her ankles at the small of his back.

He lifted his mouth from hers on a guttural moan. And then he smiled. "Seven days, six nights, huh?"

"That's right," she managed on a breathless sigh.

His hips kept rolling, pressing her down, then pulling back so that she could feel him slipping away—until the very last possible second, when he thrust in to fill her again. "We need to make the most of the time we have."

"Yes," she said on a bare husk of breath. Because he was right—and also because *yes* was the only word she knew at that moment.

And then words deserted her completely. There was only Jason, inside her, above her, pressing her into the white bed—and then rolling them so they were on their sides, facing each other, moving together, pleasure pulsing between them, filling her with heat and yearning, overwhelming her with that desperate need for more.

He rolled again and now he was under her, taking her shoulders in those strong hands of his, pushing her up so she sat above him, looking down, feeling him so deep within her.

"Move," he commanded. "Take me."

And she did. She moved, rocking on him, lifting and sinking, stroking him with her body, taking him with her as her body rose toward climax again. His big hands slid down the front of her, clasping her breasts, squeezing them so that she moaned at the pleasure that skirted the sharp edge of pain.

His touch moved lower. He clasped her hips, holding on as she rode him. She stared down at him, and he held her gaze, never once looking away.

All thought deserted her. There was only the feel of him, under her, in her. Only the glide and lift of her body on his. Only his blue eyes holding her, owning her.

A second climax came rolling through her. She went

under, still rocking, moaning his name. His hands gripped her hips even tighter, his thumbs pressing into the tender, giving flesh beneath her hip bones. She felt him throbbing within her, his climax taking form as hers began to subside.

They went absolutely still at the same time, hips pressed hard into each other as the finish swept through them both.

He said her name so softly. "Piper."

"Jason," she responded on a faint thread of breath. "Oh, yes…"

The rest was wordless—just the two of them holding on as the endless, white-hot moment opened out into afterglow.

He laughed, a husky, knowing sound. Her body went boneless. She curved over him. He reached up and gently pulled her down. Sighing, she stretched out beside him and snuggled closer.

He was hers in every way—for now. They would be together all the way home.

Chapter Eleven

Jason's grandmother Sharilyn and her husband, Hector, lived in a Spanish Colonial one-bedroom bungalow on a street that dead-ended into Melrose Avenue and Paramount Studios.

"They moved here about five years ago to downsize a little," Jason explained as he led the way up terra-cotta-tiled steps to a long walkway with glass-fronted apartment doors on either side. Birds of paradise, yucca, elephant ears and miniature palm trees lined the walk. "Before that, they lived in a small Spanish-style cottage off of Wilshire. Like this place, it was straight out of the 1920s. That house had two bedrooms and I stayed with them there while I was going to SMC. They both like these old Spanish Revival places with stucco walls and red tile roofs."

"I can see why. This is magical. Like we've gone back in time."

Jason's grandmother, a thin woman with white hair, answered the door before they could knock. "There you are!" She held out her arms. Jason stepped right up and grabbed her in a hug. "Oh, Jason. It's so good to see you."

"Good to see you, too, Grandma. Really good."

The network of wrinkles on the woman's face deepened as she smiled at Piper over his shoulder. "Hello. Piper?"

"That's me."

"I'm so glad to meet you—come in, come in!"

They stepped right into the Leversons' living room, which was furnished with a couple of recliners, a coffee table and a green sofa. There was a small flat-screen mounted on one wall. By the windows to either side of the front door, houseplants grew in profusion, some hanging in macramé pots, others on side tables and tucked into the corners.

Sharilyn's husband, Hector, emerged from the archway that led to the apartment's tiny kitchen, where something that smelled delicious was cooking. "Welcome, you two." The old man, who was stooped and nearly bald, shuffled toward them.

There were more hugs. Piper hadn't known what to expect from Jason's grandmother and her husband. She'd felt a little on edge that Jason's mom might have said something negative about her. But whatever Meggie Bravo had told them, the Leversons welcomed her with open arms.

The old man had cooked for them. They all four sat packed close together at the small table in the nook of a kitchen, eating excellent carne asada. There were homemade tortillas, too.

Hector said he'd coaxed the recipe out of a former landlady who lived in West Hollywood. "Her name is Dolores," he said. "She's something of a real estate mogul. Dolores owned the building I lived in when I met this beautiful woman right here." He leaned close to his wife and Sharilyn gave him a peck on the cheek. Nodding at Jason, he said to Piper, "Before that one was born, his father lived in the building next door to me, which was also owned by Dolores."

The old man and Sharilyn shared a slow, private smile. Then Hector spoke to Jason. "Your grandmother came looking for your father all those years and years ago. I was a widower. I never planned to love again. But I took one look at this woman right here and knew that love wasn't done with me yet."

"I remember that story," Jason said. He was smiling, glancing between his grandmother and her husband.

Sharilyn added, "Oh, by the way, Jason. Your mother called a couple of days ago."

Piper's stomach, which had given her zero trouble for almost a week, suddenly felt queasy.

Jason's hand brushed hers under the table. She pasted on a smile to let him know she was absolutely fine and not the least bothered by anything Meggie Bravo might have to say.

"Your mother said to give you her love." Sharilyn's dark eyes shifted to Piper. "And to wish you both a great trip."

Well. That didn't sound so bad. Piper's stomach relaxed a bit. She ate another bite of her dinner. The food really was terrific, the meat rich and tender, just spicy enough.

Sharilyn said, "I love your mother, Jason. I love her like I love your dad and you and your brother and sister—and this wonderful man sitting right here beside me. With all of my heart. But she's such a mama bear. The way she's always pushing and suggesting and making plans for us, you would think Hector and I were a pair of wayward children."

Jason was nodding. Apparently, he'd heard all this before, too. "I take it she's still after you to move to one of those retirement communities she found?"

Sharilyn scoffed. "That or pack up and head for Wyoming where she can help take care of us now that we're practically decrepit. We're not ready for either of those choices. Yes, we know that eventually we will have to move again. But right now, we are managing just fine. Life's too short as it is, Jason James. I screwed up a lot when I was younger. For years, I made one wrong choice after another." She gave her husband an adoring glance. "But I've finally got the life I've always dreamed of. I'm not changing things up until I'm damn good and ready to."

Jason caught Piper's hand under the table, weaving his fingers between hers. "You do you, Grandma."

"Oh, you bet I will."

Piper braced on an elbow in the big, white bed of their cabana balcony room. Jason reached up to press his hand to the side of her flushed face. She looked rumpled and happy. And damn, she smelled good, like apples and sex, which wasn't surprising as they'd just made love. Twice. Each time was better than the last. Thinking about it had him ready to go for round three.

"I like your grandmother," she said. "Sharilyn's strong-minded and sure of what she wants."

Jason lifted off his pillow enough to press a kiss to the side of her throat. Her skin was like silk. He nipped her chin lightly.

She gave a low chuckle. "You didn't hear a word I said."

Reaching out a finger, he stroked it over the cute little muscle of her biceps. "Yes, I did. And you're right. She is strong-minded. According to both my dad and my mom— and Sharilyn herself—she didn't used to be. My grandfather was a terrible person who made her life a living hell."

"You mentioned him before, that he was not a good guy."

"That's right. Bad Clint Bravo was very bad news. It took Grandma—and my dad, too—years to get over the things he put them through. But now my dad's happy and Grandma's got Hector. Her life suits her perfectly. She doesn't let anyone push her around—not even my mother."

"Well, your grandmother is wonderful. Hector, too."

The slider was open to the balcony. Faintly, they could hear splashing and laughter from down at the pool.

Piper sat up. The covers fell away from her bare breasts. He couldn't wait to get his hands on them again—on all of her. Every sweet, silky inch. "It's warm out," she said. "Let's go swimming."

He would rather take her in his arms and kiss her sense-less. But those green eyes were shining and, hey, swim-ming with Piper was always fun.

Later, back in their room again, they dropped their wet swimsuits on the bathroom floor and shared a quick shower that led to fooling around. When they finally dried off, she pulled on a sleep shirt and laid their swim stuff on the balcony chairs to dry. Back in bed, she was as eager as he was, reaching for him, kissing him like she couldn't get enough of him. He knew the feeling. Because he felt the same.

He made himself slow down, though. He took his time with her, savoring every touch, every sweet, hungry sigh.

They had six more nights and as many days.

It wasn't enough. Not if she really did insist they go backward once they got home. He didn't get that. As though they could flip a switch and be happy relegated to the friend zone again. He seriously doubted he was going to handle that well.

But why get all tied in knots about it now? They had almost a week before they rolled into Medicine Creek again. Anything could happen in that time. She might finally let herself admit what he'd known for months now, that the two of them were a whole lot more than just friends with a baby on the way.

"So I've been thinking," he said in the morning before they went to pick up Sharilyn and Hector for breakfast. "We haven't really gone over the specifics of the trip home."

She pulled on a sleeveless top. Unfortunately, that top covered her satin bra and the sweet swells of her breasts. On the plus side, it clung. As she tugged on the hem, smoothing it, she slanted him a look. "What, you don't like this shirt?"

"I love that shirt." *But I like what's under it a lot more.*

"Well, thank you—and why do I get the feeling you have a plan for our trip?"

"Because I do. You should know right up front, though, that the shortest way home is back the way we came."

"Hello. I can read a map, too—and short isn't the goal. We're taking the *long* way back, remember?"

"All right, then. I'm thinking we go ahead and take 101 north to Monterey. It's beautiful along the coast. But we have to be careful. We can't be stopping every time the mood strikes or we'll still be in California when our six days are up."

"I can be careful."

"That grin on your face tells me you left *careful* behind back in Medicine Creek more than a week ago." She gave a husky laugh at that. He said, "Okay. So it's seven-plus hours of drive time to Monterey. How about we aim for Monterey tonight?"

"Perfect."

They packed up and checked out of the hotel. When they got to the apartment, his grandmother and Hector were ready to go.

They found a cute café a few minutes away on Melrose and took their time over the meal. Jason kind of hated to leave them. In the bright morning light shining in the café windows, his grandma and her husband looked frail. Like a strong wind could sweep them up and carry them away. Right then, he could understand his mother's concern for their care and well-being.

But then Hector laughed. The sound was rich, full of life and happiness. His grandma bent close to the old man. They shared a quick kiss. Jason decided to forget what his grandmother and her husband *should* do. Their life choices were their own.

It was hard to say goodbye, though. They ended up hanging around for a couple of hours back at the apartment. They drank lemonade and looked at the pictures in some old photo albums his grandmother dug out of the closet. The albums had faded shots of his parents and of him as a baby and even some of Sharilyn when she was young, holding his dad when he was only a few months old. Bad Clint was in some of those pictures, too. In black jeans and a black hat, Clint Bravo looked like trouble just waiting to happen.

Piper seemed as reluctant to leave as Jason was. Twice, he had to remind her that they needed to get on the road.

When they finally said goodbye, it was past one in the afternoon.

An hour and a half later, they were approaching Santa Barbara.

"I've been thinking," Piper said.

He thought, *Uh-oh*, but he kept it to himself.

She went on, "I can't just drive by and not tour Mission Santa Barbara. I'm forty years old, Jason, and I've never been there." And then she frowned. "Or if I have been there, I don't remember it. My mother and I might have toured the mission way back in the day. We went a lot of places in that VW bus…"

"So call your mom," he teased her as he merged for the off-ramp.

She scoffed. "Why?"

"Ask her if you've been here. If she says you have, we can keep going."

She gave him a playful slap on the shoulder. "Not a chance. Mission Santa Barbara, here we come!"

They wandered the mission and the nearby rose garden for a couple of hours. He bought her a Celtic cross in the gift shop, and she loved the lifelike statues of Jesus and Mary Magdalene in an alcove off the sanctuary. She pouted a little when she learned that the library archive was only open Tuesday through Thursday, and then by advance appointment only.

"This is what happens when you don't plan ahead," he teased.

"It's okay." She took hold of his arm and tipped her face up to him with a radiant smile. "I'm so glad that we stopped. Thank you."

"For you, anything." They shared a quick kiss and moved on.

When they left the mission, it was after five. They climbed in his crew cab, and she leaned across the console. "Let's get a room."

An hour later, they found a motel surrounded by sand and palm trees. It wasn't glamorous, but they could walk to the beach. And they did. They took off their shoes and strolled along barefoot as the sunset painted the sky purple and pink out over the Pacific.

"Tomorrow we'll make it to Monterey," he said firmly.

"Yeah, good luck with that." She laughed, turning toward him. Going on tiptoe, she commanded, "Kiss me."

"Anytime." He let his boots fall to the sand and captured her sweet face between his hands. The kiss went on forever. It wasn't long enough.

When she dropped her heels into the sand again, she gazed up at him, beaming. He caught her around the waist, turning her, pulling her back against his chest. They stared out at the waves together as the colors of the sunset deepened.

"I'm having the best time. I haven't been out like this, taking life as it comes, since I was nine years old." She rested her head against his chest and sighed. "I hated life in that bus. But now, with you, I kind of love just winging it, going wherever the mood takes us."

He nuzzled her hair. "Yeah, the way the mood's taking you so far, we could end up driving all night to get you home in time for work next Monday."

"Relax," She tipped her face back to him and they shared another kiss. "We have plenty of time."

Not really. Time went by too fast when you had long

distances to cover. But then again, he wanted to give her the kind of trip she would remember. If that meant driving nonstop to get home on schedule, so be it.

The next day, he drove straight through to Monterey with only one stop for a bathroom break. She'd found and reserved them a room at a beachfront hotel. But they got there at noon and check-in wasn't till four. They made good use of the time, visiting Cannery Row and the Old Fisherman's Wharf.

As soon as they checked into their room, she admitted she'd booked it for two nights. "I'm thinking tomorrow, we'll take a quick trip down to Big Sur, you know?"

He shook his head, but he was grinning. "You are so sneaky."

She grabbed the collar of his shirt and got right up in his face. "It'll be fun. You'll see."

And it was. The friendly guy at the hotel desk warned that there was no cell service through most of Big Sur, so Jason bought a guidebook with a paper map of what to see along Highway 1.

Piper leaned close and whispered in his ear. "You're going to make a great dad—willing to be flexible about where to go and when to stop, but always ready with the maps and the planning."

"No kid of mine will get lost on my watch," he replied.

As the guidebook advised, they went straight through Carmel without stopping in order to get going on the drive through Big Sur, all of it along Highway 1 with its gorgeous views of the Pacific. They found a parking space at Point Lobos and hiked for a while, holding hands, following the easy trails through coastal scrub grasses and even a gorgeous, twisted stand of rare Monterey cypress.

At one point, they got lucky and spotted a group of sea lions basking on a big rock.

Back in the truck, they headed on down the highway another thirty miles or so, enjoying the breathtaking views, stopping at Castle Rock to take pictures with the rest of the tourists.

When they decided they should turn around, Piper joked that all they did was drive. Even when they took a break and stayed in one place for a couple of days, it was only to drive some more.

On the return trip to Monterey, they stopped in Carmel-by-the-Sea. In the colorful little beach town, almost everyone they passed on the steep streets seemed to be walking a friendly dog.

"I'm beat," Piper said during the short return trip to their hotel in Monterey. "I don't think I can drum up the energy to visit the famous aquarium."

"So we'll order takeout and turn in early."

They got sandwiches and chips from a nearby sub shop and returned to the hotel, where they sat at the little table by the window to eat.

She was too quiet—and had been since they got back to the hotel.

Finally, he went ahead and asked, "Something on your mind?"

She made a thoughtful sound. "Today was so beautiful. Thank you for indulging me."

They would have some serious miles to make up, but so what? "It was a great day for me, too."

She almost smiled then—but not quite. "So... Aren't you glad I tricked you into staying here another day?"

"*So* glad," he agreed.

After they ate, he coaxed her to walk with him along the beach that was just down a sandy slope from the hotel. Holding hands, they wandered along the water's edge. The wind blew her hair back and the cool waves foamed around their feet.

"How did it get to be Thursday already?" Brushing a few strands of bright hair away from her soft lips, she glanced his way.

"It happens. You turn around and suddenly..."

"...it's tomorrow," she finished for him. "And then it's Saturday. And suddenly it's Sunday and you're almost home." She was so right. And no matter how they split up the rest of the trip, they were going to be driving eight-to-ten-hour days from here on in, Sunday included, to make it back in time for her return to work on Monday.

But it wasn't the long hours of driving that concerned him. It was the somber tone of her voice and the faraway look in her eyes. Something really was bothering her.

He stopped in midstride. Tugging on her hand, he pulled her back.

"What?" She turned and faced him.

"Talk to me."

She gazed up at him for the longest time, her eyes full of shadows. Finally, she confessed, "I don't want to go home. I just want to go on like this, you and me, headed wherever the mood takes us, with nobody to judge us. Nobody to tell us that..."

He took her shoulders and pulled her close. "What?"

"Hmm?"

"*Nobody to tell us that*...what?"

She sagged against him. "Sorry. But you know what

I mean—that you're too young and I'm too old and what do we think we're doing anyway?"

"Who said that?" He kind of wanted to go a few rounds with whoever it was.

"Well, your mother for one."

Crap. He should have seen that coming. "Look. She's sorry. Honestly, she is. She wanted to tell you so, but I asked her to leave it alone for now."

"Thank you. I don't want to get into it with Meggie, I really don't."

"I know."

She drew herself up and looked directly into his eyes. "And I will be fine, I promise. I'm feeling absurdly emotional right now, that's all. It's hormones. It'll pass."

He didn't believe that—yeah, hormones might be part of it. But there was more, and they both knew it. "Hey, now…"

She looked up. "What?" Her eyes shone with unhappy tears.

He framed her sweet face with both hands. "Say it," he coaxed. "Just put it on out there."

"Something got broken in me, Jason. I was…young and brave once, I really was. I knew what I wanted, and I was determined to have a bold life with the right man, to have kids, to have it all." She was shivering suddenly. "But then I chose all wrong. That almost destroyed me. And after that, I wasn't brave anymore. Eventually, I met Walter and I…got it all wrong again." She shivered a little and put her hand on her belly. "Ugh. I probably shouldn't have eaten all those barbecue chips."

"Come on. Let's get back to the room." He wrapped an arm across her shoulders and turned her toward the hotel.

As soon as he ushered her inside, she bolted for the bathroom. He was right behind her when she dropped to the floor and threw back the toilet seat. Going to his knees at her side, he held her hair out of the way as she lost everything she'd eaten earlier.

Once that was over, she dropped to her butt and scooted back to lean against the tub. "Well, there goes dinner." She forced out a laugh.

He rose, went to the cooler he'd left near the door in the main room and came back with the usual bottle of water.

"Always right there with what I need," she said. "Thank you." She screwed off the top and drank half of it down. "Okay, then. That's a little better." She spoke cautiously, one hand on her stomach. "I, uh, really need a shower."

"You want help with that?"

"Oh, Jason. Thank you, but no."

He didn't want to leave her. But this wasn't about what he wanted. "So you're telling me that you'd like a little time alone?"

A slow nod this time. "Yes, please."

Reluctantly, he volunteered, "I'll take a walk."

"Thank you."

So he left their room and went down to the beach again. The sunset was every bit as gorgeous as the night before, lighting the sky in purple and orange, the vivid colors reflected in the shifting sea below.

He plopped to his butt in the sand and watched the colors change as night came on. Eventually, he got up again, brushed off the sand and headed back the way he'd come.

In their room, he found her lying on the bed in a big, white T-shirt, her hair in that cute single braid. She opened her eyes as he entered.

"Sorry," he said. "I didn't mean to wake you."

Sitting up, she scooted to the end of the bed and put her bare feet on the floor. "You didn't." She held up the remote in her hand. "I was thinking of turning on the TV, but then I ended up just lying here, waiting for you. Want to watch a movie?"

He didn't, not really. He wanted to know more about what was making her sad. But that was for her to share when and if she was damn good and ready. He slipped off his flip-flops right there by the door. "Sure."

"Come sit by me." She patted the space at her side. He went to her and sat down. With a sigh, she leaned her head on his shoulder. "I'm kind of a coward. I just want to relax and watch something fun and mindless."

"I get it." Catching the tail of her braid, he gave it a tug.

Smiling now, she took his free hand, turned it over and plunked the remote in it. "You pick."

He pointed the device at the screen and started scrolling through the options. "*Guardians of the Galaxy*?"

She nodded. "Those are good. Which one?"

"Might as well go for the best."

"Ah." She tipped her chin up. "The first one…" Her mouth was right there, softly parted. Irresistible.

As if he even wanted to resist. "On second thought…"

"Hmm?" She tipped that mouth higher, a clear invitation. He tossed the remote over his shoulder. It bounced on the bed behind them and then dropped to the rug. Not that he cared where it landed. "Later for Peter Quill," she said. "Kiss me."

"Good thinking…" He claimed her mouth, taking her under the arms, pulling her with him until they were stretched out on the mattress.

What was it about kissing her? How could a kiss make everything better? These were deep questions—and right now, all he wanted was to kiss her some more. He stroked his tongue along the seam where her lips met, and she opened for him.

The sadness in her eyes earlier, the troubling things she'd said that didn't really tell him what the matter was?

He put all that from his mind.

For now, it was just the two of them, Jason and Piper, alone on a big, comfortable bed. The three long days of driving ahead of them, followed by an iffy future at best for them as a couple, and in time a baby that would change his world completely?

He let all that go. It would still be there to stew over in the morning.

"Be right back," he said as he rolled off the bed and started tearing off his clothes.

"Hurry," she urged him.

And he did, pulling his shirt off over his head, shoving down his jeans and briefs and kicking them away.

A moment later, he was back on the bed with her, gathering her into his arms. "I like this shirt," he whispered against her parted lips.

"It's a plain white T-shirt. Extra-large. Nothing special about it," she chided as her fingers, cool and soft, brushed at his temples.

"Oh, it's special, all right." He eased his hand up under the hem of the shirt, letting his palm glide over her thigh, teasing her a little with his hand between her legs, rubbing at the sweetness beneath her silky panties, then tugging at her shirt again. "This shirt is special because you're in it."

She chuckled. "I know that look. I won't be in it for long."

"Smart girl."

"Yes, I am. And don't you forget it."

He pulled back to look at her.

"What?" she asked.

"Panties first, I think…" He slipped one finger under the elastic at her left hip.

"Here. Let me help you." She eased her hand between their bodies and took the other side. Together, they pushed them down.

When those panties reached her knees, she lifted both pale, shapely legs straight up toward the ceiling. He whipped them off and tossed them toward a chair—and after more careful consideration, he saw that he didn't need that big, white shirt off.

Not yet anyway.

Instead, he scooted down the bed. Before she could lower her legs back to the mattress, he was between them, guiding them to rest on his shoulders. That put his face right where he needed it—with one smooth, white thigh to either side.

He started kissing her again, light kisses at first, bringing his fingers into play, too. She moaned and called his name, tossing her head on the pillow, begging him, "Please, Jason. Yes, Jason. Oh, please, just like that…"

He followed her instructions to the letter, kissing her and stroking her until her moans grew more desperate. With his mouth and eager fingers right there, he could feel the moment her climax began, a flutter that quickly built to a pulse.

She moaned and tossed her head from side to side. He

went on kissing her, stroking her, as she soared over the edge of the world.

"Jason…" She reached down and tried to get hold of his shoulders. "Oh, please…"

He knew what she wanted. Still, he waited, letting her hit the peak and start to come down before sliding up her body, wrapping his arms around her and rolling them so he was on the bottom.

She blinked down at him, gasping. "Yeah?"

"Oh, yeah. No doubt." He eased a hand down the back of one perfect thigh.

She sighed as she swung that leg over him.

"Up you go." He took her by the waist and boosted her over him, until she straddled him on her knees.

She did the rest, reaching down between them, positioning his aching hardness just where they both wanted it. Her green eyes held his. "It's only fair that I torture you at least a little…"

As if he was going to make a peep of complaint. "Have at it, sweetheart."

And she did. Wearing the smile of a wayward angel, that braid hanging over her right shoulder, a rope of red silk against the cotton of her big white shirt, she took her sweet time, bending close, lowering that clever mouth onto him.

Time flew away as she tortured him so sweetly with that perfect mouth of hers.

And finally, when he hardly knew his own name anymore, she sat up again and reached down between them to position him just so.

Once she had him in place, she lowered her body by fractions of degrees. It took her forever to claim his full length. Until then, he existed in the sweetest, most perfect sort of agony, trying not to groan, not to toss all dignity to the wind and beg her outright to let him all the way inside.

When she finally had all of him, he took that white shirt by the hem on either side. "Arms up."

"Yes!" She shot her hands skyward.

He tugged that shirt up and over her head, balled it between his fists and then flung it in the general direction of the door.

She was laughing as he reached for her—but the laughter didn't last long. He pulled her down on top of him and took her mouth.

That kiss was endless. And all the while, she rocked on him.

The past, the future—all those days ahead with the question marks in them. Days when she might be his or might be lost to him. Days when he hoped to become a good father, a loving one, both protective and wise...

For right now, he let all that go. There was no future. No past. No questions. No doubts.

Just Piper all around him, taking him, owning him, riding him to the sweetest place where pleasure took over and there was only right now.

Chapter Twelve

When Jason woke, it was still dark. A glance at the blue numerals on the clock by the bed told him it was almost 3:00 a.m. Beside him, Piper stirred and tossed her head from side to side. She moaned, an unhappy sound.

"Piper?" he whispered.

He reached out to soothe her, but pulled his hand back when she spoke in a pained, pleading voice, "Don't… No… Stop it…"

"Hey…" Through the shadows, he could see that her eyes were shut. Her face seemed strained, her sweet mouth was twisted.

She struggled as though someone held her captive. "I don't want to do this, Brandon. It's too dangerous! Let me go!" Right then, she sat straight up in the bed. Her eyes popped open, wide and terrified. "No!"

He sat up beside her. "Hey…" She flinched when he touched her. Raising both hands, he showed her his palms. "It's okay. It's just me…"

For a moment, she stared at him, eyes blank. Then she crumpled. "Oh, Jason…" She swayed toward him. He took her in his arms and held her for a while, stroking her hair, rubbing her back.

"I'm okay," she said at last, and gently pulled away.

"I'll turn on the light…" He hesitated. But when she didn't object, he reached over and flipped the switch on the lamp by his side of the bed.

He sat up, propped his pillow behind him and adjusted the blankets. She did the same. For several awkward seconds, they sat there in silence. She was still breathing too fast. He didn't want to do anything to freak her out more than she already was.

Finally, she reached over and put her hand on his. He laced their fingers together and held on as her breathing slowed to a more normal rate.

"I guess I owe you an explanation," she said.

He lifted her hand and pressed his lips to the back of it. "No you don't. I want to hear whatever you have to tell me, but not because you feel you have to explain yourself."

She gave him the softest, sweetest smile then. "But I do have to explain. Because I care about you. Because we're having a baby. Because I need you to understand."

"Okay, then."

They pulled up the blankets, getting comfortable.

Finally, she leaned her head on his shoulder and said, "I dated now and then in high school and during my four years at Wyoming State, but nothing serious. Then I met Brandon McAdams at the University of Washington. I got my master's in library science there. Brandon was kind of a big deal, a high achiever, you know? Lettered in academics, baseball and football. All the girls were after him, but he was with me, the nerdy library science major. I was wildly in love with him…" Her voice faded to nothing.

He waited, wondering if she'd changed her mind about saying more.

But then she went on. "The thing about Brandon was

that he got a thrill out of taking things one step too far. Being with him was exciting. When we hiked, we always had to take the most challenging, dangerous trails. I went skiing with him once. He pushed me to try a run I wasn't ready for. I wiped out and ended up in a cast for six weeks. He loved a challenge, loved to take chances. I still have nightmares about him pressuring me to do stuff I wasn't ready for or comfortable with. The dream I just had is the worst one, the worst thing he ever did to me."

Jason wrapped an arm around her and pulled her closer.

"It happened here in California," she said.

That surprised him. "You mean here in Monterey?"

"No. Until this trip with you, I'd never been south of Sacramento. But Brandon's parents owned a cabin up in Placer County, on the American River. I had just finished my first year at UW the summer Brandon I and drove down to his parents' cabin from Seattle for Memorial Day weekend.

"We arrived on Friday afternoon. His parents weren't there yet. Brandon and I went down to the river for a swim. It was cold, deep and swift. We climbed up a rocky cliff until we came out on a promontory far above the racing water. He wanted to hold hands and jump. I could see boulders in the churning current below. I knew it wasn't safe. When I wouldn't take his dare, he pushed me in and then jumped in after me…"

It took considerable effort, but Jason kept his breathing slow and even. "The guy was a psychopath."

She made a low, humorless sound. "Yeah, you could say that. I didn't hit the rocks, but I got caught in the current. I almost drowned. He pulled me out, performed CPR…

And when I coughed and came to, he sat back on his heels, grinning. 'See? It all worked out just fine,' he said."

"Tell me you punched him in the face."

"No, I did not. And it wasn't because I took the high road. At the time, I was still coughing up water, barely able to breathe. When I could manage words again, I said I wanted to go back to the cabin. We went. Then his parents arrived. They'd always seemed kind of cold and distant, like I wasn't good enough for their precious, perfect son. I just wanted to get away from him and from them. But we were up in the mountains, almost eight hundred miles from Seattle, and I didn't have a car.

"Somehow, I got through the weekend, but I was miserable, scared of my own boyfriend and very pissed off. As for Brandon, he put on a good act for his parents, but as soon as we were in his car driving back to Seattle, he hit the roof, calling me rude and self-indulgent and other names I would rather not repeat. I just sat there, silent, waiting to get away from him. The drive took twelve endless hours. When he dropped me off in Seattle at my studio apartment, he pulled the latch on the trunk. I jumped out and got my suitcase. Then I leaned in the passenger side window—and broke up with him, right there on the street."

"Good for you."

"Yeah. I thought so, too. I thought I was home free."

He didn't like the sound of that. "But you weren't?"

She shook her head. "Brandon was furious. His eyes were…feral. He said, '*You* don't break up with me. *I* break up with you.' I said he could call it what he wanted. But he and I were done. I headed for my building…" She paused. Her breathing was agitated.

"Take your time," he whispered.

She nodded. "He, uh, he left his car right there in the middle of the street and followed me up to my apartment. I was really scared by then. I didn't know how far he would go, what he would do. I got to my door, and I told him to leave. He wouldn't go. He ripped my purse off my shoulder and dug around in it until he came up with my keys. Then he dangled them in front of my face. When I grabbed for them, he whipped them away.

"He said, 'I'm coming in and before I go, you're going to understand how things work around here.' By then, I was beyond scared. I didn't know what he'd do. I screamed."

"Tell me someone came."

She nodded on a ragged little breath. "The guy next door, a middle-aged guy, came out of his place and said, right to Brandon, 'What the hell's going on here? What do you think you're up to, mister?'"

"And...?"

"It was like my neighbor had flipped a switch. Brandon dropped my purse and keys and put up both hands. 'Not a thing,' he said. 'Not a thing.' And he took off without another word."

"Did he leave you alone after that?"

She nodded. "I think he actually realized that he'd gone too far. The summer went by, and I never saw or heard from him. I had a job there in Seattle and I was taking classes, too. When the fall semester came, I saw him on campus more than once. He looked away. So did I."

"I would say you got lucky."

"Oh, yes I did."

"But, Piper, what happened, what you just described—both the nightmare, and the reality. There was nothing lucky about what that guy did to you."

"Yeah. I know. I haven't had that dream in the longest time, though. I kind of thought I was done with it." She scooted down under the covers, pulling her pillow with her. He stretched out on his side, facing her.

They were quiet together. The story she'd just told him still had him wanting to punch a hole through a wall—or better yet, go looking for the guy who'd almost drowned her.

He should probably just let her go back to sleep. But he wanted to know more—everything about her. Whatever she was willing to share with him. "So… Walter?"

She gave him a strange, wry little smile. "Yeah. You're catching on about Walter, aren't you?"

"You've said that Walter made you feel safe—and I'm guessing you needed safety, after what happened with that douchebag in Seattle."

She tucked her hands under her pillow. "I didn't date anyone else while I was at UW. Then I got my first job as a librarian, in Billings. I was there for two years, and I made some friends. But if a guy asked me out, I tried to be nice about it, but I always said no. Then there was an opening in Medicine Creek. I took it and I met Walter."

"I get it. Walter was good, right? He was what you needed."

"Oh, Jason…" Her eyes were all shadows, bottomless.

He wanted to touch her—stroke her hair, caress her cheek. But he kept his hands to himself. "What? Say it."

"No. Walter was not what I needed, though at first I really believed it would work with him, that I *had* found what I needed in him. Back when we first started dating, I told Walter everything about the awfulness with Brandon.

Walter said he understood. He said that what I had with Brandon wasn't love. He said, 'I'll show you what love is.'"

"That's a little…"

"Smug?" she asked with a groan.

"Yeah. *Smug*'s a good word for it."

"Well, Walter was kind of smug. But he did show me what love could be—up to a point. He was a good, steady man who treated me with consideration and respect. But whatever that special connection is between two people, Walter and I didn't have it. He was kind and he was gentle, but I didn't know his heart at all. And I never really showed him mine. We just went through the motions. We got through the days together, not exactly miserable, but never really happy, either—I mean, we'd agreed we wanted kids, but I never got pregnant naturally. And neither of us pushed to find out why."

"Sweetheart…" He touched her cheek and smoothed her hair.

She gave him the saddest little smile then. "The last couple of years, we rarely had sex. We were old friends who shared the same house. And when he died, I felt sad, I really did. But then slowly I came to realize that I was so much happier on my own. I like my life. Just as it is. I really do."

He wanted to argue, to tell her that it could be better, richer, with the right person. But he doubted she'd believe it just because he told her so. "This—all that you just told me—it's what you meant last night, on the beach, when you said that you made two wrong choices…"

"Yes." She held his gaze, unblinking. "Two wrong choices—Brandon and then Walter. I didn't get it right with either of them. I don't think that I know how to get it right. I don't think I'm cut out for a real, deep, successful relationship. I just don't know what I'm doing when it comes to all that relationship stuff."

"Hey." He nuzzled her cheek. "Don't sell yourself short."

"Oh, I'm not. Honestly. I keep hoping to get you to see that I'm perfectly happy being single and I'm done with trying to understand all the coupling-up crap. Being half of a couple just doesn't work for me. I'll be a single mom like my mom before me and there's nothing wrong with that."

He really wanted to argue with her, to insist that she shouldn't give up on love. But he'd tried that already, back at the end of April, when he'd cornered her at the diner. Arguing with her about love hadn't worked then.

Why should it work now? And anyway, wouldn't that only make him more like Brandon and Walter? The last thing she needed was another guy mansplaining away all her valid concerns.

"You're right," he said, choosing his words carefully. "Your mom did a great job raising you and there is no reason you can't do the same with our child. You're going to be a terrific mom."

She gave him a sly smile. "You're refusing to argue with me."

"I am. Will you please let me get away with that?"

"Oh, Jason. I have to admit, there is no man quite like you."

"I'm thinking that's a good thing. Right?"

"It is, yeah." She scooted a little closer. "It's a very good thing."

Now her lips were right there, inches from his. He couldn't help but claim them.

With a sigh, she snuggled closer.

He wrapped her up in his arms and deepened the kiss.

* * *

Piper woke with a start. She was leaning against the passenger-side window as they sped along I-5. Her neck had a crick in it and there was drool down her chin. She swiped the drool away, brushed her hair out of her eyes and glanced at Jason over there behind the wheel. As usual, he looked like every woman's dream of a smoking-hot cowboy. A quick glance at the speedometer told her that they were sailing along at sixty-eight miles an hour.

"Hey there, sunshine." He grinned at her and tipped his hat.

"How long have I been asleep?"

"An hour or so."

Flatland spread out in all directions. Far off, she could see the gray humps of mountains. With a yawn, she asked, "Where are we?"

"In the Sacramento Valley five miles from Willows, California. Halfway to Grants Pass." They were staying in Grants Pass, Oregon, for the night. She'd booked them a room before she conked out against the window.

Her stomach growled. "How about stopping for lunch?" she asked hopefully.

"Sure. Check your phone for a good place?"

"Will do."

They ate fat roast beef sandwiches at a cute little deli in Willows. In no time, they were back on the endless, flat highway.

"I'm happy to drive," Piper offered.

"I'm good staying behind the wheel unless you really want to take over."

She didn't. He drove on.

She grabbed a pillow from the back seat and napped

some more. When she woke again they were still in California, just passing Red Bluff. She smoothed her sleep-tangled hair back over her shoulder and asked, "Whose idea was it to take the long way home?"

He glanced her way and then focused his eyes on the road again. "I see no upside to answering that question."

She faked a frown. "You're no fun. But at least there are a few more hills around here—and I really do have to pee."

They stopped at a gas station and then got right back on the road.

It was still afternoon when they checked in at the hotel she'd found in Grants Pass. Their room had a balcony and a gorgeous view of the Rogue River.

After dinner, they took a little stroll around the hotel grounds. And later, back in the room, she kissed him eagerly and pulled him down onto the soft sheets of the big, comfortable bed.

Their time together was flying by. They only had one more night on the road after this. And she wanted his arms around her far too desperately for this love affair they were having to be almost over.

The next day, they drove 595 miles from Grants Pass to Spokane, through the vineyards and farmlands of the Willamette Valley, past Portland, and then northeast through the Columbia Gorge.

Her stomach started churning before they crossed into Washington. She asked Jason to pull over.

On the side of the highway right there in the glorious Columbia River Gorge, she threw up. Cars went by fast enough to make the crew cab rock behind her. Didn't even faze her. She rinsed out her mouth with the water from the bottle Jason handed her.

"My turn to drive," she said.

She drove the rest of the way to the KOA campground just beyond Spokane where Jason had reserved them a spot for the night.

"Like old times," she teased as they got ready to bed down in the tent.

"Old times, only better," he added. "Because this time we're zipping the sleeping bags together."

She climbed in the double bag with him and spooned back against him wearing her big turquoise T-shirt with an open book and Just One More Chapter printed on the front. When he trailed a finger up her thigh, taking the hem of her big shirt along with him, she smiled. And when he pulled that shirt off over her head, she raised her arms high.

A sleeping bag on a thin foam pad didn't make a very comfortable bed, but she hardly noticed. She was far too busy enjoying every last minute with Jason. They tried to be quiet, but at one point, some guy at the next campsite over whistled and suggested that they get a room.

Snickering like a couple of naughty kids, they whispered, "Shh," to each other. And then snickered some more.

Sunday morning came much too soon. They had ten hours in the crew cab ahead of them. After breakfast at a coffee shop right off I-90, they headed for home.

She drove first, through the Idaho towns of Coeur d'Alene, Kellogg, Wallace and Mullan. They rolled on into Montana. She stayed behind the wheel through Haugan, Saint Regis and Superior. A few miles out of Missoula, she had to pull off in order to lose what was left of her breakfast.

Jason handed her the usual bottle of cold, delicious water and took over behind the wheel. They stopped in Missoula for gas and a bathroom break and then kept going to Butte, where they got off the highway long enough to find the Hanging Five Restaurant, a family-style establishment that served cinnamon rolls as big as Piper's head.

She wanted one so bad. But she was way too likely to gobble the whole thing. And with the morning sickness situation, she couldn't be sure all that buttery, sugary goodness would stay down the rest of the way home.

Jason pulled her close with an arm around her shoulders. "I support you, whatever your choice."

With a sigh, she passed on the cinnamon roll and settled on an excellent turkey club sandwich instead.

From Butte, it was a little over five more hours to Medicine Creek. Jason drove and Piper alternately napped, read, fiddled with the radio and kept him company.

They talked about safe things—his life on the ranch, her plans for the library. She got him talking about his chain saw art.

He said he used to whittle. "But I like the big statement of a chain saw carving. A ten-foot red cedar dragon isn't something you can set on a shelf and forget until you have to dust it again."

He mentioned the carvers he'd met over the years, often at competitions. "Several carvers I know live on the West Coast. One's in Santa Cruz, as a matter of fact."

"We should have stopped in to see him..."

"Her," he corrected. "Molly Taft is her name."

"Is she good?"

"Her work is exceptional—and as for stopping to see her, I thought about suggesting that." He glanced her way.

Her skin warmed at the look in his eyes. "I think you would like Molly."

"So why didn't you mention her?"

"I wanted you all to myself." His voice was rough in the best sort of way. He turned his gaze back to the road.

Her throat felt thick. She swallowed to push down the knot of emotion. Their two weeks had whizzed by so fast. It almost didn't seem possible that they were already almost home.

Too soon, they were leaving Billings behind, then Lockwood and Toluca. And suddenly, they were passing the Crow Agency and then Garryowen, a town with a population of two, where the Battle of the Little Bighorn began. It wasn't far from there to the Wyoming border. Sheridan went by in a blur.

Twenty minutes later, Jason pulled the pickup to a stop in front of her house. He turned off the engine.

Panic rose inside her, a hot ball of desperation—to get out of the truck and flee up the front walk, to make it into her house before she burst into a flood of ridiculous tears and begged the man behind the wheel for more time, at least a few days. Another week. And then another...

More time for the two of them, more time for this heat and joy and wonder between them to burn on.

But that was just foolish. They had an agreement. And she was determined to stick by it.

She grabbed the door handle in a death grip and stared across the console at his beautiful, beard-scruffy face. Those blue eyes regarded her so calmly, like he had a clear purpose, like he knew what to do next.

Too bad she didn't. "Thank you." She sounded downright frantic. That wouldn't do. Sucking in a slow breath, she let it all the way out before drawing in one more and giving him what she hoped was a warm smile. "It was such a great trip. And you know, I'll just grab my stuff from the back and—"

"I'll get the stuff and walk you to your door."

"Jason, it really isn't—"

"Yeah, Piper. It's necessary." He was out of the truck before she could think of a way to stop him. She jumped out, too, and met him at the back, where he grabbed her suitcase and the big duffel with her camping clothes and gear in it. "Lead the way," he said.

So she did, striding swiftly up the walk, fumbling to get her key out of her shoulder bag and then finally managing to stick it in the lock. She pushed the door inward onto her small entry hall. Home. It all looked so perfectly peaceful, spotless and neat.

When she stepped inside he was right behind her.

"Just put those down. Thank you again. I'll take it from here."

He set both bags on the floor. But instead of leaving, he shut the door.

She took a step back. "Jason, I…" All she had to do was say, *please go*, and he would. It shouldn't have been that difficult.

Oh, but it was. She needed him to go. But his leaving was the last thing she wanted. Already, she ached for him, for their time together these past two glorious weeks.

How had it flown by so fast? Two weeks gone in what felt like an instant, a kaleidoscope of sweet moments, spinning and glittering, then suddenly tunneling down to this…

The two of them at her door, saying goodbye—or trying to anyway.

"Give me your hand," he said.

Without the slightest hesitation, she did. His fingers
closed over hers and it felt like a lifeline, like everything
that really mattered was now held, warm and hopeful, between their joined hands.

He pulled her closer. She failed to object.

A moment later, she was captured in the perfect prison
of his big arms. She looked up at him, whispered his name.

He took that as an invitation to lower those beautiful
lips of his to hers.

She kissed him. How could she not? She kissed him and
she wished they could stay like this forever holding each
other so tight, her soft breasts to his hard chest, her mouth
opening under his. She needed him to go, but this kiss…

She never, ever wanted it to end.

When he finally lifted his head, she stared up at him
and tried to summon the gentle words that would send
him on his way.

"You really want me to go?" he asked, his voice rough,
low, thrilling. A hot shiver coursed through her. No, she
didn't want him to go. What she wanted—what she needed—
was to keep on feeling the way she felt whenever he touched
her.

But that wasn't the deal. She opened her mouth to tell
him to go.

And instead, she surged up on tiptoe, reaching for him.
He met her halfway, kissing her wildly as she ran her
hands up over his hard shoulders and strong neck. His
hat was in her way. She took it by the brim and tossed it

over her shoulder. There. Now she could thread her fingers into his dark, thick hair.

Her feet left the floor as he scooped her up against his broad chest. She wrapped her legs around his waist and felt him, hard and ready for her. That only made her clutch at him tighter and kiss him more deeply.

The stairs were right there, a few feet from the front door. He lifted his head and asked, "Your bedroom?" in a rough, low voice that promised unearthly delights.

And then he waited, giving her yet another opportunity to stop this madness now.

"Upstairs," she instructed breathlessly, "first door on your left."

And up they went.

A minute later, he was carrying her into her room and straight to the sleigh bed she'd found at a yard sale and painted snowy white. Gently, he set her on the turquoise-and-white duvet.

She stared up at him. His eyes were all pupil, his mouth fuller than ever, deep red from their kisses.

Without a word, by silent mutual agreement, they undressed. She kicked off her hiking sandals and dropped each piece of clothing to the floor by the bed. He followed her lead, toeing off his boots and tossing his clothes to the rug, too.

And then, when they were both naked, she reached out her arms again. He came down on the bed with her.

Their kisses grew more desperate, even hungrier than on the way up the stairs. The summer sunlight slanted in through the filmy white curtains. It was so good with him, always had been. Every time, starting with their first night back in April.

She reached down between them, wrapped her fingers around his hard, ready length and guided him into her, crying out as he filled her. He whispered her name as he covered her lips with his.

They moved together, arms wrapped around each other. Her mind was spinning. The world seemed full of golden light. She could go on like this forever—and oh, she wished she could. She wished that this moment might never end.

Too soon, she felt her body rising toward the peak. With another cry, she sailed out into fulfillment, finding that sweet spot where the tension tightened so perfectly, then burst wide in a shower of glorious sparks. For several sweet moments, he held her good and tight. Her breathing slowed and she sighed in completion.

He didn't leave her. Instead, he continued to hold her. He kissed her cheeks and her throat, and then covered her mouth again as he began to move inside her once more.

Her body responded. She wrapped both legs around him, hooked her feet at the small of his back and lost herself to everything but the flow of perfect sensation.

That time, he rode the crest with her. She went over into free fall, and he followed right behind. The pulsing within continued for the longest time.

But at last, the hurricane of pleasure mellowed, leaving her breathing like she'd run a hard race, still twined around him, holding him so tight, wishing that she didn't have to let him go.

Slowly, she came back to herself. He eased his weight off her. But he didn't leave her—not yet. He rested his head on her shoulder. As for her, she was still holding on to him, not quite able to take her hands off him, though she knew she needed to put a little space between them.

It would be so easy to freak out right now. This was not the way it was supposed to go, not what they'd agreed on. She should have said goodbye to him downstairs at the door.

He was stroking her arm, lazily letting his fingers drift down into the crook of her elbow and lower, to the tender, pale skin of her inner wrist. It felt so good, their bodies pressed warm and close. She had matched her breathing to his.

Peace. Yes. Peace was the essence of this moment. She didn't want to give this up.

And really, why should she?

"Jason?" She kissed him on his scruffy cheek, using her teeth a little, soothing the scrape with more brushing kisses.

"Piper..." He turned his head enough to meet her lips with his.

They opened at the same time, tongues coming out to play, tangling, wet. She loved kissing him. He made kissing an art—spontaneous, playful, delicious and fun.

It came to her then, the answer to this ongoing problem. So simple. And it could work. She knew that it could.

She clasped his big shoulders, pushing him away just enough to break the sweet, endless kiss. "Jason..."

He looked at her with a slow smile. "Yeah?"

She lost her train of thought as she gazed at him. He had the longest eyelashes. What was it about really good-looking men? Why did they always have lush, thick, beautiful eyelashes that any woman would envy?

And where was she? Right. "I've been thinking."

"Yeah?" He guided a swatch of hair off her forehead and back behind the shell of her ear. "About what?"

"I don't want to give this up—you and me, like this. Jason, it's so good. I don't want to go backward."

He made a lazy, happy sound. "Tell me about it."

"So, remember that day at the diner way back in April? You suggested that we could try being friends with benefits?"

His brow crinkled a little—in thought? Or was he actually frowning? "I remember."

"Well, I think you were right. I think that might work. I mean, I would have my life. And you would have yours. And, you know, later, when the time comes, we'll work things out to take care of our baby.

"Oh, but Jason, I do want the sex, too. I really do. It's so good with you. And it could be so simple. I'll keep my house and you'll have yours. We won't be a couple. We're not getting married or anything."

"Let me get this straight. You want me to be your friend—*and* your booty call?" He didn't sound all that excited at the idea.

"Well, yes, for as long as it works for both of us. I mean, whatever happens will just happen. You might…meet someone else eventually. If you do, well, I'll miss the sex. But we will still be friends and co-parents. And you know how it goes, it could be that this thing between us will just fade away in time, and we'll both be fine with that. Because, honestly, who knows what happens with this stuff? I certainly don't."

The way he looked at her then, as though he was the older one, wiser and more experienced in…everything. And she was the youngster, green and untested, struggling to figure out how life really works.

"There's only one problem with your plan," he said.

"Problem?" She blinked at him, confused. "But *you* were the one who suggested it first."

"That was then. Things have changed."

"Well, okay. How so?" she asked.

"Damn. Piper…" Instead of giving her an answer, he wrapped his hand around the back of her head and moved in close again for a quick, hard kiss.

When he pulled away, she stared at him, completely bewildered. "Jason. What are you getting at?"

"You're not going to like it."

"Just say it, already."

"Fine. You can lie to yourself all you want to, but the friends-with-benefits solution? That ship has sailed."

"What are you talking about?"

"You're in love with me, Piper. You're in love with me deeply, completely and forever."

She gasped. "That's not true."

"Yeah, it is. And if you think your college boyfriend broke you, then you ought to give some serious consideration to how you'll feel the day I show up at your door to let you know there's someone else."

Piper could not believe what he'd just said. "You don't know what you're talking about. How many times do I have to tell you that I'm not doing that? I'm not falling in love with you or with anyone. Not ever again."

He didn't argue. Instead, he sat up and asked gently, "You want me to go?"

Did she? "You have no right to start telling me what's in my own heart."

"True." He rose and started picking up his clothes.

She stared at him, furious—and yet also bereft. "And now you're leaving, just like that?"

He pulled on his jeans, then sat on the bed to put on his socks and boots. "Do you want me to stay?"

"I… No. No, really. This is not working. You should go."

"Okay, then." He yanked his T-shirt on over his head. Finally, he rose. "I'm out of here."

Stunned, she stared after him as he left her bedroom. The sound of his boots echoed on the wooden stairs.

She never heard the front door open or click shut. He must have gone out very quietly. But he really was gone. Because a minute later, she heard his truck start up and drive away.

Chapter Thirteen

"So, what's up with you and Medicine Creek's hottest librarian?" asked Ty.

Knocking back a big gulp of champagne, Jason tried to decide how to answer his nosy second cousin.

The two of them stood under a giant ash tree next to a pretty rail fence. Beyond the fence, cattle grazed peacefully on rolling, green Rising Sun Cattle Company land. Far off to the west, the Bighorn Mountains rose, gray and craggy, poking into the wide, blue Wyoming sky.

It was a perfect Saturday afternoon for an outdoor wedding, and two hours ago, Ty and Sadie McBride had tied the knot. Jason wore his best black Western suit coat, matching dress pants and a white shirt with a string tie. His black tooled boots were buffed to a fine shine.

Ty nudged him with an elbow. "I mean, I thought she might be here with you today, you know?"

Jason continued to consider his reply. *Mind your business* had kind of a nice ring to it.

Then again, hauling off and punching Ty in the mouth held a special kind of appeal—not because Ty's questions were in any way deserving of a fist to the face. More because Ty looked so happy, and Jason was envious as hell that his cousin had the woman he wanted and a lifetime ahead of him with Sadie at his side.

Ty clapped him on the back. "Sorry, cousin. Anything I can do—anything—you just say the word."

"Thanks," Jason replied through clenched teeth. Because it would be all kinds of wrong to beat the crap out of his well-meaning cousin on the man's wedding day.

"Isn't it spectacular?" June Copely, in a blue sequined cocktail dress that clung to her generous curves, wrapped a plump arm around Piper's waist. It was an hour before the doors opened on the Medicine Creek Library's Annual Gala and Silent Auction. They stood in the atrium-like space near reception just beyond the wide entry hallway. "Jason is so talented."

Piper stared at the life-size Tyrannosaurus rex carved of white pine. The dinosaur had its mouth open, displaying hundreds of sharp, powerful teeth.

"It's impressive," she agreed, and wanted to cry. She missed him so much. There was an ache in the center of her chest, a gaping hole through which all her happiness had somehow leaked out. She kept reminding herself that cutting it clean was for the best.

But it didn't feel like the best. It felt like she was missing what made life worthwhile.

June was still admiring the T. rex. "You think it'll give the little ones nightmares?"

"Are you kidding? They'll love it."

June laughed. "Oh, yes they will—and thank God for Hunter Bartley." A year ago, Hunter and his reality show, *Rebuilt by Bartley*, had raised the ceilings and pushed out the walls on the main entrance and the reception atrium.

Even after those renovations, it had still been necessary to do some fancy maneuvering to get the enormous carving into the building. But now it stood proudly in the center of the atrium. "If it weren't for Hunter we never could have gotten this big boy in the door."

Two hours later, the event was in full swing. They had an excellent turnout. It seemed like just about everyone in town had shown up this year.

Guests of all ages wandered among the stacks and along the rows of tables set up with donated goodies for auction. They sipped sparkling cider and placed their bids.

Starr was there with Cara in her arms and Beau at her side. Piper greeted them.

"We missed our morning at the Perfect Bean last month," Starr chided.

Piper made a sad face. "I hate when that happens. Next week? I can do Wednesday at ten."

"I'll meet you there," replied Starr as Cara held out her arms for a hug.

Piper took the little girl, kissed her velvety cheek and chatted with Starr and her husband for a few minutes. When they moved on to check out the auction tables, Bobby Trueblood appeared, his mom right behind him.

The little boy grinned up at Piper. "Hi, Mithuth Wallath." He had two teeth missing in front and he looked about three inches taller than he was back in April.

"Bobby! How are you?"

"Real good. I *like* that big dinothaur!" he exclaimed.

Behind him, Maxine laughed. "We checked out three books on dinosaurs last week. He can't get enough."

"There's a stack of good ones available on the auction table," Piper reminded her.

"I thaw them!" Bobby grinned wider. "We bidded on them."

"Excellent." Piper nodded. "Good luck." Right then, Bobby's little sister peeked out from behind Maxine. Piper greeted her. "Nice to see you, Reina." The wide-eyed child raised her hand in a shy wave.

A moment later, Maxine herded the kids toward the refreshment tables in the open area between the children's and teens sections.

Piper watched them go—and spotted Jason for the first time that evening. He stood at the table with the paper plates, plastic cutlery and beverages on it, a foam cup in his hand, talking to Carolyn Kipp. About Jason's age, Carolyn ran the front desk at Don Deal Insurance Agency right there in town. She was pretty and friendly. Piper liked her.

Or she had until right this minute.

Jason glanced up suddenly. It was like he had radar.

Their eyes locked. And that hollow space inside her? It ached harder with emptiness.

She turned away.

Somehow, she managed to avoid eye contact with him for the rest of the evening. He was the star of the event. His T. rex brought a final bid of $10,000. There was fierce competition for it. And in the end, it went to some big spender from San Francisco who'd moved to town five years ago and built himself a giant house on the banks of Crystal Creek—a house that would now have a T. rex in the backyard.

The weekend crawled by. On Monday, Jason called her. Like the big, fat coward she was, she let it go to voice mail. And then she put off playing his message back.

Tuesday, he texted her. She avoided looking at that text for a couple of hours. But she was three months pregnant. They were having a baby together. He'd made it clear from the beginning that he intended to be part of everything that had to do with their child.

She forced herself to read the text.

When is your next doctor's appointment? It should have been last week, right? And do you have a date for the thirteen-week ultrasound? That's coming up soon. Call me. I mean it.

Though it broke her heart all over again to have to see him or talk to him, she made herself call him back.

The first words out of his mouth were, "Did I miss one of your visits with Dr. Hayes?"

Her heart ached all the harder at the sound of his voice. The pain was made even worse because she'd broken her agreement with him that he would be in on everything involving the baby—and judging by the banked anger in his question, he knew that she had. "Yes. I went last Thursday."

Silence echoed for several seconds before he spoke again. "We had an agreement, Piper."

"I know we did. I'm sorry. It won't happen again."

He seemed to be thinking that over. Finally, he said, "So, then, I have your word on that?"

"Yes. I won't leave you out again."

"All right. The next ultrasound?"

He was going to be there for that. He was going to be there, and she would have to see him, to have him right there beside her through the procedure. That was going to be painful.

But what was the alternative? To shut him out? She could probably do that, insist that he stay in the waiting room. He might even accept her decision. But her baby had a father who wanted to be involved. She needed to put on her big-girl panties and be glad for that.

"Piper? You still there?"

"Uh, yes. The ultrasound is this Friday at eleven in the morning. Up in Sheridan, same as before."

"I'll drive you."

At least that much, she could fairly object to. "No. I'll meet you there."

"Fine."

She swallowed. Hard. "All right. I'll see you then."

"Wait. Anything new at your appointment with Dr. Hayes?"

"No. Really. Everything's fine. The baby is fine. I'm doing well."

"Can you send me the after-visit summary?"

She started to argue that there really was nothing he needed to know. But why? Arguing would only stretch out the agony of this phone call. "Sure. I can email it to you."

"That'll work." He rattled off an email address. She grabbed a pencil and pad from the kitchen junk drawer and wrote it down. "How's your morning sickness?"

"Actually, it's better. I'm finally through the first trimester, so that makes sense, right?"

"Yes, it does. And I'm so glad to hear that you're getting past feeling sick all the time." His voice was softer now. She didn't know if his sudden gentleness made her feel better—or all the worse. Really, when would she stop missing him? When would she stop hurting at the sight of him, the sound of his voice, the mere mention of his name? He said, "And that leads us to my next question…"

She pulled out a chair at her kitchen table and dropped into it. "There's another question?"

"Yeah, Piper, there is." His tone had cooled again. "You're at three months and it's time to tell my family that in January we're having a baby."

Oh, sweet Lord. This was her life now. She was not her mother, getting pregnant by a stranger at a rock festival, blithely walking away to raise her baby on her own.

Nope. She was having a baby with a responsible man who lived in her hometown. And he would damn well demand to be there for every step of this process—he and his large, loving extended family. He had a *right* to be involved. And it was good for their baby that he demanded that right.

But at this particular moment in time, she just wanted to stretch out on the sofa with her eyes closed and an ice pack on her forehead. "Listen, Jason?"

"Yeah?"

"I need to think that over."

"It has to happen. My family *will* know. There's no getting around it."

"I realize that. I promise you I do. I just, well, it's a lot all at one time."

"What's a lot?"

"Everything."

"Piper, are you all right?" His voice had gentled yet again. He really was worried about her.

"Yes!" It took everything she had in her not to burst into tears. "I'm fine, I'm just…adjusting, you know, to the way things are. And I'll see you for the ultrasound on Friday. We can decide then about how and when to tell your family."

He said nothing for several seconds. She braced for his objections.

But then he agreed, "All right. We'll talk about it then. Goodbye for now."

And that was it. He was gone. She shoved her phone halfway across the table and put her head in her hands.

The next day, she met Starr at the Perfect Bean. It was just the two of them. Beau was watching Cara at home with the help of old Daniel Hart, who was like a father to Beau and a grandfather to Starr and Beau's kids.

Piper sipped her masala chai, and they spent the first few minutes talking about what a success the auction had been and what was coming up next at the library.

Then Starr got around to the elephant in the room. "So, you and Jason…?"

Piper stared across the cute cast-iron café table at her friend and hardly knew where to begin. "There's something you probably should know."

"Omigod. What happened? Are you all right?"

Piper leaned across the table and lowered her voice to keep it just between the two of them. "He wants more. I can't handle more."

Starr slowly sipped her coffee. When she set the cup down, she suggested, "Don't sell yourself short."

Piper almost choked on her chai. "Jason said the same thing to me one of the times I tried to explain to him why I've got no idea how to have a real relationship with a man."

Starr leaned even closer. "Jason's a good man. You're

both adults. The age difference doesn't have to be a big deal if you don't let it. As for the past—meaning Walter and whatever happened before you met Walter. That's over. Let it go."

"Oh, Starr…" She reached out.

Starr was right there, taking her hand, holding on tight. "Piper. I get that you're afraid. But you should see the look in your eyes when his name is mentioned. I'm just going to say it. You're in love with him."

"I…"

"Hey. It's okay. I get it. Sometimes the words are hard to find. But I do know Jason. He's one of the good guys."

"You're right." Piper put her hand on her still-flat belly. When she glanced up again, Starr was watching her fondly. Right then, Piper wanted to tell her about the baby. And why shouldn't she? It really was time to start sharing the good news with people she cared about. "And listen, there's another thing…"

"Let me guess…" Starr leaned that extra few inches so that she could whisper in Piper's ear. "You're having Jason's baby and you're just now getting around to telling me about it."

Piper's stomach lurched. She breathed through her nose and the queasy feeling faded. "How did you…?"

"You know your mother is not real big on keeping secrets, right?"

"My mother…" Piper slowly shook her head. "Right now, I don't know whether to laugh or cry—my mother." She groaned and leaned toward her friend so the conversation could remain just between the two of them. "I mean, she's always saying that secrets are destructive. I guess

I should have made her promise to keep quiet about the news until Jason and I were ready to let people know."

Starr whispered, "You're how far along?"

"Thirteen weeks on Friday—and yes, I will start showing soon. It's about time to begin letting people know that there's a baby on the way."

"You're going to be a wonderful mom."

"I will try my best."

"There is no doubt about it. You will be a great mom. And I'm hoping you'll think about maybe telling Jason how you really feel?"

Her stomach was suddenly swooshy again. She took another deep, slow breath. "I will. I'll think about it."

Starr beamed. "That's what I wanted to hear."

Emmaline answered the door in a paint-spattered smock, her acres of graying red hair gathered and twisted up in a giant pile with the aid of a tie-dye scarf. She had a dab of yellow paint on her nose. "There's my girl."

It was a little after six. Piper had come straight from the library. "Hey, Mom."

Emmaline pulled her in for a hug. "You came at the perfect time. I just finished a painting and I've made your favorite sticky tofu bowl."

Piper waited until they were sitting at the table to bring up what Starr had told her. "Mom. I saw Starr this morning. She knows I'm pregnant and when I asked her how she knew…"

Emmaline shrugged. "Yep. I told her. You didn't want me to?"

"Well, Mom. We were waiting until the three-month mark, just to be sure everything was okay."

"I'm sorry, my love. I didn't get the memo on that. I won't tell anyone else until I get your say-so. And if you ever have another baby, I won't say a word about it until you give me the go-ahead."

"Great. But... How many people did you tell?"

"Hmm. A few. Mostly my artist friends. They're thrilled—for you, for me. And for Jason, too."

"So that means just about anyone in town might know by now."

"Yes, it does—and the baby is fine, right?"

Piper nodded. "Last week, Dr. Hayes said that things are looking really good."

"Wonderful. And as far as my telling people, you do realize they're all going to find out one way or another anyway, right?"

Piper suppressed a giant sigh. "Yes, Mom. But it really was my news to share."

"You're absolutely right. It won't happen again. I won't tell anyone else until you give me the okay."

"Thanks." What more could she say? The damage, if there was any, had already been done.

"So. How is Jason? You should have brought him with you tonight. There's plenty of food." Emmaline ate a chunk of the perfectly seared and sauced tofu.

As for Piper, right now she just wanted to cry again. She ate some rice, taking her sweet time about it.

But stalling did her no good.

Her mom studied her face and just *knew.* "Oh, my baby." Emmaline set her napkin by her plate and pushed back her chair. "Come here." She pulled Piper from her seat.

Piper didn't even pretend to resist. She went gratefully

into her mom's open arms. "I sent him away," she confessed, breathing in her mom's familiar earthy scent.

Emmaline held her close and rubbed her back. "It's not the end of the world. Sometimes a woman just needs a little space."

"I don't know what I needed. I mean, the truth is I had all these doubts and fears and bad memories of what happened with Brandon, of how wrong Walter and I were together. I got scared that it couldn't work with Jason, either, that I wouldn't know how to try again, to really be with him. To love him the way he deserves to be loved. I didn't know how to take the next step, so I, um, insulted him and then broke it off with him."

Her mom asked gently, "Insulted, how?"

Piper pulled back enough to give her mother a scowl. "Look. I don't want to go into detail, okay?"

"I understand." Her mom spoke softly, soothingly. "And whatever happened before, now you will fix it. You will go to him and tell him how wrong you were and ask him to please give you another chance."

"Oh, Mom…"

Emmaline took her by the shoulders and looked her squarely in the eyes. "Nothing's unfixable—unless you give up and don't even try."

That night, Piper called her dad. He answered on the first ring. She had him put her on speaker so that Nia could join the conversation. And then she told them that they were going to be grandparents again.

Her dad got all choked up and Nia said maybe they would be showing up in Wyoming earlier than originally planned.

"I'm thinking that we'll try early spring, if that works for you?" suggested Nia.

Piper said, "Yes. It'll be so great to see you. Just come whenever you can."

When she hung up, she almost called Jason to tell him that she'd called her dad about the baby.

But then she thought how he was still waiting for her okay before he told Meggie and Nate. He might be put out with her, that she hadn't even given him a heads-up before sharing the news with her dad.

She dropped the phone on the counter and promised herself she would reach out to him tomorrow.

That night, very late, Jason woke to the sound of heavy rain drumming on the roof. In his bed by the window, Kenzo stirred, his tags jingling as he gave his neck a scratch.

Jason rolled over and tried to go back to sleep, but the drumming overhead seemed to get louder, waking him every time he started to drop off. He thought of Piper—no big surprise. The beautiful, frustrating redhead who was having his baby was never far from his thoughts.

Was the rain invading her dreams tonight, too?

He would see her Friday, the day after tomorrow, for the ultrasound. And he'd get to see his baby again, too—his baby who was now, according to Google, as big as a Meyer lemon.

Thoughts of the baby always made him smile.

The rain kept coming down. Now he was starting to feel kind of antsy. He turned on the lamp, swung his feet to the floor and headed for the john.

When he returned to the bedroom, Kenzo was out of

his bed. The dog stretched and yawned, then dropped to his haunches and stared up at Jason hopefully.

"You're kidding me, man. It's pouring down rain out there."

Kenzo whined again. He needed to go out.

"Just don't say I didn't warn you. I'll let you out, but I'm not going out in that frog strangler with you."

He followed the eager dog into the two-story great room and was almost at the front door when his bare foot landed in a puddle of water. "What the…?"

Kenzo whined again.

"All right, you got it." He let the dog out, turned on the wagon wheel chandelier hanging from the rafters above and spotted the leak right away, way up there at the peak.

Last winter during a blizzard, they'd lost a couple of big branches off the Douglas fir ten feet from the house. Those branches had sounded like boulders when they hit the roof and then loudly tumbled the two stories to the ground. Apparently, they'd done some damage.

He mopped up the water, then got a bucket from under the kitchen sink and stuck it below the drip.

By morning, the rain had cleared off. He got busy gathering eggs and feeding horses. After stopping for breakfast, he and Joe went to work burning ditches. In the process, Jason told his baby brother about the leak. They'd put on that roof together, he and Joe and their dad.

"I want to get up there," he said. "Locate the leak, diagnose the problem. I'm thinking the flashing at the roofline was damaged when those big branches hit last winter."

Joe nodded. "I'll spot you."

It was almost one when Jason got back to his place. He made himself a sandwich and ate it standing at the sink.

Figuring now was as good a time as any to get a look at the roof, he gave Joe a call. His brother said he'd be over in twenty minutes.

That gave Jason time to hop in his crew cab and drive to the storage shed where they kept the ladders. He loaded up a lightweight aluminum nineteen-footer and headed back to the cabin. Kenzo was right there with him, panting contentedly in the passenger seat.

Jason thought of Piper. Because every damn thing in the world reminded him of Piper lately. Right now, it was his panting dog sitting in *her* seat.

Sometimes a man got lucky. He found a woman and the two of them were just right for each other. They had that special combination of commonality and disparities. They took pleasure in a lot of the same things, but they also helped each other. Where one lacked, the other had more than enough to pull them through any difficulty.

He and Piper were like that. Together, they could have the best kind of life—if only she'd get out of her own way long enough to see the truth of who they were to each other.

Joe was waiting on the deck. Jason parked as close as he could to the steps. He hauled the ladder out of the back and Joe helped him get it in place, fully extended, with the base effectively braced in position at the far end of the deck, so that the ladder could lie flat against the steep slant of the roof on the two-story central section of the house.

Jason put on his Rockport work shoes and his grip gloves and up the ladder he went. Just as he'd suspected, the flashing was damaged along the ridgeline.

Mentally ticking off what he'd need for the repair, he started back down. He was off the roof and on the second-to-last rung a few feet from the deck floor when Joe said, "Here comes Mom. Looks like she's headed for the barn."

He heard the sound of her pickup's engine and glanced that way at the same time as he took the next step down and missed the last rung. Tipping over backward, he hit the deck, his head bouncing hard against the wide-plank boards.

Everything went black.

Chapter Fourteen

Piper was reviewing her report for the upcoming board meeting when the phone on the desk rang. "This is Piper."

"You have a call from Meggie Bravo," said Marnie Fox, who was out in front, stationed at the circulation desk today.

Piper's heart was suddenly racing. She couldn't think of anything good that Jason's mom might want to say to her.

But whatever it was, Piper would deal with it. If she was ever going to have a chance with Jason again, getting along with his mother would be part of her job. "Put her through."

A moment later, Jason's mom said, "Hello, Piper?"

"Hi, Meggie," she cautiously replied. "What can I do for you?"

Meggie made a nervous sound. "Hmm. Well, first of all, I would like to apologize for my behavior that night you came for dinner. I have no excuse for myself. I'm overprotective sometimes, though my grown children are very capable of taking care of themselves and of making their own adult decisions."

An apology? Meggie Bravo had called to say she was sorry? Warmth bloomed in Piper's chest. "Well, I…" She struggled to come up with the right words. *Any* words. "Thank you."

Meggie jumped right in. "Oh, don't thank me. I'm the one in the wrong. I need to apologize. And I *am* apologizing. I hope that eventually, you can forgive me."

"Of course I can forgive you…" Right then, Piper guessed what must be going on here. Meggie knew about the baby. She'd heard it from one of Emmaline's artist friends—which was fine. Piper said sincerely, "I completely understand that you only wanted what's best for Jason."

"That's true. But I was hasty and judgmental and—"

"Meggie." Piper decided to just lay the cards right out on the table. "It's okay. I get it. With the baby coming, you're worried I'll try to keep you from being involved in your grandchild's life, and I want to reassure you right here and now that I would never…"

Meggie's gasp cut her off. "There's a baby? You and Jay are having a baby?"

Piper groaned. "You didn't know?"

"No! I had no clue."

"Oh, Meggie. Now I'm the one who's sorry—for laying the big news on you so badly. My mom has been telling her friends that Jason and I are having a baby. I assumed that one of them must have told you."

Meggie laughed. "Oh, Piper…" And then a sob escaped her. "This is wonderful news. I can hardly believe it…"

"Well. Um, now you know."

"Oh, yes I do. I can hardly believe it. I really can't. This news does make me so happy."

"I'm glad."

"But, Piper, I want to make it very clear that I called because my son loves you and because I was wrong and I want to make it right with you—not because I'm getting a grandchild, after all."

Piper was smiling now. "Yes. I understand. And I am so happy to hear from you."

"When are you due?"

"Mid-January."

"Is everything going well?"

"It is. No issues so far—except quite a bit of morning sickness, which seems to be tapering off now that I'm moving into the second trimester."

"Excellent. I simply… Well, I'm downright thunderstruck over your news."

"Thunderstruck. I hope that's a good thing."

"Oh, Piper. Yes it is. It is very, very good. Now I'm doubly glad I called. I've been concerned about Jay, I really have."

"Concerned…how?"

"Well, he's been more and more distant the past couple of weeks since you two came back from your trip. I've worried that something might have gone wrong between you, and if it has, I know I'm at least partly to blame. I've promised him I would stay out of it, and I tried. Piper, I really tried."

"I believe you. And it's okay. I'm *glad* that you called."

"That's such a relief. Thank you."

"The truth is, Meggie, I broke it off with him."

Meggie sighed. "I'm sorry to hear that."

"I, uh… Well, I got a little overwhelmed and messed everything up. I'm planning to reach out to him, to see if we can…" Where to go with this? How to even begin?

"Hey. Piper, it's okay. I realize I'm not the one you need to talk to about this—which brings me to the main reason I called."

The main reason? "What do you mean? What reason?"

"Let me just start by saying that Jason is okay."

Her heart was suddenly throwing itself at the cage of her ribs. "What happened?"

"He's all right now. But a couple of hours ago, he fell off a ladder."

She let out a cry. "No!"

"Yes. I'm happy to say that he didn't crack his skull, but the fall knocked him out. He was unconscious for several minutes."

Piper jumped up so fast, her chair flew back and hit the bookcase behind her desk. "Where is he? I need to—"

"Hey, now…" Meggie said in the voice she probably used to soothe agitated ranch animals. "It's okay, honestly. He has a mild concussion and a nasty bump on the back of his head. But he's all right. He's here, with me and Joe, up at the hospital in Sheridan. I mainly called because I was thinking that if you wanted to be here, too—"

"I do, Meggie." Her whole heart and soul were in those words. "Very much."

"Well, all right. That's great. Come on up. I'll wait for you out in front."

At the hospital, Piper parked a bit crooked and ran for the main entrance. Meggie was right there in front of the glass doors as she'd promised she would be, wearing old jeans, a faded long-sleeved shirt and dusty rawhide boots, her gray-streaked dark hair pulled back in a low ponytail. She held out her arms and Piper went into them.

"I'm so glad you called," Piper whispered as Jason's mom held her tight.

Meggie pulled back smiling. "Me, too." She took Piper's

hand. "Come on. I know a certain cranky cowboy who will be so happy to see you."

They waited at Reception until a nurse came. "I can take you back," the nurse said. "But Jason's brother is with him. We don't usually let three visitors into our small exam rooms all at the same time."

"Just give us a minute with Jason, please?" Meggie coaxed. "I'll make sure that two of us clear out quickly."

The nurse led them through a door and into a narrower hallway and a smaller door labeled Exam Room Three.

In the cramped room, Jason's brother sat in a guest chair fiddling with something on his phone. Jason himself, in a floral-patterned hospital gown and thick socks, was stretched out on the exam table. Even fully extended, the table was too short for him. His stocking feet hung off the end. He seemed to be sleeping. His head was turned away from the door and he'd thrown an arm over his eyes.

Peering closer, Piper could make out the bump on the back of his head. She longed to launch herself at him, grab him close, promise him he would be all right—and beg him to give her just one more chance.

Joe looked up. "Hey, Piper," he whispered so quietly, she understood his words more by the movement of his lips than by the sound. His mouth stretched wide in a giant smile. "Good to see you." He nodded in Jason's direction. "He's conked out. It's so boring in here and he's not supposed to read or strain his eyes."

Jason stirred and mumbled, "Not now, Joe. Let me sleep…" But he didn't turn his head. His big arm remained covering the top half of his face.

Joe kept right on whispering. "Don't worry. The doctor

said napping is fine. Just ask him a simple question when he wakes up. If he answers clearly, he's okay."

With a pointed look at her younger son, Meggie shot a thumb over her shoulder.

"Yes, ma'am." Joe got up and followed Meggie out, pulling the door silently shut behind him.

Now it was just the two of them. Piper stared down at the man she loved, the father of her baby, the man she'd honestly believed she would never find.

Jason slept on, his big chest rising and falling with each breath.

Quietly, Piper moved the chair Joe had been sitting in closer to the exam table. Then she sat down and waited for the man on the table to open his eyes.

Apples.

Still half-asleep, Jason drew in a slow breath through his nose.

The concussion must have made him delusional. He could swear he smelled Piper's shampoo. He drew another slow breath and let it out with care. Yep. The scent of apples, clean and sweet and delicious.

Definitely delusional. No doubt about it.

And how damn long would it be before someone came and said he could go? He'd been cooped up in this tiny room for too long now. They'd poked and prodded and asked him a million questions, all of which he'd answered clearly and correctly. Yeah, his head hurt. But there was nothing more they could do for him here. He wanted to go home and stretch out in his own bed.

He rolled fully onto his side toward where Joe sat, drew his legs up onto the dinky exam table and opened his eyes.

He was fully expecting to see his brother sitting there, fooling around on his phone.

But it was Piper in the chair instead—Piper, in a green skirt and a white silk shirt, right next to him, up close and personal.

He groaned. Maybe he was worse off than he'd thought.

"Hey," the vision said with a slow, sweet smile. "How're you feeling?"

He blinked. Twice. But each time he looked again, she was still there. "Uh, Piper?"

"Yes?"

"Are you really here?" He reached out.

She took his hand. Real. Her touch was real. And then she brushed her soft lips against his skin. "I am here, yes. Your mom called me. We made peace. I told her about the baby. She said you'd been hurt and asked me if I wanted to be here with you. I couldn't say yes fast enough."

He closed his eyes at the wonder of all that. "If you're not real, don't tell me, okay?"

"Oh, Jason." She bent close. He felt her breath on his cheek. "I am real, I promise you." And then her lips were there, pressed to his cheek, so soft, so absolutely perfect.

He turned his aching head just enough to capture those lips with his own.

That kiss lasted a long time. When he opened his eyes again, he said, "Ask me a simple question."

She gave a soft laugh. "I love you. I was wrong. I don't want to be without you. And here's the question—will you give me another chance?"

"Oh, hell yes."

She laughed. "You are so easy."

"Hey. Cut me some slack. I have a head injury."

"Oh, Jason…" She looked at him like he was the answer to all the questions in her heart. He'd fall off a ladder every day for a chance to see her like this, with nothing but love and hope in those green eyes of hers.

"I love you, Piper. You're it for me. You're everything."

"Well," she said in a sweet, breathless whisper. "I'm really glad to hear that. Because I feel the same way about you—but then you already knew that. You said as much two and a half weeks ago. Right before you walked out my door."

"I was hurt," he said gruffly.

"I'm so sorry. Please forgive me."

"You know I do."

There was a tap on the exam room. A nurse came in. "Jason, how are you feeling?"

Wincing as his injury pressed against the exam table, he turned his head toward the woman at the door. "My head hurts some. But overall, I feel good." He gave Piper's hand a squeeze. "Real good."

"What day is it?" asked the nurse.

"Thursday, July 18."

"Excellent. You ready to go home?"

"Yes, I am."

"Go ahead and get dressed and we can let you out of here."

Piper didn't want to be apart from him—which was just as well because Jason said he wasn't letting her out of his sight.

Joe took the crew cab back to the ranch. Jason rode with Piper to her house, but only long enough for her to pack a bag. At the Double-K, Nate and Meggie's cousin Sonny had fixed the leak in Jason's roof and put the ladder away.

They had dinner at the main house that night. The mood was festive. Meggie broke out the bubbly in celebration of the news that she and Nate were going to be grandparents. Piper opted for ginger ale because of the baby— and Jason did, too.

They all raised their glasses high when Nate offered the toast. "To Jason and Piper and the little one we can't wait to meet."

Piper spent the night in Jason's bed spooned up nice and close. And early the next day, they returned to the hospital together for her thirteen-week ultrasound.

It was a revelation. Piper cried happy tears. Their lemon-size baby girl waved her arms and kicked her feet. They could see her brain and her heart. She looked healthy and so active.

That night, in bed, she said, "I don't think it's possible to be happier than I am right now."

Oh, but it was.

Two weeks later, Piper moved in with Jason at the Double-K. She put her house in town up for sale. It sold in mid-August to a young couple from Houston.

On Labor Day, she and Jason shared a picnic at that special spot where he'd taken her once before, under a willow tree by Crystal Creek. He knelt on their picnic blanket and asked her to marry him. As soon as she said yes, he slipped a vintage-style ring on her finger. It was just what she would have chosen for herself, with an oval diamond flanked by two gleaming emeralds. When she threw her arms around his neck, he scooped her up, carried her out into the creek and dunked her good and proper.

They were married on Thanksgiving Day in a simple ceremony at the Rising Sun Ranch, with Jason's big extended family all around them. Piper's filmy pearl-white dress had an empire waist that flowed out and down over her giant belly. Her mom, an ordained minister of the Unity Church, officiated.

And when Jason took her in his arms to kiss her, he whispered, "I love you."

"And I love you," she answered. "Deeply, completely and…"

"Forever," he finished for her as his lips met hers.

Piper wasn't feeling quite so romantic on that brutal day in January when their daughter decided to be born. In fact, she was scared to death.

Outside a blizzard had descended. The world was a frozen landscape of wind-driven white, making a trip to the hospital impossible. Piper tried her best to put a brave face on the situation, but she really had planned to cap off her advanced-age pregnancy by having her baby in the hospital, where the professionals would know what to do if anything went wrong.

She labored for hours, with Jason and Meggie taking turns coaching her. Piper cried. She moaned. She screamed at the ceiling—and at Jason and Meggie, too. At one point, when she was feeling completely exhausted, she even called Dr. Hayes. He offered suggestions and encouragements. Piper screamed at him a few times, too. As the hours went by, she doubted her ability to do this, to make it through.

But then finally, at 1:10 a.m. on the twenty-fifth of

January, her little girl let out that first furious wail. Jason caught her and laid her on Piper's chest.

Meggie bustled out into the great room, giving the three of them a little time alone together as a new family.

When Jason's mom returned, she tied off the cord with two sterilized shoelaces, and then cut the space between. A bit later, as the baby nursed for the first time, Jason and Meggie discussed names.

Piper said, "You two can talk it over all you want. I already know her name. It's Megan Emmaline. What else could it be?"

Meggie started crying then. "It's only from sheer happiness," she reassured the new parents.

"Come here, Mom." Jason grabbed her in a hug.

Later, during a break in the storm, Nate and Joe came over. They each got to hold little Meg. And then they took the exhausted new grandma back to the main house.

"You did it," said Jason reverently, as he climbed into bed with Piper and their newborn daughter.

"*We* did it," she replied.

On the floor, Kenzo whined.

"Fine," Jason muttered. "But only this once."

Kenzo jumped up on the mattress and settled, like the gentleman he was, down at the foot of the bed.

Jason nuzzled Piper's nose and pressed a kiss at her temple. "I keep thinking of that first night back in April. That was a great night. My dream come true."

She gave a tired little chuckle. "I made it very clear that it was one night and one night only."

His grin was smug. "And look at us now."

She touched his beard-scruffy cheek. "Together. With our little girl…"

"You didn't make it easy, though."

She laughed then, but softly so as not to wake the baby. And then she said sincerely, "I should have trusted you sooner."

He shook his head. "You needed the time."

"I did, yes. And that's why we took the long way getting here."

"The long way is the best way," he said. And then he kissed her, a slow kiss, but light as a breath.

* * * * *

Watch for Sarah Ellen Bravo's story,
coming in October 2024,
only from Harlequin Special Edition.